"Cas
you have or **.**

"I won't be holle

"I expect not. Bu
could and I'll hear them."

He meant the kids could call for him. "Why would they need you when I'll be right there in the same tent or whatever you want to call it?"

"No reason. Just as there's no reason to get all prickly about it."

"Prickly?" She swallowed hard. "If I am it's because you make me sound like I can't manage on my own."

He held up his hands in a sign of protest. "It never crossed my mind."

"Well, then. So long as we understand each other." She headed back to her site.

He chuckled softly and followed her. "Oh, I get it."

She ignored the note of triumph in his voice. How could he possibly comprehend? He had no idea of the events that had shaped her life and made her want nothing half as much as she wanted to be independent. Self-sufficient. "I don't need anyone," she muttered.

"Sounds mighty lonely to me."

Books by Linda Ford

Love Inspired Historical

The Road to Love
The Journey Home
The Path to Her Heart
Dakota Child
The Cowboy's Baby
Dakota Cowboy
Christmas Under Western Skies
"A Cowboy's Christmas"
Dakota Father
Prairie Cowboy
Klondike Medicine Woman
**The Cowboy Tutor*
**The Cowboy Father*
**The Cowboy Comes Home*
The Gift of Family
"Merry Christmas, Cowboy"
†*The Cowboy's Surprise Bride*
†*The Cowboy's Unexpected Family*

*Three Brides for Three Cowboys
†Cowboys of Eden Valley

LINDA FORD

lives on a ranch in Alberta, Canada. Growing up on the prairie and learning to notice the small details it hides gave her an appreciation for watching God at work in His creation. Her upbringing also included being taught to trust God in everything and through everything—a theme that resonates in her stories. Threads of another part of her life are found in her stories—her concern for children and their future. She and her husband raised fourteen children—four homemade, ten adopted. She currently shares her home and life with her husband, a grown son, a live-in paraplegic client and a continual (and welcome) stream of kids, kids-in-law, grandkids and assorted friends and relatives.

The Cowboy's Unexpected Family

LINDA FORD

HARLEQUIN® LOVE INSPIRED® HISTORICAL

If you purchased this book without a cover you should be aware that this book is stolen property. It was reported as "unsold and destroyed" to the publisher, and neither the author nor the publisher has received any payment for this "stripped book."

Recycling programs for this product may not exist in your area.

ISBN-13: 978-0-373-82955-2

THE COWBOY'S UNEXPECTED FAMILY

This edition published by arrangement with Love Inspired Books.

www.LoveInspiredBooks.com

Printed in U.S.A.

Owe no man anything, but to love one another.
—*Romans* 13:8

To families. To my children and their children.
May you build sweet memories,
establish worthwhile traditions and grow in love
and care for each other. I wish this for all families.

Chapter One

Eden Valley, Alberta
Summer 1882

Cassie Godfrey's dream was about to come true. She could see it there before her eyes. She could smell it, and practically taste it. Twenty-five years old and she was finally about to become self-sufficient.

"I'm not sure this is a good idea." The cowboy sitting next to her sounded worried but she dismissed his concern. She'd heard all the arguments she cared to hear.

"I'll be fine." She jumped from the wagon seat and headed to the back where her things waited to be moved to her new home. Only one small problem remained. Or perhaps it was a large problem.

She had no house.

Roper Jones climbed down slowly, reluctantly. "Where you planning to sleep?"

"Eddie lent me a tent." She'd spent the winter at Eden Valley Ranch where Eddie Gardiner was boss and had recently married Linette. When Linette had discovered Cassie living in the Montreal train station after the death of her husband, she had gathered Cassie under her wing and taken her to Eden Valley Ranch with her. After Linette and Eddie married, they'd insisted Cassie was more than welcome to remain and share their big house but it was time for Cassie to move on. For months, ever since she'd reached the Eden Valley Ranch, her dream had been growing. There was a time she thought a secure future meant depending on a man, but she'd grown to see she didn't need a man to take care of her. She could take care of herself. It had become her dream and that dream was about to be realized.

"You're mighty determined." Roper's chuckle sounded a tiny bit regretful. He hoisted the tent and a couple of bags from the wagon and headed for the little patch of land Cassie had persuaded Mr. Macpherson to sell her. He'd been reluctant about selling to a woman but she pointed out she was the head of her household—although she refrained from mentioning it was a household of one—and a widow, which entitled her to file on a homestead.

"Guess if the government would allow me to own one hundred and sixty acres for a homestead, I can buy a small lot." Her words had persuaded him, and no one else had raised an objection.

Roper set her things on the ground and leaned back on his heels. "Cassie, this doesn't seem like a good idea to me. Why not come back to the ranch?" His grin did nothing to erase the disapproval in his eyes.

She planted her feet on her own piece of land and sighed. "I realize you're only wanting to help but believe me this is exactly where I want to be and what I want to do." She turned full circle, mentally measuring the boundaries of her lot. It lay behind Macpherson's store, close enough that she could supply the bread for his store, once she had a stove, as part payment for the lumber for her house. Yet it was far enough to be out of sight of the freight wagons, stagecoaches and riders passing the store.

Roper followed her visual inspection until they'd both gone full circle and ended looking at each other. He was a pleasant enough man with a ready smile tipped a little crookedly at the moment. Stocky built, solid even. A good head of brown hair mostly hidden under his cowboy hat. A square face. His hazel eyes were always full of kindness and hope, though she'd gone out of her way to make it clear he need not pin any hope on her.

"Why must you insist on this foolishness?" He swung about to indicate the vast open prairies, the rolling foothills, the bold Rocky Mountains. "Ain't nothing but nothing out here. A few cows. A few cowboys. A store. A settler or two."

Her gaze took in the wide land and for a moment rested on the mountaintops that seemed to poke the blue sky. As always they made her feel stronger, and she brought her mind back to Roper's concern. "And Mr. Macpherson," she added, "just a holler away."

"Who's to protect you from wild animals? Either the four-legged or two-legged kind?"

"Indeed. And who has protected me in the past? Sure wasn't my dead husband." She'd been so afraid sleeping in the railway station. "Nor my dead father. Certainly not my still-living grandfather." She made a grating sound of disbelief.

"Must be the good Lord 'cause it sure ain't your good sense."

"Think what you will." She turned away to examine the stack of belongings. "Thanks for bringing me to town and unloading my stuff."

"You're telling me to leave?"

"Don't recall saying so but shouldn't you get back to the ranch?"

"You're bound and determined to do this?"

She faced him squarely. She would reveal no flicker of doubt. "I'm bound and determined."

"Nothing I say will convince you to reconsider?"

"Figure you about said it all and still I'm here."

But he didn't move and she avoided looking at him. He'd already made his opinion clear as spring water. As had Linette and Eddie.

"It goes against my better judgment to leave you here alone."

"This is something I have to do." She didn't bother explaining her reasons, afraid they would look foolish to anyone else. But she was through feeling indebted to someone for her care.

He pressed his hand to hers. "Cassie, at least let me help you set up some kind of camp."

The weight of his hand, the warmth of his palm, the way he curled his fingers around hers made her realize how much she would miss him. But when he reached for the tent, she grabbed his arm to stop him. "I'll be fine. Don't worry about me." Even though she had pointedly ignored him all winter it was comforting in some strange, unexplainable way to know he was there, on the periphery of her world.

But she would not depend on anyone. She'd long ago learned the cost of doing so. She had to make her own security. She fussed with the ropes around the rolled-up canvas tent. "I plan to manage on my own."

He edged past her, shuffled toward the wagon, never taking his eyes from her.

She did her best to keep her attention on the pile of belongings at her feet but couldn't keep from glancing his way when the wagon creaked as he stepped up.

He sighed loud enough to make the horse prick up its ears. "Look, it ain't like I'm asking to be your partner or anything like that." He grinned as if to inform her he considered the idea plumb foolish. "Just want to make sure you're going to be okay."

"I'm going to be just fine." She lifted her hand in farewell.

With a shake of his head, he drove away.

She watched until the trail of dust hid the wagon. Only then did she turn and face her predicament. She had land of her own. A nice level bit of ground with trees surrounding it and the river a few steps away.

She had plans to support herself, and a tent to provide temporary shelter. She had a pile of lumber that would become her home.

There was only one small hitch.

She had no notion of how to transform that pile of lumber into a house.

First things first. She would erect the tent and prepare camp.

Three hours later, she had managed to sort out the ropes and stakes for the tent and put it up. Sure it sagged like a weary old man but it was up. She'd unrolled her bedding along one side and slipped her derringer under her pillow. Whatever Roper thought of her she wasn't foolish enough to be unprepared.

Macpherson had provided a saw, hammer and nails with the lumber. She carried them to the pile of lumber and stared helplessly. She had no idea how to begin.

God, I know there must be a way to do this. Surely you can help me.

But she heard no voice from the clouds, nor did

she feel a sudden burst of inspiration. As usual she'd have to figure it out on her own.

Roper muttered to himself as he headed toward the ranch. Stupid woman. If he didn't know better he would think she was crazy in the head. But he'd watched her all winter, seeing the pain and defiance behind her brown eyes and wanting to erase it.

From the beginning Cassie had been as prickly as a cactus. Over the winter she'd mellowed. Her black hair had gone from dull and stringy to glistening and full. Morose, even sour, at the start, she'd started to laugh more often.

He shook his head and grunted. But she'd changed in other ways, too. She'd grown downright stubborn and independent.

He adjusted his hat to suit him better and swatted away an ornery fly that wouldn't leave him alone.

Growing up in an orphanage he'd learned if he helped people, made them laugh, life was more pleasant for everyone. He'd become adept at smoothing out problems in order to maintain peace.

He ached that Cassie refused to let him help in any way.

"Shoot. Best thing I can do is forget all about her." Something else he'd grown good at—letting people go. He'd learned the hard way not to expect permanence. Still he'd be giving Eddie every excuse known to man to ride to town until he was certain she was well settled. In fact, he'd leave the job and stay in town if he could think of any reasonable excuse. After all, he had no particular ties to the ranch. To any place for that matter.

But he could think of no reason to hang about town other than to make sure Cassie was safe and happy. Seems she was only too happy to see him gone so maybe he'd accomplished one of his goals.

A dark shape on the trail ahead caught his eye and he blinked. He pulled the horse to a halt and stared. Rubbed his eyes and stared some more.

He'd seen mirages of trees and water but he'd never seen a mirage of kids. He squinted hard. Three kids. Four, if that squirming armload was another.

He called to them as he edged the wagon forward.

The huddle of young 'uns left the trail and ran toward the trees a distance away.

"Now hold up there."

The kids picked up speed.

Roper quickly secured the reins and jumped to the ground, breaking into an awkward trot. His bowed legs weren't made for running but he didn't let that slow him much.

One of the kids hollered, "Hurry."

Another started to cry.

He couldn't bear to hear a kid crying and he slowed. But just for a moment. Kids didn't belong out in the middle of nowhere all alone. It wasn't a bit safe. He forced his legs to pump harder and closed the distance.

The biggest one turned and faced him, a scowl on her pretty little face. "Leave us alone!"

He skidded to a halt and took their measure. The girl looked about twelve, maybe a little older. She held a trembling younger girl maybe two years old. Roper couldn't see anything of the little one but the fine golden hair and impossibly tiny shoulders. Then there was a boy a year or two younger than the older girl. And between them, face full of fear and defiance, a young lad of maybe six or seven. The look on each face held a familiar expression…

one he had seen time and again in the orphanage that had been his only home. It spelled fear. And trouble.

He held up his hands knowing the bunch wasn't ready to see the folly of their attitude. "I mean you no harm but I can't help wondering what four young 'uns are doing out here halfway between nowhere and nothin'."

The eldest two exchanged glances, and a silent message passed between them. The boy answered. "None of yer business."

Roper backed off a step but rocked on the balls of his feet, ready to grab them if they tried to escape. "Long way from here to someplace." They'd been headed away from Edendale so he guessed that wasn't their destination of choice. "You might get a little hungry and thirsty."

The girl glared at him. "We don't need no help."

He sighed. Where had he heard that before? And he didn't like it any better from the lips of a young gal with nothing more than the company of three younger kids and a gut full of determination than he had hearing it from Cassie. "How about you let me give you a ride at least?"

Again that silent communication. The young lad signaled to the older girl and they lowered their heads to hold a confab.

He waited, letting them think they were in control but he had no intention of turning around and leaving them there.

They straightened, and the oldest answered, "We'll accept a ride. For a little ways."

"Best we introduce ourselves," Roper said, and gave his name. "I work on a ranch over in the hills there."

Three pairs of eyes followed the direction he indicated and he could see their interest. He turned to the kids. "Now tell me who you are."

The big girl nodded. "I'm Daisy. This is Neil." She

indicated the older boy, then nudged the younger one. "Billy, and Pansy."

"Suppose you got a last name."

"Locke."

"Well, howdy." He held out a hand but they shrank back. He waited, wanting them to know he meant them nothing but kindness. Finally Neil grabbed his hand and gave a good-size squeeze. The boy had grit for sure. Guess they all did to be out here alone.

He led them to the wagon. They insisted on sitting together in the back. He climbed to the seat but didn't move.

"Mister?" Daisy sounded scared.

He shifted to face them. "It might help if I had some idea where you want to go."

Again a silent discussion then Daisy nodded. "We're looking for our pa. He set out to get himself some land close to the mountains. Maybe you heard of him. Thaddeus Locke."

He'd heard of the man. One of the only settlers in the area. Last time he'd been mentioned in Roper's hearing was last fall. "Where's your mother?"

"She died. Before she did, she made us promise to find our pa." Daisy's voice quivered but she held her head high.

"Well, let's find him, then. Mr. Macpherson will know where his farm is." Macpherson knew everything about everyone within a hundred miles. 'Course that didn't mean more than a couple hundred people, not counting Indians. Roper turned the wagon about.

"You don't know where our papa lives?" Neil asked.

"Can't say as I do." The kids murmured behind him and he glanced over his shoulder. Little Pansy rested her head against Daisy's shoulder, big blue eyes regarding him solemnly, unblinkingly. The kid had been aptly named with eyes as wide as the flower. "We'll soon be at Macpherson's store." The collection of low buildings clung to the trail ahead, trees of various kinds clustered behind the buildings. His gaze sought the little area behind the store. As they drew closer he saw Cassie had almost managed to get the tent standing, but it swayed like a broken-down old mare. He chuckled. Wouldn't take more than a cupful of rain to bring it down and soak everything inside, including her if it happened while she slept. The canvas flapped in the wind. Fact was she might not have to wait for rain to topple the tent. A breeze made by bird wings would do the trick.

"Whoa." He jumped down and went to the back of the wagon.

Already Neil was on his feet with Pansy and he helped Daisy to the ground as Billy scampered down to join them. All four regarded him with wary eyes.

He pushed his hat farther back on his head and returned their study. "Your ma would be proud of you." Where had that come from? The words must have been dropped to his tongue by the good Lord because the three older kids beamed, and Pansy gave him a shy smile that turned around in his heart and nestled there. "Now let's find your pa."

They trooped into the store. Macpherson leaned across the counter talking with another man. Roper recognized the North-West Mounted Police officer, Kipp Allen. "Howdy, Constable. Didn't see your horse outside."

The man nodded a greeting. Even though he lounged against the counter, he had a way of holding himself that let you know he saw clear through you. "He threw a shoe. He's down at the smithy." His eyes shifted to the young 'uns and he straightened, his gaze watchful.

Roper paid him no mind. "Macpherson, these here are

the Locke kids looking for their pa, Thaddeus Locke. I'll give them transport if you tell me where I can find him."

Macpherson blinked. Just once but enough for Roper to wonder what secret the man had. "Best you be asking the constable."

Roper shifted to meet Allen's study. "I'm asking."

The Mountie's eyes softened and he faced the children. "I'm sorry to inform you that your pa passed away last winter. I buried him on his property."

Neil and Daisy drew in a gasp.

Orphans. Just like him. Roger remembered well the loneliness, the discouragement of it. How many times had he held his breath and watched a man and woman come to the orphanage for a child? Waiting. Wanting. Hoping. Never chosen. The matron tried to comfort him. "People want to know your background." But he had no background. No name. Only what someone had given him after he was discovered as a squalling infant on the doorstep. "You'd do well to forget about a home and family," she'd said.

He tried to heed her advice and turned his attention to helping others. Making them laugh. Teaching them how to smile for strangers so they would be chosen. Helping others find a home helped him find his joy and satisfaction.

But as he grew older and left the orphanage he forgot the matron's sound advice. Until it was too late. He learned the hard way that his background mattered more than who he was. After that experience he knew he would never belong in a forever family.

Small whimpers brought Roper's attention back to the children. Billy's eyes were wide as dishpans. Pansy stuck her fingers in her mouth and burrowed against Neil's shoulder.

"What...how'd he die?" Neil squeaked out.

The Mountie closed the distance between himself and the children. Roper automatically stepped away, out of respect for the sorrow visibly carved on their faces.

"Son." The man clasped Neil's shoulder. "I regret to have to tell you that he froze to death. Near as I can figure he went out in a storm to check on his animals and got turned around trying to get back to his cabin." He let the news sink in. "I have admiration for a man who is willing to face hard things rather than shirk his responsibilities. You kids can be proud of him."

Although the kids seemed to welcome the praise, Roper couldn't help wondering if staying safe for his family wouldn't have been more responsible than worrying about a couple or three animals.

The Mountie straightened. "We'll see you get back to your mother."

"Mama's dead." Billy blurted out the announcement, then sobbed into Daisy's dress.

"I see. What other family do you have?"

Daisy's mouth worked silently for a moment. Life had dished out a lot of bad news for them. No doubt she reeled inside, making it difficult to recall things.

"Mama had a brother but we haven't heard from him since I was Billy's size."

"Do you know where he was at the time?" The Mountie pulled out a little notepad, ready to jot down the information.

"We were living in Toronto then. It was before Papa decided we would do better to move West. He always wore a suit. I think I remember Mama saying he was a lawyer. Maybe. I can't be certain."

"Do you remember his name?"

"Jack. And Mama's name before she married was Munro."

"Can you spell it?"

Neil answered. "I can. I saw it in the Bible." He spelled it.

The Mountie wrote it down, closed his notepad and stuffed it into his breast pocket. "Fine. We'll locate him for you. In the meantime, we'll have to find a place for you to live." He turned to Roper. "I expect Mrs. Gardiner would take them in."

"Normally, yes." His boss's wife shared her home with anyone who needed it. "But she's been awfully sick. The boss has been plenty worried about her. I 'spect he'd say no to the idea."

"Then I'll have to take them back to the fort."

"And then what?"

"No one will likely take four but we'll split them up between willing families. Or..." He didn't finish the thought.

But Roper knew.

Send them to an orphanage.

Daisy stepped back, Neil at her side. They pressed Billy behind them and Pansy between them both holding her tight.

"We aren't going," Daisy said.

"We're sticking together," Neil added.

And then Roper heard himself say, "I'll look after them."

The kids relaxed so quickly he was surprised Pansy didn't drop to the floor.

Billy poked his head out between his older brother and sister. "You will?"

"Now wait a minute." The Mountie held up his hands. "You live in a bunkhouse when you're not out on the range. You expect to bunk these children with you or carry them on horseback across the mountains?"

"Well, no." Put that way it sounded pretty dumb. But something about their predicament forced him to speak and act on their behalf. "But I'll think of something." Eddie wouldn't object to giving him some time off. If he did, there were other ranches that could use another cowhand. His smile tightened. Eddie was a good boss. Roper liked working for him. But he wouldn't let these kids be sent someplace they weren't wanted. No siree.

The sound of a pounding hammer came from behind the store. The corners of his mouth lifted. "I know a young woman who will help me care for them." If he could make her see what a good arrangement this was for all concerned. It was perfect. God sent. He could help Cassie get set up. In return, she could help care for the kids until the uncle came. Then he'd be at ease about moving on and letting her run her business.

The assurance in his voice caused the Mountie to study him carefully. Then he shook his head. "'Fraid I can't simply take your word for it." He turned to the kids. "I'll find a wagon and be right back for you." He headed for the door.

The kids pressed tight to each other, fear vibrating from them.

Roper leaped forward, catching the Mountie before he could open the door. "Constable, there's no need for that. Give me a chance to make arrangements." He bored his eyes into the Mountie's but the man had more experience staring down people and Roper thought he'd blink before the Mountie finally relented.

"Tell you what. I've got to check on my horse and finish my business here. That'd give you enough time to arrange things?"

What he meant was that was how much time he'd allow Roper and his silly idea. "It's all I need."

"I'll be back shortly." The Mountie pushed past him, and strode down the street.

Roper wanted to holler at him to take his time but knew the Mountie would do as he chose. Instead, he turned to contemplate the kids and his predicament. All he needed was a convincing argument. But if Cassie got all independent and resisted the idea, what would he do? He needed help from the good Lord and he uttered a silent prayer. "Come on, kids. I think I know just the place for you." As he shepherded them out the door, he prayed some more. If ever he needed God's help—and he had many times in his life—it was now.

Chapter Two

Cassie had heard a wagon stop at the store but she paid it no mind. Her thoughts were on other things.

She pulled out a length of wood and dragged it to the site she'd chosen for the house and laid it alongside the other three she'd put there. She still had no idea how to proceed. Did she build the floor and put the walls on top? Did she make the walls and build the floor inside? How did she put in the windows?

She sat down on the stack of lumber and stared at the four pieces of wood. If she had the money she'd hire someone to do this. Someone who knew what they were doing. Someone who would expect nothing in return but his wages. But she was out of funds. Roper's offer to help flashed across her mind but she dismissed the idea. She did not want to be owing a man for any reason. She bolted to her feet. She'd ask Macpherson what to do, and she'd do it. By herself.

Her mind set, her back stiff, she turned and staggered to a stop as a wagon drew up before her property.

Roper jumped down, leaving a boy on the seat. She thought she glimpsed two or three more kids in the wagon but she must be dreaming. Why would Roper have kids with him? She supposed the boy could be headed out to work at the ranch, though he looked too young to have to earn his way in life. But if Roper took him to the ranch Eddie and Linette would see he was properly treated. He could be a companion for Grady, the four-year-old boy Linette had rescued on her ocean voyage from England.

Roper crossed the grassy property and stopped two feet from her. "See you're about ready to move into your house." His grin mocked her.

"Check back in a week or so and your grin won't be so wide."

He glanced at the lumber on the ground. "Guess you know what you're doing."

What he meant was, *You're lost in the fog.* "I was about to ask advice from Macpherson. Who are those kids?" Three pairs of eyes peered at her over the edge of the wagon and the boy on the seat watched with unusual interest.

Roper removed his hat, scratched his head until his hair looked like a windblown haystack then shoved the hat back on, adjusting it several ways until he was satisfied.

She'd never seen the man at a loss for words. "Roper, what are you up to? You haven't kidnapped them, have you?"

"Nothing like that." He stared at the wagon and the kids, who stared right back.

"Well, what is it like?" She alternated between watching Roper and watching the kids as wariness continued to creep across her neck like a spider.

He faced her so quickly she stepped back, as much from his bleak expression as from being startled. "The kids' mother is dead. They came West hoping to join up with their pa but they just heard he's dead, too."

Cassie's heart dipped low, leaving her slightly dizzy. She remembered what it was like to hear your pa had died, recalled what it felt like to suddenly be homeless.

"I said I would keep them until their uncle sends for them. Or comes for them."

"Roper, how will you look after four children?"

"I will."

She didn't bother pointing out the obvious arguments. "Why are you here?"

He gave her a look rife with possibilities and she didn't like any of them. "I know how to build a house. I could put this up for you in short order."

"We've had this discussion."

He snatched the hat from his head. "Hear me out. What I have in mind is a business proposition." He paused, waiting for her response.

"I'm listening." The word *business* appealed to her. She had every intention of becoming a successful businesswoman.

"I plan to take care of the kids until the Mountie finds their uncle. But I can't do it alone. If you helped I would pay you by building your house." He grinned, as pleased with himself as could be. "I'll stay here, in a tent, as long as it takes me to build it."

She stared at him, turned to study the kids who listened intently. She wanted to help. Not for Roper's sake but because her heart tugged at her. She knew how uncertain the children would be feeling right now. She hoped their uncle would welcome them, unlike her grandfather who had never welcomed Cassie and her mother. He'd made it clear every day how much it cost him, though the way he'd worked Ma she knew he'd gotten a bargain in the arrangement. Cassie didn't want the children to feel as lost as she had felt, but if she went along with Roper's suggestion would he end up thinking he had the right to control her life? She would never give up her dream of being self-sufficient.

The youngest boy sank back in the wagon. "She don't want to help us," he muttered.

The words were slightly different than the ones that had echoed in her head from the time she was nine until she'd run off to marry George, but the ache was the same. The need to be accepted, to feel secure.

Before she could reason past the emotion, she turned to Roper. "It's a deal." She held out her hand, and they shook. He held her hand a moment longer than the shake required, his eyes warm and thankful. She clamped her lips together and tried to deny the feeling that the two of them had stepped across an invisible line and entered strange new territory.

He released her hand and turned to the children. "Come on, kids. You're staying here."

They scrambled from the wagon and edged their way over to face Cassie. She felt their uncertainty like a heat wave.

She wanted to ease that fear. "You'll be safe here as long as you need."

The oldest girl teared up. "Thank you. Thank you."

The oldest boy's expression remained guarded. Cassie knew he wouldn't easily accept words; he'd have to see for himself they were more than empty promises.

Roper introduced them all and at Cassie's request they gave their ages: Daisy, thirteen; Neil, twelve; Billy, six; and Pansy, two.

Cassie quickly assessed them. They seemed weary and afraid but not defeated, especially Daisy who appeared competent in her role as mother, her watchful brown eyes never leaving her siblings.

Neil, too, seemed strong though not yet grown past childhood. His brown hair was in need of a cut, she noted as he stared at Cassie with the same deep brown eyes as Daisy.

The two younger children were both fair-haired, like their older sister, and blue-eyed and clung to their older siblings.

They all shuffled their feet and grew exceedingly quiet as the Mountie crossed from Macpherson's store.

"You kids ready to go?"

Cassie shot Roper a look full of hot accusation. He had neglected to say anything about the NWMP having a claim to these children. What else had he not told her?

"Constable, they'll be staying here with us." Roper included Cassie in his announcement.

The Mountie looked about slowly, taking in the pile of lumber, the tiny sagging tent and likely a whole lot more. His gaze stopped at Cassie. "Are you in agreement with sheltering these children temporarily?"

She nodded, too nervous to speak as he studied her. His look seemed to see a whole lot more than the tight smile she gave him.

His gaze again went to the tent.

Roper stepped forward. "I guarantee they'll be as safe and dry as any kids setting out with their folks in a wagon."

He might as well have said things would be a little rough.

The Mountie didn't answer for several minutes then shook his head. "This is most unusual. Two unmarried people caring for a family. However, I've had reports about a group of Indians stirring up trouble and I need to check on them before I head back to the fort. Should be gone a few days. I'll leave the children in your care until then. When I get back, I'll make my decision." He donned his Stetson to indicate the interview was over and headed back to the store.

Tension filled the air after he left. Cassie searched for something to ease the moment, but as she glanced about, the enormity of the situation hit her.

"Where is everyone going to sleep?" She waved her hand toward her tent that grew more bowed with each puff of wind. Obviously that wouldn't be sufficient.

The kids considered the tent. As if the thought of so many inside was too much for it to contemplate, the tent collapsed with a heavy sigh.

Billy giggled. "It got tired and laid down."

For some reason his words tickled his brother and older sister and they pressed their hands to their mouths, trying to contain errant giggles. They failed miserably and stopped trying.

Pansy's eyes widened and she gurgled at their amusement—a sweet pleasing sound that brought a smile to Cassie's mouth.

Their reaction was likely the result of all the emotion of the past few hours, Cassie reasoned. She glanced toward Roper. As he met her gaze, he started to chuckle.

"I don't see what's so funny about the prospect of sleeping out in the open." But there was something infectious about the laughter around her and she could no longer keep a straight face.

They laughed until she was weak in the knees and had wiped tears from her face several times.

As if guided by some silent signal they all grew quiet at once.

"I'll put up a temporary shelter," Roper said. He headed toward the pile of lumber.

Neil sprang after him. "I can help."

"'Preciate that. Let's find something to build half walls with."

"Half walls?" Cassie asked.

"Temporary but solid. I'll get some canvas from Macpherson to cover the top. It will be warm and dry until we get the house done."

Neil grabbed the end of a board that Roper indicated.

Cassie trotted over and reached for a second board.

Roper caught her shoulder and stopped her. "I can handle this."

Did he think he could simply take over? "We need to discuss our arrangement." She edged away from the children so they wouldn't hear the conversation. "I want to be clear this is only while the children are here."

"Cassie, that's all I expect." Something about the way his eyes darkened made her think of retracting her words. But only for a quick second.

"I don't need or want help for my sake."

He lifted his gaze to the sky as if seeking divine help then grinned at her.

She gave his amusement no mind. "I'd pay you if I could."

"You take care of the kids." He tipped his head toward the quartet. Neil had joined the others and they regarded her warily. "I want nothing more."

"Good. So long as you understand completely."

"You've made yourself more than clear. Now about the children…"

"Of course." She had no idea how she could manage until they had some sort of shelter and a stove, but she'd keep her part of the bargain and care for them. She squared her shoulders as she joined them. "When was the last time you ate?"

"We're not hungry," Daisy said but the way Billy's

eyes widened with hope and little Pansy stopped sucking her fingers, Cassie knew Daisy did not speak for the others. "I'll make tea." She headed for the tent to retrieve her stack of dishes. She lifted the canvas and crawled inside, fighting the billows of rough material. A moment later, she backed out with her hands full.

Billy giggled.

"Shh," Daisy warned.

He sobered but the way his lips trembled tickled the inside of Cassie's stomach.

"I feel like a bug crawling out from a hole." She grinned and ran her hands over her hair.

"Pretty big bug." Billy's smile flickered and sputtered to an end as Daisy poked him in the back.

"He doesn't mean anything bad. He just hasn't learned to think before he speaks." Daisy's stare dared him to say anything more.

"Have, too."

Cassie chuckled. Obviously the boy didn't seem inclined to listen to Daisy's warnings, silent or otherwise. To distract him, she said, "Billy, why don't you gather up some firewood?" There was plenty of it lying about. Neil had gone back to helping Roper so she asked Daisy, "Could you help with these things?" She indicated the kettle and the box of supplies.

Daisy jiggled Pansy farther up on her hip and grabbed the kettle.

It was on the tip of Cassie's tongue to suggest that Daisy put her sister down but she wondered if either of them were ready to be separated and decided to leave it be.

It didn't take long to get a fire going and hang the kettle over it. Roper paused from his work to drag logs close.

"Benches," he explained, and she thanked him.

She took the biscuits and jam out of her provisions and when the tea was ready she called Roper and Neil. The other children hovered beside the fire, Pansy still riding Daisy's hip.

Roper hung the hammer over the board walls he had started and squatted to begin a mock fistfight with Neil. "You hungry, boy, or do you want to stay here working?"

"I'm hungry." Neil batted Roper's harmless fists away and tried to jab Roper's stomach.

Roper bounced away on the balls of his feet, still throwing mock punches.

As Neil laughed, the other three watched, their expressions relaxed, the guardedness gone from their posture.

Cassie studied them. Strange how the kids seemed to feel comfortable with Roper. Maybe because he was always laughing and teasing. Didn't he know there were times to be serious? Times to think about the future?

The pair reached the campfire.

"I haven't a cup for everyone until I unpack some boxes." She indicated the crates nearby. In one of them were dishes purchased from Macpherson that she planned to use when she served meals to people passing through in need of a feed and willing to pay for it.

"We'll share," Daisy said and offered a drink to Pansy from her cup. "Neil and Billy can share, too." Her look ordered them to agree without fuss and they nodded.

Cassie dipped her head to hide her smile. Daisy had taken on the role of mother. She didn't have much choice but Cassie wondered how long it would be before the others, especially Neil, decided otherwise. Still smiling she lifted her head and encountered Roper's gaze. He darted a glance at the kids and winked at her.

Winked! Like she was a common trollop he found

on the street. Her cheeks burned. Her heart caught fire. How dare he?

He left his perch by Neil and plopped to the log beside Cassie. "My apologies. I didn't mean to offend you. I meant only to signal that I understood the way you'd read the children." He kept his voice low as the kids shared their drinks. "Neil and Daisy are both strong. So far they work together for the good of all. I hope it continues until their uncle arrives."

Cassie stumbled over her thoughts. She'd misread his action and now she was embarrassed and uncertain how to undo it. Best to simply face it honestly and move on. "Apology accepted and please accept my own regrets for being so quick to jump to offense."

He nodded but the air between them remained heavy with awkwardness.

"Those biscuits for eating?" Billy asked, eyeing the plate of biscuits and jam.

"Billy." Daisy grabbed his arm. "Mind your manners."

Neil watched Cassie with a look of uncertainty that made her forget any lingering embarrassment. How well she understood that look. Even more, she knew the fluttering in the pit of one's stomach that accompanied it. She wanted more than anything to put a stop to the kids feeling that way—and equally as much to lose the memory of that sensation.

"Billy, you're right. I've forgotten my manners as the hostess. Thank you for reminding me." She grabbed the plate and handed it around. "Take two," she insisted. She stopped in front of Neil. "We don't know each other and you might not be here long enough that we ever do but while you are here, you are safe. I expect each of you to be cooperative and polite but I'm not about to change my mind when you slip up. I won't kick you to the curb." She chuckled softly and glanced toward Macpherson's store. "Guess it might be a little hard seeing as there isn't even a street let alone a curb." She returned her gaze to Neil. "What I'm trying to say is you can trust me."

Neil held her gaze for a heartbeat then took two biscuits. "Thank you."

She didn't expect to win his approval overnight but it was a start. She held the plate and the remaining biscuits out to Roper.

He shook his head. "Give them to the kids. I'll go out early tomorrow and rustle up some more food."

Seems she would be depending on him far more than she cared to. Her whole goal had been to be free of obligation and debt. She ached to say it again but not while the children were listening.

The kids finished their food, handed Cassie their cups and quietly thanked her. They sat on their crude log benches, fingers twitching, their gazes darting about and long sighs escaping their lips.

Their restlessness made her skin tingle. "Go ahead and play while we have some more tea." She refilled Roper's cup and they watched as the kids hurried away to the other side of the walls Roper had constructed. As soon as they were out of sight, tension grabbed Cassie's muscles. This was a far cry from what she'd planned. Her agreement to work with him felt like a walk back into the very thing she meant to escape. "How long do you think it will take to contact the uncle?"

"I wouldn't venture a guess. Why? You already wishing I was gone?"

"You make me sound rude and ungrateful. I'm not. I just have plans. Goals. Don't you?"

He stared off in the distance for a moment, his expression uncharacteristically serious. Then he flashed her a teasing grin. "Now that you mention it, I guess I don't. Apart from making sure the kids are safe."

"I find that hard to believe. Don't you want to get your own ranch?"

He shrugged, his smile never faltering. "Don't mind being free to go where I want, work for the man I wish to work for."

She wanted him to admit to more than that. "Wouldn't you like to have a family of your own?"

The corners of his eyes flattened. The only sign that he wasn't still amused. "I never think of family."

She puffed out a sigh. "Family can be a pain."

He shrugged again. "Wouldn't know. Never had any except for the other kids in the orphanage." He laughed. "An odd sort of family, I guess. No roots. Changing with the seasons."

She didn't answer. Her grandfather had made the word *family* uncomfortable for her but that was different than what Roper meant. She didn't know how to respond to his description of family. With no response coming to her mind, she shifted back to her concern. "Roper, about our arrangement. I—"

He chuckled. "I know what you're going to say but this isn't about you or me. It's about the kids."

"So long as you remember that."

"I aim to. I got rules you know. Like never stay where you're not wanted. Don't put down roots you'll likely have ripped out."

She guessed there was a story behind his last statement. Likely something he'd learned by bitter experience but she didn't bother to ask. "I plan to put down roots right here." She jabbed her finger toward the ground.

"That's the difference between you and me." The

grin remained on his lips but she noticed it didn't reach his eyes.

She studied him. "I'm guessing taking care of other people's business is another of your rules."

He laughed out loud at that. "Seems I got more rules than I realized."

Whispers and giggles came from behind the wooden walls. "Do you think they'll be okay?"

"You did good in telling them they'll be safe here." His grin seemed to be both approving and teasing.

How did he do that? Never quite serious. Always positive. Certainly different than how her grandfather had been. Thinking of the older man, she shifted her concern to the children. "They will be safe as much as it lies within me to make it so." And they'd never be made to feel like they were burdens. Not if she had anything to do with it.

"Good to know." He eased to his feet. "Watch this." He tiptoed to the half walls, glancing back at her with a wide grin. He held his finger to his mouth to signal her to silence then he edged around the corner and jumped into the children's view, yelling wildly.

Pansy screamed, Daisy gasped loudly enough for Cassie to hear her, and then started to laugh. Neil let out a yell. At the same time Billy hollered and ran diagonally across the lot.

Next thing she knew, Roper was tearing after Billy. "I'm going to catch you."

Billy looked over his shoulder, saw Roper bearing down on him and ran so fast his short legs could have churned butter. Not far behind Roper, Neil joined the pursuit.

Cassie jumped to her feet. What were they doing? Had Billy done something to annoy Roper? Was Neil trying to protect his brother? Aiming to protect the kids, she picked up her skirts and ran toward them.

Roper caught Billy and lifted him into the air. "Gotcha." He plopped the boy on the ground, knelt over him and tickled him.

Cassie slowed to a halt. It was only play!

Neil reached them, and threw himself on Roper's back. Roper flipped to his stomach, Neil still clinging to him.

"You got me. Oh. Ow. Let me go."

Both boys piled on him, tickling and play fighting. At least she hoped it was play and by all the laughing she guessed it was. She knew little about play. Seemed her whole life had been work and if not work, then soberness and trying to please. Fun did not fit into either category. Somehow she thought it was that way for all children. Apparently Roper didn't agree.

Daisy joined her, Pansy again riding her hip. "Don't worry. The boys won't hurt him."

"I was worried about the boys."

They looked at each other and laughed. Pansy gave a shy smile from the shelter of Daisy's neck.

Cassie gave the little gal some study, taking in her wondrously big blue eyes that, in a few years, would bring grown men to her beck and call, and her fine blond hair that could use a combing. Suddenly she realized all the children were travel soiled. They would need baths and food and clean clothes and—

The enormity of the task she had taken on hit her like a falling pine. How could she possibly manage?

She sucked in air to relieve her anxiousness. It was a business arrangement that would result in having her house built, she told herself. It would help her achieve her dream. It was temporary and two of the kids were big enough to lend a hand. She could do this. She pushed her shoulders back as if stepping into a harness, and like a horse leaning into a load, she turned toward the fire.

Daisy followed on her heels. "I intend to do my share around here."

"Fine. Let's get the dishes done then heat water for baths."

"I guess we are pretty dirty. Mama would scold us for sure." Her voice quivered.

Cassie faced her. "I expect she would be proud that you've managed so well."

Daisy nodded. "Roper said Ma and Pa would be proud of us."

"Indeed."

She washed the few dishes, handing them to Daisy to dry. Pansy sat at Daisy's side, content to watch. As soon as they'd washed and dried the last cup, Cassie dragged out the big tub.

Roper saw her intent and he and Neil hauled more water from the nearby river.

As the water heated, Roper finished the walls and somehow built a frame for the roof on which to drape the canvas he purchased from Macpherson. With Neil's help he brought over the stove Cassie had ordered and set it up in the new shelter.

Cassie eyed it with joy. She'd be able to start baking bread for Macpherson and paying off her loan a lot sooner than she'd anticipated.

With the kids helping, Roper soon had Cassie's bed roll in one corner of the shelter, furs and blankets arranged for the children next to her bed. The stove and a crude table he'd put together made an area where she could work and feed the kids.

They dragged the tub under the canvas and filled it with water.

"I'll bathe Pansy," Daisy insisted.

Cassie didn't protest. She hadn't ever bathed a baby. Nor a two-year-old. Her heart clenched as she recalled her hope for babies. Twice she'd thought she'd welcome an infant into her arms but twice it wasn't to be. They had never drawn breath after their births.

She turned away, unable to catch her breath, and slipped outside before anyone noticed.

Roper found her there. "What's wrong?"

"Nothing." She stared toward the sun dipping behind the mountains and breathed slowly, evenly.

He gently touched her shoulder. "Are you regretting your decision?"

"It was an act of God."

His fingers tightened on her shoulder. "Are you talking about the children?"

She closed her eyes and pushed back a groan. Of course, he meant the children in the tent. "No, I don't regret my decision. It will benefit me to get my house up as soon as possible."

"You didn't mean the kids, did you?"

His quiet question, the gentleness in his voice tugged at her soul, made her want to wail out her pain. But she'd learned to hide her hurt, bury her feelings. She didn't know any other way of dealing with life. "I better go check on them."

He blocked her retreat. "I think they can manage quite well without us. Let's go for a walk."

"I'm really too tired."

"I want to show you where I'll set up my camp in case you need me for anything."

She stiffened her spine. "I think I can manage."

He chuckled. "I'm sure you can but this is a business deal, remember? The kids are my responsibility."

Somehow he had taken her elbow and herded her toward the river and a grove of trees.

"I'll take the tent that collapsed on you and pitch it here." He pointed. "If you need me, you have only to holler."

"I won't be hollering."

"I expect not. But I feel better knowing anyone could and I'll hear them."

He meant the kids could call for him. "Why would they need you when I'll be right there in the same tent or whatever you want to call it?"

"No reason. Just as there's no reason to get all prickly about it."

"Prickly?" She swallowed hard. "If I am it's because you make me sound like I can't manage on my own."

He held up his hands in a sign of protest. "It never crossed my mind."

"Well, then. So long as we understand each other." She headed back to her site.

He chuckled softly, and followed her. "Oh, I get it."

She ignored the note of triumph in his voice. How could he possibly comprehend? He had no idea of the events that had shaped her life and made her want nothing half as much as she wanted to be independent. Self-sufficient. "I don't need anyone," she muttered.

"Sounds mighty lonely to me."

"You can be lonely with people around." Thankfully they had reached camp and he didn't get a chance to respond.

The sound of giggling stopped them, and they listened.

"That's about the happiest sound in the world." Roper seemed pleased, content even.

"How can they be happy? Their parents are dead. They're orphans." Their lives were full of uncertainty.

"A person can be as happy as they make up their mind to be."

She'd heard the words before. "Linette said the same thing when we first arrived at the ranch." She didn't believe it was that simple any more now than she had then. People made demands of a person that made happiness impossible. It was why she intended to survive on her own.

"I figure you might as well choose to be happy as miserable."

She heard the shrug in his voice. "Sometimes it isn't up to you."

"I suppose you're right in the sense that our lives are in God's hands and ultimately we have to trust Him. But knowing that makes it easy to enjoy life, don't you think?"

Grateful for the dusk that hid her expression, Cassie murmured a sound that could be taken as agreement if he chose to interpret it as such. But inside, protests exploded. Didn't God let man have a choice? Because of free will, not all men lived by God's rules. Not all people were kind. Not all of life could be enjoyed.

She realized Roper was waiting for her answer. "Sometimes you have to work to get what you want from life. I trust God to help me achieve my goals." Saying it out loud solidified it in her mind. God had given her the opportunity to own a plot of land and now, by caring for the children, she would get her house built much faster, and no doubt better, than she could have done it. God had given her what she needed. She would apply all her skill and strength to making it work. "Now if you'll excuse me, I need to take care of my share of the responsibility."

"And I need to get my camp set up while I can still see." Still, he hesitated as if he wanted something more.

She searched her mind but could think of nothing more she needed to do. "Good night, then."

"Good night. Call out if you need anything." He turned and strolled away.

She watched until he dipped down toward the creek, out of sight. Yet she felt how close he was, how ready to come to her rescue.

He would soon learn she could manage on her own.

Chapter Three

Roper tethered the horse nearby then pitched the tent. When he finished, it had a nice taut roof line. He gathered up firewood and built a fire.

He stretched out on the bank, stared at the flickering flames and listened to the murmur of voices from up the hill. Everyone was secure and happy. He'd managed to deal with two issues at the same time. He could help Cassie put up her house and keep the kids safe and together.

More than that, he'd played with the boys and seen them relax. Now to do the same for the girls. Daisy took her responsibilities so seriously it might take her a while to let go. But Pansy could well prove the greatest challenge of them all. She was so young. So shy. He smiled up at the star-laden sky as he recalled how she ducked her face into Daisy's shoulder when she made eye contact. She was comfortable enough to laugh only when Neil or Daisy held her.

But Roper wanted to see her comfortable enough to let Cassie and himself hold her and play with her.

All he had to do was gain her confidence.

He also meant to get Cassie to stop trying so hard.

What was she aiming to prove, anyway? Everyone knew she could do whatever she set her mind to. She was like a stubborn badger in that way.

He'd once watched a furry little badger digging a hole, dirt flying faster than a man could shovel. The badger encountered a rock in his path and simply dug around it.

Cassie was almost as belligerent as a badger, too.

Why didn't she accept life and enjoy it? Made no sense to fight it all the time.

He smiled as he thought how to deal with the quintet up the hill. In the morning he'd spend some time playing with them so they'd forget their troubles.

His breath eased out in a long contented sigh. He'd struck a great bargain in getting Cassie to agree to help him with the children in exchange for him putting up her house. He chuckled into the dark. What had she planned to do with that pile of lumber without his help? He could picture her fashioning a structure as shaky as the tent she'd put up.

Why was she so prickly about accepting help? He could build a good solid-frame house in a matter of days.

Mentally he planned the construction. He might have to drag it out longer than necessary in order to care for the young 'uns until their uncle made arrangements. But Cassie would know if he purposely dillydallied. He'd need a solid explanation she'd accept.

He sat up briskly and drew his knees to his chest. "Of course. That's the answer." She'd need a cellar to store her supplies in. It would take him a few days to dig one. Satisfied with his plan, he lay back again.

The sounds from up the hill subsided. Everyone was tucked in for the night. He kicked sand over the fire and went into the shelter of his tent. But he didn't immediately fall asleep as he normally would. Instead, he thanked God for the opportunity to take care of both Cassie and the youngsters.

Next morning Roper was up with the dawn and bagged four partridges. He dressed them and roasted them over his fire. By the time he heard Pansy's shrill voice, the birds were ready for breakfast and he marched up the hill.

Neil and Billy were outside, bleary-eyed in the morning sun.

"Morning, boys. I brought some breakfast in case anyone's hungry."

Both pairs of eyes immediately lost all sleepiness.

"I'm hungry," Billy said.

"Never mind him. He's always hungry." But Neil's gaze didn't waver from studying the roasted birds.

Daisy led Pansy from the tiny abode. As soon as the little one saw Roper, she lifted her hands to her sister and insisted on being carried.

What would it take to get the littlest one to warm up to him? At that moment, Cassie stepped out, head down as she fingered her hair into submission in a ragged bun. Her distraction allowed him plenty of time to study her. Her black hair glistened like sun off water. She had a leanness to her that once made him think her frail. She'd soon disabused him of that notion. She was about as frail as a sapling clinging tenaciously to the side of a mountain in the midst of winter storms and summer heat. His heart sunk to the bottom of his chest. He'd had little success getting her to warm up to him.

Cassie grew still and sniffed, catching the scent of his offering. She lifted her gaze—full of interest until she saw him. Then the interest faded to resistance.

Must she always be so prickly?

"Brought breakfast," he murmured before she could say anything.

She opened her mouth, glanced around at the expectant children and closed it again as if she needed to reconsider her reaction. "I expect the children are hungry. I've got a few more biscuits, as well." She ducked back inside and reemerged with a pan to put the birds in and tin plates for everyone. "I dug out the dishes from my supplies." She passed around plates for each.

"Guess I'll need to build us a table and benches." He slipped the birds from the spit as he talked and wiped his knife on his pant leg before he set to carving them.

The children watched in total fascination. Even little Pansy, although she kept her face pressed to Daisy's shoulder, watched his knife slice off portions, drool wetting her sister's dress. Seems it had been a few days since this bunch had had a good feed. He put a piece on each plate and Cassie added a biscuit. The youngsters perched on logs but no one took a bite.

Roper sent Cassie a questioning look. She shrugged. Then her mouth pursed as if she realized something. "I expect you're all waiting for someone to say grace."

Four heads nodded.

"Ma said we should never forget to thank the good Lord for His mercies," Daisy said.

"I sure am thankful for breakfast," Billy said. "It smells awfully good." He swallowed hard.

Roper blinked as every pair of eyes turned to him. "Me?"

"You're the man," Neil pointed out. "Ma said it was a man's job to lead the family. I said grace when Pa was away." His chest swelled with pride then sank again. "But I'm just a kid."

The expectation of these youngsters made Roper

want to stand tall. Yes, he was a man. One who seldom thought to say grace when he was out on the trail and this wasn't much different. Not that he couldn't. But at the cook shack, Cookie or her husband, Bertie, said grace. It had been a long time since he'd spoken a prayer aloud. In fact—

"I could do it if you want I should," Neil offered in an uncertain voice.

"No, I'll do it."

The children reached for each other's hands. Billy reached for his hand on one side. That left Roper with one hand to extend toward Cassie. He hesitated. Would she refuse this gesture?

Daisy gave them both a look that was half scolding and half confused.

He reached for Cassie's hand and she slipped hers into his as she darted a look at him from under black eyelashes. One eyebrow quirked as if daring him to read more into this than he should.

A grin threatened to split his face.

She sighed, and nodded toward the cooling food.

Still smiling, he bowed his head. Suddenly his mind went blank. What did Bertie or Cookie say? He should be able to remember. Cookie, especially, bellowed the words loud enough to brand them on his brain. "Dear God. Thanks for the food. Thanks for health and strength." Cookie normally said more. Sometimes a whole lot more but he must have paid more attention to the aroma of the food waiting his attention than the words because they had disappeared. "Amen."

The children attacked their food.

He didn't realize he held Cassie's hand in a deadly grip until she jerked his arm to get his attention. With an unrepentant grin, he freed her. He held her gaze for several seconds before she huffed and turned to her food. He got a kick out of teasing her.

A few minutes later the children finished and stared at the slower adults.

He felt their unasked question. "What?"

Neil and Daisy exchanged a silent look that spoke volumes.

"Spit it out." He swallowed the last bit of biscuit and put his plate on the ground before him. "You might as well say what's on your mind. After all, we're going to be together for a time." He figured it would a few days for the Mountie to take care of his business. He hoped he could then persuade the man to leave the children with them while he contacted the uncle. Daisy nodded. "Ma made us promise we'd make sure the little ones are raised right and that we continue some of our practices that both Ma and Pa held as important."

He guessed Daisy was going someplace with this information but he had no idea where and turned his questioning gaze to Cassie, wondering if she got the drift, but she merely shrugged.

"What practice did you have in mind, Daisy?"

Daisy glanced at Neil who nodded encouragement.

She took a deep breath. "Ma, and Pa before he left, always read to us from the Bible after breakfast. And they prayed for us to have a good day and be safe. You could be like Pa."

Roper stared. He guessed he looked as surprised as he felt. Being raised in an orphanage, he had no knowledge of this kind of thing. Of course, he knew families had traditions but he thought that meant trimming the Christmas tree or going to Grandma and Grandpa's house for Sunday dinner.

He swallowed hard and clamped his lips together. The idea of playing pa to these youngsters…

It sounded mighty appealing but he had no idea how it was done.

He managed to find his voice. "I got no Bible."

Daisy turned to Cassie. "Do you?"

She nodded. "I'll get it." She hustled to the shelter, and disappeared from sight. They all stared after her.

Roper had to wonder if the children felt as awkward as he. But likely not. This was familiar to them.

Cassie returned and handed him a Bible bound in brown leather. He trailed his fingers over the soft cover.

"It was my husband's."

He lifted his head to meet her gaze. He knew she'd been married before. Their first introduction referred to her as a widow. Yet holding this solid proof of a lost love did something unsettling to his insides. "You sure you don't mind us using it?"

She shrugged. "It doesn't do much good tucked in the bottom of a bag, now does it? Besides, the children have made a request. Shouldn't you try and fulfill it?"

He opened to the first page. *Presented to George James Godfrey on the occasion of his sixteenth birthday by his loving parents.*

Swallowing a lump of guilt, feeling as if he had inadvertently ventured into private territory, he quickly turned the page. *This certifies that Cassie Ann Muddbottom and George James Godfrey were united in Holy Matrimony.* He sputtered back a snort of laughter. *Muddbottom.* Some of his mirth leaked out. He felt Cassie's considering look and flipped the page. *Births and deaths.* He should not read this. It was too personal. But his eyes did not obey his brain. *Baby boy Godfrey. Baby girl Godfrey.* She'd had two children? Where were they? The answer lay in the record before him. They were born and died the same day. *Oh, Cassie. I had no idea.* If they'd been alone he would have spoken his sympathy. Maybe even risked her ire by pulling her into his arms and patting her back.

Instead, he sucked in a gulp of air and continued turning pages till he got to the pertinent stuff. He cleared his throat and read, "'In the beginning God…'" He read to the end of the chapter then slowly closed the book.

The children sighed as if content. The feeling lasted about thirty seconds before he realized they waited for him to pray for their safety throughout the day. Just as their pa had.

He sat up taller and squared his shoulders. He wasn't their pa, but he could do this. "Let's pray." They all bowed their heads. Even Cassie. His throat tightened as he glanced at them. Maybe this was how fathers felt, though he wasn't sure how to describe the feeling. Protectiveness, or responsibility or… He swallowed back a lump at the word that sprang to his mind. Joy. Joy at such a privilege. It was his first real taste of being part of a family and he rather liked it. Even as a portion of his brain reminded him of one of his rules. *Don't put down roots. You'll only have them ripped out.* It wasn't a lesson he cared to repeat.

He ducked his head before anyone wondered what took him so long. "Dear God in heaven, who made the earth and everything in it, please watch over us today. Keep us safe. Help us be happy. Amen."

Daisy got to her feet, shifted Pansy farther up her hip and gathered up the dishes with her free hand. "I'll wash them."

Neil headed for the water bucket. "I'll fetch more water."

Billy glanced about. "What should I do?"

"Get more firewood," both older children said at once and the entire family set to work.

Roper fingered the Bible on his lap. He wanted to say something to Cassie about her losses. But he didn't want to upset her. Seemed being reminded of two dead babies and a deceased husband just might do that. But he enjoyed sitting by her side and didn't want her to leave. "Do all families do that?"

She jerked and seemed to gather herself up from some distant spot. "Do what?"

"Read the Bible and pray each morning. Is that what all families do?"

She turned then and considered him with such brown-eyed intensity he had to force himself not to squirm.

"I'm guessing they didn't do so in the orphanage?"

"Nope. We stood for grace. Ate quietly and without complaint even when the food was thin gruel, then gathered our dishes and carried them to a big tub before we marched to our classrooms."

"No Bible instruction?"

He chuckled at the idea of wasting time on such an activity. "On Sunday we were given religious instruction. When I was about ten there was a sweet old man who came in and told Bible stories and made it seem like fun. A lot of us became believers when he was there. But he only came a couple of years. The rest of the time we had stiff preachers who intoned a sermon for us." He realized his voice imitated their mind-numbing monotone and he grunted. "Haven't thought about it in a long time. I remember the sessions were so boring some of the little ones would fall asleep. If they were caught they'd be punished. I made sure they didn't get caught."

Her eyes sparked with curiosity and a warmth that sent

satisfaction into his soul. He liked having her regard him with eyes like that.

"What did you do?"

"To keep them from getting caught? If we were allowed to sit where we wanted, I sat with the little ones and played finger games that didn't attract any attention but kept the little ones watching." He illustrated by having the fingers of one hand do a jig on the back of the other. "It was nothing special but they had to keep alert to see when I'd do something."

"And if you couldn't sit with them?"

"Then it was harder. But one of the things I did was send a tap down the line. Everyone would pass it on to the little ones."

"Seems you felt responsible for the younger children."

He considered the observation. "It wasn't really responsibility. Not like Daisy. It was more like I wanted everyone to be happy."

Her grin tipped the flesh at the corner of her eyes upward. "I think you haven't changed a great deal."

He tried to think how he felt about her evaluation. He decided it was true and he didn't mind that she'd noticed something he did without thinking about it. "Back to my original question." He tipped his head to indicate the circle where the children had sat. "Is it normal? You have a family. Is that what you did?"

Her eyes darkened. The smile fled from her face. What had he said to bring such distress to her face? Whatever it was, it had been unintentional.

But how could he undo it when he was at a loss to explain it?

The ground beneath Cassie's feet seemed to tip as a thousand memories crowded her mind. "My father died when I was nine so I don't recall much about being a whole family." Except she suddenly did. "I remember sitting on my father's knee as he read aloud. We were in a rocking chair. A lamp glowed nearby so it must have been evening. Mother was in the kitchen so it was just me and…" She stopped the words that had come from nowhere. Just her and those comforting, secure arms. "Just me and my father." The memory ached through her. She concentrated on breathing slowly and deeply. She forced strength into her voice. "Seems I recall my father reading to me at night. He heard my prayers before Mother tucked me in and kissed me good night."

"Didn't you keep doing the same things after he was gone? I guess I would…both to honor him and preserve the memory."

"Things changed after he died." Her grandfather didn't allow such extravagances. *The child is big enough to put herself to bed. I'm not supporting you to spend time coddling her.* She pushed to her feet. "I better get to work." She went to join Daisy at the dishpan. "I'll dry," she said to the girl.

Roper strode away in the direction of Macpherson's store. She wouldn't watch him go. Nor voice any curiosity about why. But hadn't he said he'd build her house? Shouldn't he be doing so? He liked to make everyone happy, did he? She sensed it was more than that. Seems he had a need to make sure people were well taken care of. Well, she silently huffed, she had no need of his help. She'd learned to depend on no one. She had all she needed right here on this little bit of land. She glanced about at the piles of lumber, the neat little shelter Roper had erected. Yes, she'd accept his help in exchange for providing care for the children. But she'd never make the mistake of expecting it nor of counting on it.

Daisy persuaded Pansy to sit on a log at her side as she dried the dishes. "I want to thank you for allowing us to stay here and I promise we'll do our best not to be any trouble."

Children are nothing but trouble. The words reverberated through her head in her grandfather's harsh voice. How could such a coldhearted man raise a son who turned out to be a loving father? Why had the better of the two died? Seemed bitterly unfair in her mind.

She hated that these children should feel the same condemning words hovering in the background and vowed she would not do or say anything to make them real. She dried her hands on the towel and turned to Daisy. With her still-damp hands, she clasped the girl's shoulders and turned her so they were face-to-face. "I don't consider you the least bit of trouble. In fact, it would be mighty lonely if I were here by myself." Yet that was exactly what she intended once the children were gone. "Besides, isn't it to my benefit? I get help to build my house."

Daisy considered her steadily, then, satisfied with Cassie's assurance, nodded. "Still. I wouldn't want you to regret it."

"I promise I won't." As she returned to her task a flash drew her attention to the side. Roper stood with two spades over his shoulder, so new and shiny the sun reflected off them. He stared as if he'd overheard the conversation. She favored him with a challenging glare, silently informing him not to read anything into her confession of loneliness. It was meant to reassure the children, not give him an argument to pursue.

"What's with the shovels?" Far as she could figure he needed to wield hammer and saw, not shovels.

He moved closer so she saw the green glints in his

eyes. "Got to thinking. Didn't you say you plan to bake bread for the store?"

She nodded even though he knew the answer.

"And feed travelers?"

She didn't bother to nod again.

"Seems you might be needing a cellar. You know. To keep things cool in the summer and stop your canned goods from freezing in the winter. So me and Neil are gonna dig you one."

No way could she hide her surprise and she knew he read it on her face by the way he grinned in satisfaction. He held her gaze for several seconds.

She tried to tell herself she didn't notice the way his eyes flashed pleasure at coming up with an idea that seemed to please her. Tried to convince herself he was only doing what he always did—making sure people were happy. But try as she might she couldn't deny a little start of something both sweet and reluctant. It was sweet to have someone appear to care about what might please her. But she dare not let herself think past that. A woman in her situation could do no better than maintain her independence.

Still grinning, Roper called Neil and handed him a shovel. Together they marched to where she'd marked the boundaries of her house and began to dig.

An hour later they'd made little progress.

She began to suspect digging a cellar hole would consume an inordinate length of time.

Had that been his reason for suggesting it? Not concern for her at all but only an excuse to hang around and do for her what she preferred to do for herself?

He'd always balked at her independence.

She glanced about at the children. Daisy brushed Pansy's hair and talked softly to her. Neil worked alongside Roper trying his best to dig at the same pace as Roper, which was impossible yet Roper told the boy how well he was doing. Billy carried the dirt to the designated area. How could she tell Roper she suspected him of delay tactics?

She didn't need or want him trying to take care of her.

Chapter Four

As Roper and Neil dug, Cassie turned her attention to other things. First, she had to prepare meals for the children and Roper. With the stove set up in the little shelter, she could bake, using this time to her advantage to start paying off her debt at Macpherson's. She mixed up a hearty stew of meat and vegetables and as it simmered, she cut lard into flour for biscuits. By noon, she had several dozen baked and cooling.

"This place is steaming hot."

She turned at Roper's voice behind her and brushed a strand of hair from her burning face. "I'm baking."

"Both yourself and biscuits, I presume."

She grinned at his teasing.

"You need a breeze going through here." He ducked outside and made a racket on the wall. Then the canvas rolled up and blessed cool air blew through the shack. Roper peered through the opening. "I can roll it down at night."

"Oh, that feels good." She fanned herself. "I didn't realize how hot it was."

He came in again and eyed the biscuits covering the table. "You've been busy."

"Dinner is ready." She reached for the pot then realized she had no place to put it.

Roper grabbed a towel and took the pot. "Come see what I made."

She wrapped a selection of biscuits in a towel and followed him outside. "A picnic table. Perfect. Now we can eat outdoors in comfort."

He set the stew in the middle of the table. "I thought you could use it for feeding travelers, too."

"Thank you, but—" Oh, dear. How were they going to manage working together if he constantly took care of her when she was determined to take care of herself?

Though, on her own, it would take a little longer to build a house and get herself organized. Macpherson understood she'd take time to get established.

"Just part of the business deal." His dismissive tone warned her not to make a fuss about it.

She stifled a sigh. She might as well take advantage of all this arrangement offered. So she tucked away her resistance as Daisy passed around the plates and cups.

Cassie waited for the children to sit, then chose a place that wouldn't put her near Roper. She didn't want to be forced to hold his hand again during prayer. But as soon as she was seated, Neil and Billy slid down on the bench opposite her and made room for Roper to edge in and sit directly across from her, an unrepentant grin on his face. He'd correctly read her attempt to avoid him.

She barely restrained herself from wrinkling her nose at him but let him guess at the silent message in her eyes. *Don't think I've changed my mind about wanting to keep this businesslike.*

He winked, and when he saw her draw her eyebrows together in affront, he sighed. "Cassie, don't be looking for offense when none is meant."

She forced a smile to her lips but figured it looked as wooden as it felt.

Roper wagged his head in mock frustration. "Cassie, Cassie, what am I going to do with you?"

She tipped her chin. "You could try saying the blessing so we could eat before the ants find us."

The children giggled.

Roper chuckled. "Very well." He eagerly reached for her hand, giving her a look that said he enjoyed her discomfort. Then he bowed his head and uttered a few words. "Amen."

When she jerked her hand free, his eyes practically glittered with triumph. Oh, bother. By overreacting to an innocent, meaningless touch of hands, she'd given him reason to think it meant more than it did when she only wanted to remind him this was a business deal.

They ate in companionable silence except for Pansy who fretted.

Daisy hushed her. "She needs a nap."

"Finish your meal, then put her down," Roper said.

"And the dishes?"

Goodness, the child had an overblown sense of responsibility. Cassie patted her hand. "I can manage a few dishes."

Daisy nodded gratefully, scooped up her little sister and disappeared inside the shack. For a few minutes Daisy's gentle murmurs blended with Pansy's fussing, and then all was silent.

Roper helped Cassie clean up the table. "Daisy reminds me of you," he said.

"How's that?" She filled a basin with hot water, and began to wash the dishes. She scrubbed the plates and Roper dried them.

"She feels she has to do everything herself."

"Independence is good, especially when she has no one else." Seems that should have been self-evident even to a man like Roper, determined to help everyone he met.

"But is that true?"

"Her father and mother are dead. Who knows what her uncle will decide about their future? Seems the best thing they can do is learn how to manage on their own, expect nothing from anyone else."

"What about people who want to help?"

She couldn't tell if it was hurt or warning that made his voice so low and decided it was safest to assume the latter. "I suppose she has reason to wonder what other people want in return."

"I don't want anything but to help. What do you want?"

Maybe she'd been talking more about herself than the children. "I expect nothing from them. I hope they understand that."

"Your words are contradictory."

"Maybe so. But it seems best to count on no one but yourself." She had to change the direction of this conversation before she said more than she meant to…things she hadn't even reasoned out yet. "How long do you think it will take to dig the cellar?"

He shrugged, his gaze lingering on her as he understood her attempt to avoid explaining herself. "Depends on how hard the ground is. And I don't want to overwork young Neil. He's determined to match me shovelful for shovelful. Besides, I don't want him to think the only thing I want from him is work. In fact, I've decided to take a break for some play." He paused. "If you have no objection."

"Of course I don't." Did he think all she cared about was work? "The children should certainly be allowed a little fun."

Maybe he was right. She seemed to know little about how to play.

"You'll join us, won't you?" Had he read her mind and determined to teach her?

"I have biscuits to deliver to Macpherson's."

"You might wake Pansy if you go into the shack."

Cassie scrambled to find an excuse to avoid joining Roper and the children. Before she could, Roper waved to the boys.

"Who wants to play a game?"

Neil and Billy perked up and raced toward him. Daisy slipped from the shack and hesitated.

"You, too." Roper waved to her. "Everyone's going to play." He shot Cassie a challenging look. "Play refreshes the soul."

Cassie swallowed hard.

"Come on. We'll go down by the river so we don't wake Pansy."

The boys ran after him, while Daisy followed more slowly, cautiously, as if uncertain she should let herself play.

It was Daisy's hesitation that convinced Cassie to join the parade. Daisy was still young enough to enjoy a game or two. She shouldn't let her responsibilities take away that pleasure. So Cassie linked arms with Daisy. "Let's see what he's up to." She could feel the girl relax beneath her touch.

Roper glanced over his shoulder and grinned.

Cassie knew he'd heard her and, furthermore, she guessed he might have some inkling as to her motive. Though she felt a strong urge to wrinkle her nose at him, she hoped the toss of her head convinced him of her lack of concern for his opinion.

Roper waited until they all reached the bank of the river. "Who knows how to play Sneak Up on Granny?"

No one said they did.

"I'll be granny. You line up there." He drew a line in the sand. "I'll stand here." He went about twenty feet away. "When I turn my back, you try and sneak up on me. When I shout 'stop,' don't move because when I turn around and see you moving, you go back to the start."

"What's the point of the game?" Cassie refrained from saying it sounded silly because she recognized the voice in the back of her head as that of her grandfather. *Waste of precious time.* For that reason alone she would play the game and waste as much time as she pleased.

"If you can sneak up on me and touch my shoulder without me catching you moving, you get to play granny."

Cassie snorted. "Great. I've always had a hankering to play granny." She drew her lips in, hunkered over like an old woman and smacked her gums loudly.

The three children giggled and Cassie knew a sense of satisfaction. Was this how Roper felt when he made others happy? She shot him a look, wondering if her surprise showed.

Their gazes caught and held, and the look of triumph in his eyes seared away something she couldn't identify. Didn't want to acknowledge. All she would admit was it felt good and right to make the children laugh. It seemed fitting to see them enjoy life.

She would not listen to the strident voice of her grandfather telling her to stop wasting time.

The children toed up to the line he'd scratched in the ground. She did the same as Roper took his place ahead of them.

"One, two, three." He counted, turning his back.

Neil raced forward. Billy took a giant leap. Daisy tiptoed.

Cassie took one cautious step, and then another.

"Stop."

Neil skidded but not in time. Billy was in midair and landed with a thud.

Roper chuckled. "Boys. Back to the start."

Daisy and Cassie grinned at each other. He hadn't caught them.

"One, two, three." He turned away again.

Billy and Neil tried to make up for lost time but Cassie edged forward, knowing she must be ready to stop quickly.

"Stop."

Again the two boys were sent back to the start amid groans.

Roper gave Cassie and Daisy a long stare as if daring them to waver. Neither of them did.

They continued. Cassie was within two feet but Roper called stop so often she daren't move. She tensed. One step was all it would take. As soon as he began to turn away, she leaped forward and reached out to clap his shoulder. At the same time he hollered stop and turned to face her, and they collided.

She staggered, off balance and about to fall, until he caught her, his hands warm on her arms as he steadied her.

She looked deep into his hazel eyes, saw his concern over bumping her. Her heart beat a frantic tattoo against her breastbone. Longing rose up within her, a hunger to be valued and appreciated. To be cared for.

No, she told herself. Such feelings were a weakness she would never allow herself. She'd learned far too well how they made her vulnerable. She shook free from his grasp. "Guess I'm granny now." Surely he wouldn't notice the trembling in her voice.

"Guess so." His voice grated as if his throat had grown tight.

They returned to play although she had little interest. She wasn't a bit sorry when Pansy's cry brought an instant end to their game as Daisy rushed back to get the little one.

The rest trooped after her.

"I'm going to take biscuits over to Macpherson's and see if he can sell them." Cassie headed for the little shack as if she had a sudden deadline.

"Come on, boys. Let's get that cellar dug." Roper sounded as cheerful as ever.

Why had she wasted so much time? It was Roper's fault. Something about him enticed her to forget her responsibilities and goals.

All winter she'd avoided him as much as possible without being rude. Or maybe sometimes, especially at first, she hadn't cared if she happened to be rude. All she could remember of the first few weeks at the ranch was the pain of her losses and despair at how desperate her situation was.

When Linette had found her sleeping in the train station in Montreal she'd cajoled, enticed and begged Cassie to accompany her West on her trek to meet her future husband. Cassie had agreed because it had seemed better than her current situation. Anything would have been better. She didn't know she would end up in a tiny log cabin, barely big enough for one adult let alone three adults and a child. Even worse, Eddie was not expecting to marry Linette and said he had no intention of doing so. Not that Linette was deterred. She said she would prove to him she'd make an ideal pioneer wife.

Cassie smiled. The attraction between Linette and Eddie had been obvious from the first but it had taken the pair most of the winter to acknowledge what the rest of them saw.

She pressed her palm to her chest. She missed Linette. And Grady.

She missed Cookie, too. From the beginning, the big-hearted woman seemed oblivious to Cassie's sharpness and showed her nothing but kindness. Slowly, between Linette and Cookie and the gentle attention of the cowboys at the ranch, Cassie's wounds had healed. She'd gone from thinking she had no choice but to accept whatever kindness and protection a man would offer to knowing she could live life on her own terms.

It wasn't something she meant to give up. She had a life to live. Work to do. A business to establish.

She filled a large bowl with biscuits, covered it with a clean tea towel and headed over to Macpherson's store. A couple of cowboys lounged against the counter as she stepped inside. Within minutes most of the biscuits had been purchased.

Macpherson snagged one of the biscuits for himself and tested it. "These are good. Reminds me of my daughter, Becca. She used to bake the best biscuits. Many a man stepped into the store solely to see if she had any baking on hand."

Cassie couldn't remember much of what she'd heard about Macpherson's daughter. "She moved away, didn't she?"

"Married herself a fine young man, Colt, and adopted two orphaned children. They have themselves a little ranch northwest of here. I expect them to visit this summer."

Cassie chuckled. "You're obviously proud of them."

"A fine bunch." He indicated the crumbs of biscuit on his fingers. "Bring me more of these as soon as you can. You set up to bake bread yet?"

"I'll start today."

Glowing with satisfaction she returned to her place. Oh, didn't that sound good! *Her place.* A business about to take off. A house soon to be constructed, thanks to Roper's help.

She ground to a halt at the corner of the shack and watched Roper digging her cellar. Her house. Her cellar. Her land. It seemed Roper was contributing far more to this arrangement than she. What would she owe him? Nervousness quivered in the pit of her stomach. She didn't like to owe anyone. She sucked in air to calm the fluttering, and reminded herself that it was a business agreement. So he could help the children.

Or was it an excuse so he could take care of her?

He glanced up, saw her watching and slowly straightened.

Her eyes must have given away her doubt and confusion for he climbed from the hole and strode toward her.

She shook her head to clear it, and ducked into the shack where she made a great deal of noise pulling out a bowl so she could set the yeast to rise.

"Cassie? Something wrong?" His voice came from the doorway.

"The biscuits sold like hotcakes. Macpherson was very pleased. Asked if I could start providing bread." No doubt she sounded falsely cheerful.

It took only three steps for him to close the distance between them. "That's good news. So why do you look so troubled?"

She could deny it, tell him he must be imagining things. But her doubts had a tenacious grip on her thoughts. She straightened and slowly faced him. "Why are you doing this?"

He looked around, not knowing what she meant and searching for a clue. "Doing what?"

She waved her hand around the little shack, then pointed to indicate the activity beyond the canvas walls. "Everything. Why are you digging a cellar? Offering to build my house? What do you expect in return?"

He stepped back and his eyebrows knotted. "Cassie Godfrey, you are one suspicious woman. I told you what I want—to help the children. I grew up in an orphanage. Never knew anything about family. I saw kids ripped from their siblings. Do you think I could stand back and let that happen to these youngsters when I could do something to prevent it?" His voice had grown harsh. "I'm more than willing to dig your cellar and build your house if it enables me to help them. I thought you understood that."

She sighed. "Family isn't the ideal dream you seem to think it is."

"And yet I doubt it's the curse you seem to consider it." He swung about and strode from the shack.

She stared after him. Was that what she thought?

Her earliest memories had been pleasant enough but then… She shook her head. She didn't know what she thought. Except that she intended to have a batch of bread ready to deliver tomorrow.

She set to work, pausing only to make supper and hurrying through the meal so she could return to her baking, though, if she admitted the truth to herself, she wasn't half as busy as she acted.

She simply did not want to face Roper any more than she must and feel guilty about his accusing looks. No.

She'd keep busy running her business and she'd not allow anything to divert her from her purpose.

As soon as breakfast was over the next morning, Roper headed for the cellar hole, his insides burning with frustration. Prickly Cassie, always seeing ulterior motives. She'd avoided him last evening. He'd hoped for a change in her behavior at breakfast but she'd slid her glance over him as if he were invisible.

"I hope my bread turns out," she murmured as if nothing else mattered.

Before he reached the cellar, he veered off toward the river. In his present frame of mind he wasn't decent company for a young lad. He grabbed his rifle. They could always use fresh meat. On second thought…

He hitched the horse to the wagon.

Neil appeared at his side. "Whatcha doing?"

"Need to take the wagon back to the ranch and get my saddle horse." Eddie had told him to help Cassie if she'd let him so he wouldn't have been concerned when Roper didn't immediately return.

"You coming back?"

At the sound of fear and uncertainty in the boy's voice, Roper's anger fled. "I'm not about to ride out on you." He clamped his hand to Neil's shoulder. "I said I was going to build Cassie's house and I will. I said I would look after you until your uncle came and I will. Never doubt it. But I need a saddle horse to hunt meat for us."

Neil nodded.

Billy and the girls watched him from the trees. "I'll be back. Take care of yourselves and help Cassie." He spoke out of his own heart's desire. He wanted to take care of them all…but Cassie didn't want his help.

He closed his eyes and willed his inner turmoil to

settle. He had nothing against a woman having a business if she had the hankering. But Cassie's desire went beyond what was necessary or expedient. She seemed set on proving something. He had no idea what.

"You gonna tell Cassie you're going?" Neil asked.

"I'll let you."

"You should tell her yourself," Daisy interjected, sounding quite certain.

The four watched him closely.

"Ma always said—" Neil started.

Here we go again. Them wanting him and Cassie to act like their ma and pa. He didn't want to disappoint them but he had no idea how to be a pa any more than he had a hankering to put down roots. A no-name cowboy didn't expect to belong any place for long. As he'd said to Cassie, he liked being able to say when, where and with whom. "If it will make you happy." He knew his voice revealed his frustration as soon as Daisy clutched Pansy closer and Neil reached for Billy's hand. He was getting as prickly as Miss Cassie.

If such a little thing eased their minds, he could do it graciously. "You're right. I should tell her." He flashed them a grin as he tromped back up the hill to the shack where pots and pans clattered. Hat in hand, he paused in the doorway.

Cassie glanced up, saw him and pointedly returned to her work.

"I'm going to take the wagon back to the ranch and get a saddle horse."

Her hands stilled. He felt her indrawn breath.

"Do you want to come along? You and the youngsters?"

She didn't look directly at him but he caught a flash

of eagerness. Then it disappeared, and she grunted. "Thought you were taking the wagon back."

"Uh-huh." Of course, he couldn't bring them back on a saddle horse. "Eddie might be willing to lend us a wagon."

"No need. I can't go. I've got work to do." She nodded at the bowl of dough and set of bread pans. "Check and see how Linette is, though, if you don't mind, and say hi to Grady for me."

"I can do that. You'll be okay until I get back?"

That brought her about so fast he chuckled.

"I think I can manage just fine, thank you."

"See you later, then." He was still chuckling as he returned to the wagon and bid the youngsters goodbye.

Later, he pulled the wagon onto the Eden Valley Ranch property and drove past the ranch house. From the dining room window overlooking the yard, he saw Linette watching and waved. At least she was feeling well enough to be up and about.

Eddie trotted from the barn. "Roper. Nice to see you back. Are you here to stay?"

"No. Sorry, boss, but you won't believe what I've been doing."

"Tell me about it. No, wait. You better come to the house and tell Linette at the same time."

Roper jumped from the wagon and fell in step with Eddie as they headed up the path to the house. "How's Linette?" When he left, Eddie was worried that she was so sick.

"She's fine."

"Good to see you grinning from ear to ear. Not all hangdog like you were when I left."

Eddie laughed. “She tells me she’s in the family way. That’s why she’s ill.”

Roper ground to a halt. He wasn’t sure how a man should respond. “You seem happy.” The idea of family filled him with a queasy feeling. It seemed an unnecessary risk.

“I feel like I’m walking on air.”

“You don’t mind that she’s sick?”

“Linette assures me it’s normal and temporary as her body adjusts to the new life growing in her.”

Roper grinned. “Eddie Gardiner a papa! Now won’t that be something?” He couldn’t wait to tell Cassie the news.

Eddie grinned wide enough to split his face. “It will certainly be something to behold.” They reached the house and Eddie threw open the door.

Linette waited in the entrance, the picture of health.

“You’re looking good,” Roper said.

“I’m feeling fine. Better than fine.” She sent Eddie a look full of love and adoration.

A hollow hunger hit Roper’s gut and sucked at his soul. He pushed away the feeling. It was enough that Eddie and Linette were happy, he told himself. He was glad for them.

Linette led the way into the cozy room with big windows allowing a view of the ranch buildings. “Have you been with Cassie all this time?” she asked as they sat at the big table.

“I have and you wouldn’t believe why. She sure didn’t want me to stay and help but…”

Linette served tea and cookies as he told of finding the children and his agreement with Cassie.

“Boss, I’ll be needing time off to help with the kids.”

Eddie nodded. "Take as much time as you need. Your job will be waiting."

"I'm so grateful it's worked out that way. I've been praying God would somehow make it so Cassie would get help. She's so..."

Roper sighed. "Prickly."

Linette chuckled. "Actually I was thinking independent. She once told me she didn't feel she could trust anyone. Or was it only men she didn't trust? I can't remember but once she figured out how to start her own business she was set on proving she didn't need any help."

"She's still set on doing so."

Grady burst into the room. "Hi, Roper." He looked about. "Where's Cassie?"

"I left her in town. Remember, she said she was going to live there."

Grady climbed to Linette's lap and snuggled close.

Roper had often observed that Linette gave the child as much comfort as he sought. Grady was fortunate. He could have been placed in an orphanage. Roper had no complaints about his upbringing—he'd been fed and housed and taught to read and write. Even been taught about God. But he couldn't remember ever having a lap to welcome him. He couldn't even imagine how it would have felt.

"We'll visit her soon," Linette promised Grady.

After a few minutes the boy got down and found a collection of carved animals to play with.

Linette leaned closer. "Tell me more about the children and how Cassie is doing."

Roper told her everything he could think of. Even remembered to mention that Cassie was taking biscuits to the store and was busy baking bread for Macpherson to sell.

"Sounds like she's getting into business sooner than she thought possible, thanks to your help."

He shrugged a little. Too bad Cassie wasn't as appreciative as Linette.

Linette turned to consult Eddie. "She'll be needing some supplies. Potatoes, carrots. Some meat. Do you think Cookie would part with some of the jarred beef she did up?"

Eddie chuckled. "I think if I mention sending something for Cassie, Cookie will load a wagon to the limit." He turned to Roper. "Come along. Let's see what we can find."

They found plenty. Enough to see Cassie through much of the summer unless she started feeding huge crews. Roper took time to visit with Cookie and Bertie and the cowboys still around the place, then headed back to town with a full wagon and a saddle horse tied to the back.

Roper didn't mind in the least that he'd returned with the wagon he'd meant to leave at the ranch. His only regret was he hadn't insisted Cassie come with him. Next time he would.

He glanced back at all the supplies. It eased his mind to know she'd have plenty of provisions even when he couldn't bring in game. There was no way she could reject these gifts. Because he wasn't taking them back.

The wagon rattled as he drove toward home.

Home? Guess he was so used to calling any place he hung his hat home, so it naturally followed this was home for the time being. But the word had a more satisfying feel to it than a hat rack. Probably because he had youngsters to care for and a house to build.

Suddenly he realized it was the closest to home he'd ever known even if it was only temporary. Something pinched the back of his stomach. A sensation of intermingled regret, sorrow, hope and—

He'd long ago learned the futility of wishing upon stars or anything else, so he abandoned that way of thinking and turned his thoughts to estimating how long it would take to dig the cellar at the rate they were going.

Lost in his planning, he was surprised when he reached Cassie's bit of land.

No one raced out to greet him as he pulled to a halt, which provided a sharp reminder that this was not home. Then he heard Pansy's heart-wrenching cries. He bolted from the wagon and raced toward the sound.

Chapter Five

From the moment she'd watched Roper ride away, the wagon rumbling over the rutted trail, Cassie had been apprehensive. She was alone. Unless she counted the children, Macpherson, the smithy down the road and the riders who had come to town shortly after Roper left. No, she wasn't alone. Nor was she lonely.

And Roper had promised to return. The words came from a forbidden corner of her brain.

What difference did it make if he did or not? She could manage quite well by herself. But his words of promise embedded in her mind like warm sweets.

Even her busy hands did not keep her from wondering when Roper would be back. Only, she silently insisted, so she could hear news of Linette and the others at the ranch.

She marched outside for wood, and had her arms full when something tickled her skin. "What's on my arm?" she asked Daisy who hovered nearby.

Daisy squealed and backed away. "A—A—" She couldn't speak but her eyes spoke volumes. Mostly stark fear.

Her near panic was contagious, and Cassie dropped the

load and backed away, watching as a snake writhed out from the wood Cassie had recently held close to her chest.

Cassie shuddered and swiped her hands over her chest and hair. "I hate snakes." She shuddered again and backed away from the woodpile. But she needed more wood. "Maybe Neil can get me some wood." She tipped her head toward the nearby trees. "I'm sure there's lots scattered about for the picking." But neither of them moved.

After Daisy called him, the boy stuck his head from the cellar hole that he continued to work on. "Can you get Cassie some firewood?"

He climbed from the hole. "There's a whole stack of it. Me and Roper made sure there was plenty on hand for several days."

Daisy and Cassie glanced at each other and shuddered. "There's a snake in there," Daisy said.

Neil shrugged. "Who cares about a little bitty snake? Come on, Billy. Let's get some wood for these sissies." He headed for the woodpile.

Cassie shivered. "It wasn't little. It was huge. And maybe poisonous."

Neil skidded to a halt. "How big?"

Daisy held out her arms to indicate a very large snake.

Neil edged away, reaching toward Billy and pushing him back, as well. "We'll get some from the trees." He kept his eyes on the woodpile until he was a good distance away.

Cassie could hardly contain her shudders as she returned to the shack, tiptoeing so she wouldn't wake Pansy. She opened the oven door slowly, grateful it didn't squeak. The biscuits looked fine.

In a few minutes, the boys returned with their arms loaded, and Cassie had them put some wood in the stove.

"I'm not afraid of snakes, you know," she told them

with mock confidence. Then she boldly marched to the stove and set the lid in place. "Thanks, boys, now I can get back to work."

Only it wasn't as simple as she hoped. Some of the wood must have been green for the stove smoked, the heat was uneven and she burned one side of a tray of biscuits.

The heat in the little shack grew oppressive but an hour later she had another tray of biscuits and bread baked a golden brown. She dusted her hands and looked about with satisfaction at all she'd accomplished.

Outside, sounds of the children playing came from the river. Knowing they didn't need her supervision she grabbed a spade and climbed into the cellar hole. Time to show she could manage on her own. With heartfelt determination, she set to work. The ground was hard and unyielding. After what seemed like hours, she'd made little progress. How did Roper manage to get the hole almost five feet deep in such a short time?

Roper. Who needed him? She jabbed the shovel into the ground sending a jarring shudder through her arms and into her shoulder joints. She hadn't asked him for his help. Didn't need him to dig a cellar for her. Gritting her teeth, she jumped on the top of the metal blade, bouncing until the blade edged into the rocklike ground. The wooden handle burned into her palms but she didn't relent until the dirt loosened.

Sweat beaded her forehead and soaked her chest. She ignored it. A woman must learn to manage on her own. Depending on a man made her vulnerable. Worse, it put her at his mercy. *You owe me. You have no choice. I say when and where.* Her heart threatened to burst with rage and sorrow. Her mother had jumped when Grandfather said jump. She'd given up every right even to her own opinion.

Cassie would never do the same. Never. She bent over the handle of the shovel, welcoming the pain in her blistered palms. Pain proved she was taking care of herself.

"Why don't you wait for Roper?"

At the child's voice she looked up to see Billy looking down into the hole. "I can do it myself." She tackled another bit of hard soil.

"You ain't getting much done."

"Thanks, Billy. Just the encouragement I need."

"Roper would do a hundred times faster 'n that."

"Probably he would." She grunted under a scoop of dirt. Seems each shovelful grew heavier. "But he isn't here and I am."

"He's coming back."

"Guess so. But this is my house. My cellar. My life. I can manage fine on my own."

Billy was quiet a moment. "I wouldn't like to be on my own." His voice was soft, tight with fear or perhaps sorrow.

Cassie paused, wiped her face on a corner of her skirt and grimaced at her blistered palms. "You've got your sisters and your brother so I guess you don't have to worry about it." Would siblings have made life easier for her? Likely not. They would have only given Grandfather more ammunition to use against her mother. But maybe if she had a brother or sister they could be partners—

She didn't need a partner.

Pansy started to cry and both Cassie and Billy turned toward the sound, listening as Daisy soothed the little one. Only Pansy wasn't being soothed and her wails intensified. After several shrieks, Cassie climbed from the hole and went over to Daisy who held her struggling, screaming little sister. "What's wrong?"

Daisy's eyes filled with distress. "I don't know. She

just won't stop crying." Indeed, Pansy threw her head back and refused Daisy's attempts to comfort her.

"Is she hurt?" Cassie had to raise her voice to make herself heard.

"Don't think so. I was right there and all of a sudden she started to cry." Daisy bounced her sister but the way Pansy flailed about, Cassie feared she would fling herself from Daisy's arms.

"You better sit down before she falls."

Daisy struggled to hold the crying child as they moved to the table.

"Did you see anything?" Cassie asked Neil. "Maybe a snake?" She shuddered.

Neil shook his head.

Daisy's eyes widened and she quickly examined Pansy. "I don't see any bite marks."

"What's going on?" Roper's voice startled Cassie. She hadn't heard him approach. And her relief at seeing him overrode all her fierce arguments. Only, she excused herself, because she hoped he might have a solution to Pansy's distress.

"We can't get Pansy to stop crying."

Roper reached for the little girl but she pushed him away and screeched. "Is she hurt?" he asked.

"We don't know," Cassie said, her voice raised to be heard over the toddler's cries.

Tears welled in Daisy's eyes. "If only Ma or Pa were here. They'd know what to do."

Cassie studied the three young faces, all wreathed with concern for their little sister. Each set of lips quivered. Mention of their parents under the circumstances looked like it might release a flood of sorrow.

It was a loss they would have to live with the rest of their lives and nothing would change that. Best they figured out how to do it. She pushed to her feet. "Look, there's no point in wanting things you can't have. About all you can do is fix what you can. Make the here and now work."

"How are we supposed to do that when Pansy won't stop crying?" Daisy looked about ready to wail herself.

"I'll show you."

Roper kept trying to get Pansy's attention by clapping his hands and playing peek-a-boo. Cassie figured it did little but make the child scream louder.

Seemed obvious to Cassie this was one time trying to make people laugh wasn't going to work for him. She strode over to the shack where she scooped up a plateful of biscuits, a table knife and the can of syrup and returned to the table. "Sometimes the simplest solution is the most effective. Who likes syrup on their biscuits?"

The two boys plunked down on the bench across the table from her. Both eagerly said, "I do."

She prepared them each a biscuit. "How about you, Daisy? Would you like one?"

Daisy looked doubtful.

Cassie tilted her head toward Pansy.

Daisy understood what Cassie hoped to do and nodded. "Yes, please."

Cassie prepared another biscuit and handed it to Daisy who took it with one hand and bit into it.

"Umm. Good."

Pansy watched, her cries less intense.

"Roper?"

"Sure. A man can always stand a biscuit or two." He emphasized the last word and Cassie dutifully prepared two.

She did another, put it on a plate and set it on the table to one side of Daisy. "How about you?" she asked Pansy.

Pansy sobbed—a sad sound that tore at Cassie's heart. The little girl shuddered twice, then wriggled from Daisy's arms to sit beside her.

Cassie realized they all sat motionless, biscuits held before them as they watched and waited to see if Pansy would decide to eat or continue crying.

Pansy sucked back a sob, then took a bite of her biscuit.

A collective sigh escaped and they all turned back to the food. The quiet was blissful.

"Maybe she was sad," Daisy said.

"I think you're right." Cassie thought the whole lot of them had accepted being orphans without much fuss though once or twice she'd seen them huddled together and expected they shared their sorrow with each other.

The biscuit finished, Pansy's bottom lip quivered.

Cassie jumped to her feet. "Who'd like tea?"

Three children chorused, "Me."

So she made tea, poured canned milk into the children's weak tea and waited a couple of minutes to pour stronger tea for herself and Roper.

He watched her as if he wanted to say something. His patient intensity made her nervous. Was something wrong at the ranch?

"How is Linette?"

"Looking fit as a fiddle. Practically glows with health."

"Oh, good. I was a little worried when I left but she insisted I should proceed with my plans."

"She and Cookie sent you some things." He waved toward the wagon, which she hadn't noticed until now.

"I thought you were leaving it at the ranch."

He chuckled. "Needed it again. Come see."

The children had moved away to play quietly in a circle as if afraid to get too far from each other. Pansy no longer cried but occasionally shuddered.

Cassie watched them a moment, then she followed Roper to the wagon. She nearly gasped when she saw it full of supplies. "My goodness. I can't take all this. I have to—"

Roper's smile flattened. "Manage on your own? Do you have to, or do you insist on it?"

"I can't repay it."

"Who's asking you to? Cookie, Linette, Eddie and yes, me, we just want to help. We want you to succeed, to be happy."

She couldn't look at him. The words sounded nice. Comforting even. But where did helping end and owing begin? And what was she to do with all these supplies? There were jars of canned beef—Cookie's specialty—and potatoes, carrots, turnips, pickles, onions. With all this, she would be able to start offering excellent meals to paying guests. And, tucked away in the corner of the wagon, was a batch of Cookie's excellent cinnamon rolls. Her mouth watered at the prospect.

"Don't refuse help, Miss Prickly Cassie."

She finally met Roper's eyes. The teasing and kindness she saw there made her mouth feel parched. Made her eyes watery and her throat scratchy. "Can kindness really be given without strings attached?"

She hadn't meant to ask the question aloud but it was too late to stop the words from speeding from her mouth.

Roper chuckled. "I think you know the answer." He sobered and studied her. "Seems to me someone in your past has taught you otherwise, exacted a price of some sort when they gave a gift, but there are lots of people in this world who give out of love and concern. I think you know a few if you would just let yourself believe it."

His gaze went on and on, turning over rock-solid arguments in her mind, lapping at memories of her grandfather's miserly help.

She worried her lips, unable to divert her eyes from his intense gaze. She tried to tell herself she didn't see things she longed for in his eyes. From a deep well of doubt she brought forth a snort and returned her gaze to the contents of the wagon. "I'll find a way to pay for it."

Roper sighed long and hard. "I'll let you tell Linette yourself. She said she'll visit soon. Said it would do Grady good to play with other children."

Grady. She missed the little guy and would be glad to see him. Linette, too. She was the closest Cassie had ever had to a friend. The closest she'd ever allowed. Cookie, too. Tears burned her eyes. She reached for the cinnamon buns. "The children are in for a real treat."

"I take it you're going to accept this gift?"

"Can't hardly send it back, can I?"

He chuckled. "Wouldn't make a speck of sense to even try."

"So we might as well unload it."

He grabbed a box of jarred beef. "Show me where."

They crammed most of the supplies into the shack crowding it even more. She desperately needed her house finished but her own efforts had done little to accomplish it. She stole a glance at her palms.

Roper noticed and caught her wrists. "What in the world have you done?"

She tried to snatch her hands away but his gentle hold was unrelenting. "Did some work."

"What sort of work?" His narrowed gaze filled with suspicion. "Tell me you weren't trying to dig out the cellar."

"Okay, I won't."

He made a noise rife with exasperation. "You need to

take care of these hands. Come on, I have something in my saddle bags."

"I'm fine." Again she tried to extract herself but he led her from the shack and out to the table, completely ignoring her torrent of protests.

"Sit." He nudged her so she had no choice. "And stay there while I get the ointment."

Neil left the other children and hovered close by. "You should have left the digging for Roper."

Cassie sighed. Bad enough to have Roper nagging at her. Now a twelve-year-old boy had taken up the cause. "I was only trying to help." She wasn't helping Roper. She was helping herself. It was her house, her responsibility not his.

Roper returned and knelt before her, turning her palms upward. He tsked and blew on them, cooling the heat in the blisters. But his attention did not calm her insides. He had flipped his hat to the table and she looked down at his brown hair, noting—not for the first time—the little wave that gave his hair a natural pompadour. She was a little tempted to flick her fingers through the wave and see if it flipped back into place automatically.

She swallowed hard and tried to ignore the proximity of the man. But she couldn't ignore the way he tenderly touched her hands, spreading a yellow ointment over the blistered area. "What is that?" Her voice sounded positively strangled but she couldn't help it. When had anyone been so attentive to her needs? Not in a very long time. Since she was a child younger than Neil, who rocked back and forth as he watched.

"It's something I use on my horse."

She jerked away.

He laughed up at her and captured her hands again, but his gaze remained locked on hers, edging past her hard-earned, hard-learned defenses and laying silent claim to a tender spot deep within that she had long denied—and intended to keep denying.

Correctly reading her silent defensiveness, he grinned. "Don't think my horse will mind sharing."

She huffed. "Maybe I do."

He bent back to his task. "What were you thinking? I'll finish digging the cellar. Cassie, when are you going to learn to leave the hard stuff to me? It's part of our agreement."

Again that demanding look.

Again she deflected it.

"Ma says some things are man stuff." Neil fairly burst with the need to speak his mind on the matter. "She used to say that when things were too hard for her to do. 'Man stuff for Pa to do when he got home.'"

Cassie shook her head. "I don't aim to be beholden to a man."

Roper had finished applying the ointment but still refused to release her hands. He pulled out a wad of white material and wrapped each hand.

How was she going to work with her hands bundled up in such a fashion? She'd leave the bandages on until morning then they'd come off so she could make bread.

Roper's gaze rested on her.

She didn't miss the fact that he burned with the need to say something almost as urgently as Neil. Then he ducked away to secure the end of the second bandage.

"Thank you." She tried to extricate herself from him, but he kept his fingers around her wrists. His hold was firm, yet his touch was so warm and gentle it clogged her throat with unfamiliar emotions. He perched beside her and watched her.

She studied some distant spot although she focused on

nothing in particular except the need to maintain a protective distance from the emotions threatening to rage through her.

"Cassie, I don't know what happened to make you so prickly. I don't know why you feel you must stand alone when there are those who would stand with you. I expect it was something very hurtful. I'm sorry and I pray God will heal that hurt. But hear me carefully."

When she continued to stare at nothing, he released her wrists to catch her chin and turn her to face him, waiting until she met his gaze. She immediately wished she'd continued to refuse as the kindness and concern in his face almost melted her resistance. The war inside her made her dizzy with fear and longing.

Seeing he had her full attention, he nodded. "Cassie Godfrey, we have a business arrangement. That means we each give something to this situation. You provide meals and shelter and care for the children. In return, I help with the children, dig your cellar and build your house. But hear me and hear me good. Even if we had no arrangement I would help you if you let me. I think you know that. No strings attached. No expectations except to do what Neil calls 'the man stuff.'"

She rocked her head back and forth. It sounded nice. But she couldn't trust such generosity. Best if she depended on no one but herself.

"Fine." He let her go, leaving her off balance.

She tried to clasp her hands together but the palms were too tender and she settled for folding her wrists at her waist.

"If that's the way it is at least we still have our business agreement." He headed for the cellar hole, grabbed a shovel and jumped down. In a few minutes, he pitched earth over his shoulder.

She felt his anger clear across the few feet and in the vigor of the dirt being tossed. But what else could she do? Accepting anything but business between them would give him the right to be angry at her anytime and for any reason. This way they would part when arrangements were made for the children. They would go their separate ways. It was for the best.

Scoops of dirt flew from the hole.

She did not look forward to living with Roper's anger even temporarily. She stared at her bandaged hands, remembering his gentle touch, and seemed unable to move.

Neil touched her shoulder. "You should be happy he can help you. My ma sure wished Pa was around to help her."

She nodded, her tongue suddenly wooden and unable to form a word even if she could have dragged it from her brain. She could not allow herself to be happy Roper was around for any reason—chalking up favor after favor.

Something he'd said slipped back her stalled brain.

I'll pray for you.

Ah. No wonder she was feeling out of sorts. When was the last time she'd prayed? Several days ago if she wasn't mistaken. *God, I trusted You to provide this opportunity so I could be independent. Seems I've gotten a little confused about my intentions what with the children needing help and Roper striking an agreement.* Remembering how she'd originally thought his offer of a business arrangement was an answer to a prayer, she let her tension ease out. God had provided a way she could accept help without being in anyone's debt. She would accept it with gratitude and make the best of it. *I'll just be sure to uphold my end of the bargain.*

She pushed to her feet and set to work making supper. It was difficult with her sore hands but she managed and a little later announced the meal was ready. If Roper faced her with anger she would simply ignore it and do her duty.

Hadn't she learned that lesson over and over until it was branded indelibly on her brain?

Just as she'd learned to ignore the pain of those memories.

Chapter Six

Roper tossed the shovel aside at Cassie's call to supper. His muscles burned from exertion. A satisfying feeling. And it had effectively soothed his frustration with Cassie. He knew he was right when he guessed something, or more likely someone, had hurt her badly even though she neither admitted it nor denied it. He could only pray God would heal that hurt.

He paused in the bottom of the hole to stare up at the sky. Reading the Bible every morning with the youngsters reminded him of God's love and power. It was a good habit. If he ever had a family of his own, he'd do the same thing.

Whoa! Where had that come from? He didn't expect to ever have a real family. That would mean putting down roots…trusting someone would want him to hang around forever. That wasn't possible. Besides, he liked being free to do his own thing. Seemed he had to say it louder and more often of late.

He shifted his thoughts back to his morning prayer. *Watch over us. Keep us safe. Help us be happy.* A man could wish for no more.

Calmed by his prayer, he scrambled from the hole and

jogged to the river where he ducked his head into the icy water and scrubbed off dirt and sweat.

Lacking a towel, he wiped water from his hair and shook his hands then trotted back to the table where everyone sat waiting. He grinned as he saw Cassie had carefully positioned herself across from the boys. As if he'd let that dissuade him. He sat at the end of the bench, next to Neil and nudged him over, chuckling at the scowl on Cassie's face. "Gal, I sure do like the welcoming way you have of looking at me." He hoped to bring a smile to her face or at least a flash of amusement to her eyes

He was pretty sure the flicker he saw signified uncertainty rather than amusement. Her mouth worked as if she wanted to say something but couldn't find the words. Then she turned away. "Glad to make you happy," she murmured.

He wanted to see her face better, look into her eyes and read her meaning, but she suddenly found the bench between herself and Pansy needed to be brushed off though he suspected there was nothing on it but imaginary dust.

Amusement continued to stretch his mouth. "You do make me happy," he murmured, not sure what he meant by it but knowing the words were true. He liked helping her. He liked sitting across the table from her, holding her hand as they prayed. He reached out to claim one hand now. Out of consideration for her tender palms, he wrapped his fingers around her wrist instead.

He also liked sharing the table with a woman and children. Doing what he could to ensure their safety and happiness. He knew it wouldn't last but he didn't figure to let that steal any joy from the present.

He bowed his head and thanked God for the food.

The "amen" said, the food passed, they all dug in.

"Good meal," he murmured, enjoying the tender beef,

rich brown gravy, potatoes and carrots. "You're a good cook."

"Thank you. I'm hoping others will agree." She glanced about. "I think I could start offering meals to travelers. I'll let Macpherson know."

"I'll get some fresh meat in the morning." He saw her ready protest. "You might want to save the jarred meat for when you don't have fresh."

She nodded. Again the expression in her eyes revealed uncertainty. He wished he knew the source so he could fix it. He almost laughed aloud. Yup. She'd start running to him for help in fixing her problems all right.

Maybe in another life.

"There's a snake in the woodpile," Daisy announced.

"They were afraid of it," Neil said.

Daisy gave her brother an accusing look. "So were you." She turned to Roper. "Cassie had it in her arms." She shuddered.

"It must have been in the wood when I picked up an armload," Cassie explained.

Had she turned a little pale? Roper glanced around the table, seeing an unspoken message. Ahh, he understood. The children expected him to deal with the snake. He met Cassie's gaze. Would she insist she could handle this by herself or ask for help? She ducked away but he waited and slowly she returned her gaze to him. She swallowed hard enough he wondered if she would choke. Oh, but it felt good to think she needed him. He would make her ask. Make her acknowledge the need. Perhaps if she did it once…

Would she ever realize that his caring carried no obligations?

Except to appreciate him.

He mentally shook himself. Where had that come

from? He wanted to help her for her sake not his. Maybe she needed a little prodding in asking for his assistance.

"A big snake, you say?" He made his voice sound worried. "Could have been a hognose." Not that he'd ever seen one. But he'd heard tell of them farther south. About the only poisonous snake he knew of around here was a rattler and if she'd held it in her arms—

He shuddered. It could have struck out, the bite filling her with poison. Every cowboy knew the symptoms. First, lips tingling, then a struggle to breathe then a person's muscles stopped working. Some people survived but their muscles were never strong afterward. If Cassie had been bitten, they would not be sitting around the table. He wouldn't be teasing her.

He rubbed at a spot beneath his breastbone that developed a sudden pain.

"Are you afraid of snakes?" Cassie asked him.

Neil laughed. "'Course he's not. He's a man."

"Nice to have your support." Roper squeezed the boy's shoulder. "I don't much care for the way they sneak around but I guess I'm not scared of them." He continued to wait, his eyes on Cassie.

"Would you—?" She puffed out her lips.

If only she would say the words, she'd learn that asking for a favor didn't require selling her soul.

"I'd like it if you could get rid of the snake." The words came out in a rush.

His grin stretched to its limit. "Of course I will." He rose and headed for the woodpile, two boys in his wake, chattering about how they'd take care of that nasty old snake. Roper chuckled. He guessed "they" meant him as the boys stopped a good ten feet from the pile.

He kicked the stack to alert any sneaky critters, then

picked up one piece of wood at a time, carefully searching for snakes or other things.

"There it goes." Billy jumped up and down, pointing toward the woods.

Roper saw the little green snake slither away. "Only a garter snake. Harmless as a fly." He watched it disappear. "Don't expect it will come back."

Cassie and Daisy, with Pansy safely in her arms, watched from a wide distance.

Roper replaced the wood, dusted his hands and went to face Cassie. "I doubt it will return but from now on let me get the wood."

"You planning to make wood gathering your new job?"

He understood what she didn't say. She had no intention of depending on him for this simple job. Fine. "When you get wood, pick up each piece carefully. You give him a warning and he'll be glad to get out of your way."

Again, he read confusion and uncertainty in her eyes and was at a loss to explain it. He took her elbow, pleased when she made no attempt to pull away, and guided her toward the cellar hole where they could talk away from the youngsters. "Cassie, what are you worrying about?"

"I'm not."

"Something is troubling you. I've seen it in your eyes all during the meal and even now." When she would have turned away, he caught her chin and gently insisted she face him. "Have I done something?"

For several moments she studied him, searching his eyes. He was at a loss to know what she sought.

"You aren't angry?" The words were barely a whisper.

"Me? What would I be angry about?" He couldn't imagine.

"I insisted we stick to a business arrangement between us. You seemed upset. I thought—"

"You thought I'd hold a grudge? Even go so far as to inflict some sort of punishment in retaliation?"

He waited for her answer and it came in the form of a single nod. Despite his finger on her chin she refused to meet his gaze. He slouched down until he could see into her guarded eyes. "I'm not that sort of person. You should know that by now."

Her eyes widened. A flicker of something he could interpret as both surprise and acknowledgment crossed her face.

A sigh came from deep inside. "Cassie, maybe someday you'll explain why you are so prickly. And maybe, God willing, you'll see whatever your reasons, they don't apply to me."

This time he knew the look that flashed across her face was surprise and his heart swelled with victory at the thought she might be changing her view of him.

"Now that you're in a mellow mood I have some more news from the ranch." He paused. "Could be Linette wants to tell you herself…" He considered the possibility.

Alarm made her features harsh. "You said she was okay."

"She is."

Cassie's breath whooshed out. "Then it could be that once you start an announcement, you ought to finish it." Her tone was as dry as a prairie wind. A chuckle rippled up his throat. This Cassie sure beat the prickly one of a few minutes ago.

She crossed her arms and gave him an I'm-waiting look.

He grinned. "What if Linette is disappointed not to be the one to tell you?"

She tapped a toe. "You're assuming you'd live to hear the words from her mouth."

He stared. "Live?" Then he realized she'd threatened him. In fun, of course. Delight as pure and sweet as fresh honey ran through his veins. "Why, Miss Cassie, I do believe you're intent on getting me to tell."

"I perceive that you are mighty sharp—especially for a man."

He hooted and slapped his leg as pleased as could be at her playfulness.

She quirked an eyebrow and continued to tap her toe but he knew he wasn't mistaken in observing that her eyes danced with amusement.

He forced his laughter back though it refused to leave his throat. He held his palms toward her in a gesture of defeat. "I'll tell. Just don't hurt me. Promise?"

She chuckled. "I promise. Now what's this news that you're making me wait for?"

He glanced about as if afraid someone would hear and signaled her to lean closer. No need for such secrecy but he was enjoying this playfulness too much to bring it to an end.

He whispered in her ear. "Linette is going to have a baby." His breath disturbed strands of her hair and they blew against his face. He brushed them aside, smoothing them into place.

He'd never touched her hair before. It was so silky, he wanted to run his hands over it again but she drew back and stared at him.

"She is?" She laughed. "I knew it. I told her I thought so before we left. I'm so glad for them."

Her gaze grabbed his in a triumphant look and in it he saw her joy for her friend. Her smile flattened and he saw something else…something he guessed she was unaware of. A deep sadness. He remembered the writing in her Bible—the two babies who died the same day they were born.

He acted without thinking and caught her arms. "Cassie, I read about your babies. I'm sorry. It must make you sad to hear of Linette's baby."

She swallowed hard. She stared at his chest, then she blinked and jerked back. "That's water under the bridge. I never think about it. I've got the future to consider. Macpherson is expecting me to deliver biscuits and bread to his store." She spun away and returned to the shack so fast she left a dusty blur in her wake.

Cassie thundered toward the shack. She sank to her bed on the floor, pulled her knees to her chest and rested her forehead on them. Anger and pain intermingled in her throat like a bitter medicine.

She pulled in a deep breath and held it, forcing her emotions into order. But her anger refused to dissipate.

He had no right to talk of her babies. She did not want to think of that part of her life. The joy and anticipation of the little lives. The tiny flutters of their first kicks. Their growing movements and her growing belly. With the first one, George had shared every joy. But after their little son was stillborn, he refused to allow himself any joy over the second baby.

And he'd been right to fear it would happen again. The little one never drew a breath and they buried a little girl.

Cassie rubbed at her chest but it provided no comfort.

Roper had snooped. Read words that weren't his business.

She snatched the Bible from where it rested and opened it to the page of births and deaths. Her fingers trembling, her jaw clenched, she plucked at the page, drew it toward her until it grew taut at the binding. But before the paper began to tear, she dropped the page and smoothed it. She couldn't rip it out. This was all that was left of her babies. She bowed her head over her knees and breathed hard, fighting for calmness, peace…relief.

The backs of her hands grew damp and she swiped them on her skirt then scrubbed her eyes dry. Crying accomplished nothing. Work. That was the answer.

For a second she couldn't recall what it was she should do.

Then she saw the stack of biscuits and loaves of bread. She meant to deliver them hours ago but had been sidetracked by one thing, and then another.

What kind of way was that to run a business?

She pulled to her feet, her body strangely heavy, gathered up the biscuits and bread, and left the shack.

The children played nearby and Daisy watched her.

Cassie forced a smile to her lips and hoped it looked real. She did not allow herself a glance toward the house site but heard the thud of earth hitting the ground.

Sucking in a deep breath she squared her shoulders and headed for the store. Macpherson would be pleased with her work.

Work was the antidote to foolish emotions. She needed to keep that in mind and focus on what she could do.

A short time later, Cassie rushed back from the store. "Macpherson said he expects a stage before the day is out." It was already late in the day but a rider had seen the stage on its way. "Says he'll direct the travelers this way for a meal." She laughed, hardly able to contain her excitement. Her dream would soon be fulfilled.

Her words brought Neil and Roper from the cellar hole.

"Do you need any help getting ready?" Roper asked.

Cassie sobered. She didn't want him hanging about making her remember things put to rest. Besides, she meant to manage on her own. "I have things under control." Then she remembered her manners. "Thanks." Her grin returned as she hurried to the shack. She ripped the bandages off her hands and turned her palms to examine them. They'd be fine. She didn't have time to worry about a little discomfort.

Daisy insisted on helping and Cassie allowed it. The girl needed to know she pulled her weight.

An hour later a cake stood ready to ice. A meal was cooked and pushed to the side of the stove to stay warm. The rumble of a stagecoach brought her from the shack and she stared toward the store. She watched the passengers disembark—three men and a woman. As the driver tossed down packages, a cowboy reached out to lend a hand.

Roper joined Cassie. The children clustered around. The boys bounced on the balls of their feet. Pansy ran round and round in front of them. Daisy, ever vigilant, continually darted glances at her baby sister while observing as much of the activity around the stagecoach as she could.

Cassie wanted to join Pansy in making happy, flapping circles but instead, crossed her arms and waited. "Everything is ready." Her voice seemed high, as if she worried. Well, of course she did. Her future depended on providing meals that satisfied. Word of mouth would build her reputation.

Roper draped an arm across her shoulders. "You'll do fine."

She didn't need his encouragement. Of course she'd do fine. She'd done her best.

But her stubborn defiance couldn't block the echo of her grandfather's words. *Too slow. Sloppy. You forgot*—even when nothing had been forgotten. She pushed away the uncertainty the words brought. She was in charge now. She jumped for no one unless it pleased her to do so, but for a few seconds she let the weight of Roper's arm on her shoulders anchor her to her land.

A dusty man with a ragged beard and equally ragged hat headed in their direction. She recognized Petey, the driver. Behind him came the two men then the woman clinging to the arm of the third man. Cassie could tell by the curl of the woman's lips that she wasn't pleased by her circumstances. Behind her strode the cowboy.

Cassie stepped forward, leaving Roper's strengthening arm behind. "Welcome. The meal is ready. Seat yourself." She waved toward the table. She and Macpherson had discussed a price for the meal and she'd accepted his advice on setting a fee. She held a tin can toward the guests and they each dropped in their coins.

"Where can I wash?" the woman asked, her voice demanding.

Cassie hesitated to point to the basin perched on the butt end of a log, a bucket of water beside it. She'd put out a stack of clean towels. It was the best she had to offer and totally adequate. "The washbasin is over there."

The woman looked as if Cassie had offered swamp water in a slop bucket. Cassie knew that look, though it had normally come from above a mustache. She bristled. "It's perfectly clean."

The woman sniffed. "I am not impressed with the wilderness."

"Come along, dear." The man, who must have been her long-suffering husband, urged her toward the basin. "You'll feel better after you've washed the dust from your face." He managed to edge her away.

"I'm covered with dust from head to toe. I need a full bath."

Cassie resisted suggesting she could have one in the river and turned back to the others. Instead, she caught Roper's gaze, full of laughter, and her spirits revived. How foolish to head out to the wilderness, then complain that it was wild. It was good to share her amusement with Roper. Then she snapped a mental door closed. She would not be involving Roper in the everyday aspects of her life.

The cowboy brought up the rear. He snatched off his battered hat to reveal a mane of blond hair that hadn't seen a pair of scissors for many months if Cassie had her guess.

"Lane Brownley, ma'am. Got me a little place just over there." He pointed in a vague northwest direction that could have been along the river, or toward the mountains or in the middle of nowhere. Not that Cassie cared for more specific directions. He dropped his coins in the can. That's what mattered.

"I'll gladly pay for a decent meal whenever I'm nearby, if you have no objections."

"That's what I'm here for."

His blue eyes matched the sky and shone as brightly as he grinned at her. "You and your husband got a good idea, setting up a stopping station here."

She blustered an embarrassed reply. "He's not my husband. He works for Eddie Gardiner at the Eden Valley Ranch."

"My apologies but I've seen him here several times over the past few days."

"It's the kids." She explained the orphaned children and how they had a business agreement to work together to care for them until their uncle could be reached.

Lane's eyes brightened. "Then you're planning to run this place on your own?"

She studied him without answering. Did he mean to take advantage of her situation?

Roper must have wondered the same thing. He stepped to her side and dropped his arm across her shoulder. "'Spect me or the boss or one of the boys will be stopping by mighty often."

Lane suddenly realized how his words had been interpreted and red crept up his neck. "Didn't mean it that way." He scuffled off to wash up.

Roper didn't step back but as soon as Lane bent to splash water over his face, Cassie ducked away and put a good six feet between them. From that distance she shot him a warning look. He needn't think he could make a habit of being protective.

He returned her hard look and after a moment she shifted her attention to the children.

Neil sat on a log with Pansy and Billy and watched the visitors.

Cassie waited until the guests were seated then took the potatoes to the table. Daisy brought the roast venison. They returned for the rest of the dishes only to meet Roper part way carrying gravy and carrots.

Cassie reached for the bowls but Roper shook his head. "I got them."

"But—" she sputtered.

Roper gave her a mocking grin. "Did you think I'd stand idly by and watch you and Daisy work? Nope." He took a step, then paused to face her. "Ain't gonna stand by and see some young upstart boy who thinks he's a cowboy come stomping in to make a nuisance of himself, either."

"He came to eat. He paid his money. I intend to serve him."

"And next time?"

"He pays his money, I feed him. Every time."

"Just make sure he isn't after anything but meat and potatoes."

Her nostrils flared. How dare he insinuate she would allow someone to take advantage of her? "You forget I can take care of myself." She kept her voice low so those at the table wouldn't hear but made no attempt to keep the defiance out of her words. Daisy had thankfully returned to the shack so didn't overhear this conversation. When would he realize she didn't need or want coddling? She grabbed the jug of gravy from him.

Roper put the carrots on the table, gave her a look full of judgment, then took the younger children and disappeared over the bank toward the river.

Cassie shrugged. Sooner or later he'd realize she didn't need him watching over her shoulder. She turned her attention back to her guests. "Help yourself and enjoy the meal."

The men dug in with gusto and if the way they hunkered over their plates indicated pleasure, then they enjoyed the meal.

The fine lady shivered as a fork scrapped against a tin plate. "I'd think a person charging for a meal would use real china."

Cassie smiled but didn't respond. China was fine in a restaurant but she wasn't running a restaurant.

The lady held up her hands. "I could do with a napkin."

Cassie fetched a small towel, which earned her an impatient sigh. Cassie glanced about trying to see the place as others would. The table was crude. The plates were tin. They ate outdoors. She'd been so pleased to get her business started that she hadn't thought of the deficiencies. "Once I get my place built I'll have things nicer."

"In the meantime—" The look on the woman's face said just how lacking the present conditions were.

Petey lifted his head, and wiped his mouth on his sleeve. "I remember you from last fall when I brought you out with Miss Edwards who was set on marrying Eddie. Glad they finally got hitched. You're doing okay, too, with this setup. I'll be back on a semi-regular basis and the bull trains will run until snow blocks the road. The drivers are always ready for a big feed. Once they hear about this place you'll find yourself busy as two beavers."

Cassie's tension released. "Thank you." It was hungry men who would make up the bulk of her business and they cared nothing for fancy tablecloths and napkins.

Lane leaned back with a sigh. "Best meal I've had since I left England three years ago."

"Wait. I have coffee, tea and cake." She bustled back to the shack and with Daisy's help served each customer.

The fancy lady spoke not a word of appreciation even though she ate every crumb of the piece of cake Cassie served her.

Cassie determinedly ignored the woman's constant sighs and furrowed brow. She'd grown adept at turning away such insignificant signs of displeasure. She glanced toward the river where she could hear the children playing and Roper's laugh.

A few minutes later everyone left. All except Lane. He sat with his elbows on the table watching her as she and Daisy scraped the dishes and stacked them to be washed. His attention screeched along her nerves as much as the sound of metal scraping metal.

Neil and Billy climbed up from the river, with Roper following on their heels, Pansy perched adoringly in his arms.

Cassie stared. They fit like hand and glove. Why wasn't Roper married with a baby of his own?

She choked back an unfamiliar emotion. Was it loneliness she felt? Impossible.

She shook her head to clear her confusion. It must remind her of her father and all she'd lost when he died.

Roper had been grinning down at Pansy but glanced up, saw Lane still at the table and instantly scowled. He shifted Pansy to one side and veered toward the table where he plunked down opposite Lane. "Where did you say you have this ranch?"

Lane barely pulled his gaze from Cassie and distractedly jerked his thumb over his shoulder. "That way."

"You got livestock? Farmland? Family?"

"Small herd of cows. Half a dozen horses. A pig and some chickens. Broke some land and planted oats for feed." He offered the answers in sharp bullets as if paying no attention to his words.

"Family?" Roper prodded.

"None this side of the ocean. I'm all alone."

Daisy giggled at the mournful note in the cowboy's voice and leaned close to murmur in Cassie's ear. "Think he's wanting to change that."

Cassie gave her full attention to the pan of hot soapy water as she scrubbed the dishes. She didn't know whether Daisy meant the cowboy was looking for a group of friends or if he had an eye on marriage. If the latter was his intention he'd soon learn Cassie had no such notion. But she certainly didn't object to taking a bit of his money in exchange for a home-cooked meal.

Roper reached across the table, grabbed the man's empty cup and put it among those to be washed. "Guess it's time to get back to work." But he sat at the table.

Daisy nudged Cassie but Cassie was already aware of the silent tug of war. In fact, Lane seemed the only one oblivious to Roper's broad hint to leave.

The stagecoach rattled away.

Lane finally swung his legs over the bench and pushed

to his feet. "I best get on home and see to the chores." He paused at Cassie's side. "Appreciate the fine meal. You can count on me returning." He smiled.

She smiled back. To do otherwise would be rude. Besides, she didn't object to him buying a meal. "I'll be here serving meals."

His gaze lingered then he jammed his hat on his head and sauntered back to the store. In a few minutes he came into sight astride his horse, gave a quick salute, reined around and rode away.

Roper pushed to his feet. "Thought I might have to shovel him off the bench."

Neil laughed. "Maybe you should've given him a shovel and let him help dig the cellar."

"You're jealous, aren't you?" Daisy dried a plate as she talked.

"Me?" He rumbled his lips. "Not at all but I don't see the use of a man sitting around watching everyone work."

Cassie wanted to know who he'd watched apart from her and Daisy.

Roper put Pansy down. "Come on, Neil. Let's get some more water." He paused then, and faced Cassie. She saw the guardedness in his eyes. And something more. Something that made her uncertain.

Did he expect her to reassure him? About what? That she wasn't interested in Lane? How could she be? She'd only met him a couple hours ago. She'd known Roper since last fall and constantly pushed him away. He should know it would be the same with Lane. She wasn't interested in special attention from either of them. "I need to get these dishes washed so the children can prepare for bed."

He grabbed the buckets. His strides ate up the ground until he dropped out of sight.

A few minutes later he returned with water and Pansy edged toward him. He lifted her to his knees as naturally as if they'd always been friends.

Cassie knew his naturalness came from his life in an orphanage. "Do you keep in touch with any of the children you grew up with?"

His hands grew still. He stared at the table. Then slowly he lifted his head and faced her.

She tried to read his expression. Was it wary? Pained? "I'm sorry. It's none of my business." Normally she would have added that it didn't matter to her but she couldn't say the words.

Then he smiled. Goodness, the man had a way of smiling that made her forget every cross word, every harsh thought, every determination to keep her distance.

"It pleased me tremendously to see many of the little ones taken into homes. Some of the older ones were put out to work." His grin dipped crookedly. "Sometimes they were returned as unsatisfactory, which meant they didn't work hard enough or..." He trailed off and didn't finish. "Many times the kids weren't treated kindly and found a way to leave. Sometimes they came back to the orphanage. Others simply disappeared."

She held her breath waiting for him to continue, suspecting he wasn't talking just about others. She sensed the sadness, saw the tiny telltale signs of tension in the narrow wrinkles about his eyes.

"Roper, you believe so strongly in family. It surprises me you don't have your own."

Only the tightening of the skin around his eyes revealed he'd even heard her. Once her curiosity had been unleashed it couldn't be contained. "Why aren't you married with a little girl of your own?" Her gaze slid to the child on his knee.

"I'm a man with no past. No history."

"Why would that matter? Are you afraid of what your parents might have been?"

"Not me."

She saw him jerk a little as if he'd said more than he meant. "You think it matters to others?"

"I know it does."

"I take it that's why you have a rule about not putting down roots. They'll only be ripped out."

She sat beside him, rested her palm on his forearm, feeling tension beneath his shirtsleeve. This was a side of Roper she'd never seen. "What happened?" She sensed it had been painful.

He shifted a little, obviously uncomfortable with the subject. But he didn't pull away. He turned slowly as if reluctant to look into her eyes. She held his gaze, silently promising to hear him, to help him if she could. He deserved it, trying as he always did to make everyone else happy. Who tried to make him happy?

"I worked for a man for several months when I was nineteen. The boss had a pretty little daughter a year younger. She treated me kindly. She told me her secrets of wanting adventure. Wanting to learn about the world. I believed—" he swallowed loudly "—that she cared for me. I saved my money. Had enough to buy us a train ticket to the east where I thought we'd buy passage on a ship to Europe. We'd see all the things she dreamed of. Just as soon as we were married."

He didn't go on.

She waited, increasing the pressure of her hand on his arm.

"When I told her of my plans she looked shocked. Said I'd mistaken her kindness for more than it was. She explained in a very clear way that I was not suitable. No one had any idea of my background. That simply wasn't acceptable."

"Roper, I am so sorry." She touched his cheek. "Background doesn't matter to everyone."

Something shimmered in his eyes for a moment, then he smiled and closed his thoughts to her. "I've believed for most of my life that God never closes a door without opening a window."

She stared at him. How could he believe so simply? So thoroughly? It wasn't because life had been easy for him.

"Like you." He shifted Pansy to one knee and jabbed a finger toward Cassie.

"Like me? I've never noticed open windows and doors especially in difficult situations." There'd been no escape from her grandfather until she'd met George. There'd been nothing but closed doors when her babies died. All she could do was put one foot in front of the other until it became a habit.

Daisy came over and reached for Pansy. "This little girl is almost asleep."

Cassie glanced about. "It's getting late. The children need to get to bed." She welcomed the interruption and a way to avoid continuing this discussion.

Roper stood. "Just let me point out that this business venture of yours is an open door."

She nodded. "God's given me this opportunity. I intend to make the most of it. But I won't be owing to any man over this business. Nor will I be turning away any paying customers so long as they act decently."

"Like Lane?"

She lifted her chin as she stared at him. "His money is as good as anyone's."

Her newfound freedom would not be relinquished.

Chapter Seven

Roper lounged by his campfire knowing sleep would not come while his mind twisted round and round. Why was Cassie always ready to take a contrary view about everything he said?

He regretted only one thing. He wished he hadn't talked about her babies. The mention of them had hurt her badly. More and more he began to suspect Cassie's way of dealing with things that brought pain or made her uncomfortable was to pretend they didn't exist. Instead, she worked. Work was her way of forgetting.

But working for Lane Brownley? He'd seen the way Lane watched Cassie. The man had more than a good meal in mind. He couldn't blame Lane for seeing Cassie as a woman he'd like to take home as a wife.

But he had no right to poke his nose into Roper's temporary home. Roper bolted to his feet and kicked dirt on the fire. He was not the sort of person who believed in anything but temporary.

Suddenly, he laughed. He should warn Lane that Cassie was dead set on being independent.

* * *

The next morning, Roper's irritation lingered…a fact that churned his insides. All his life he'd been able to put aside the disturbing events of a day and greet the new dawn with joy and anticipation, but not today. And that only increased his frustration.

He tried to dismiss his feelings as hunger but a hearty breakfast didn't change anything.

As he jumped into the cellar hole, he called it worry. But no amount of searching his mind yielded anything that deserved his concern.

He tried to explain it as anything but what it was.

Jealousy.

Roper jabbed his shovel into the ground and dug out a lump of dirt. He wasn't jealous of Lane. But something about Lane made his muscles twitch. The man was like a big overgrown pup.

Roper only wanted to protect Cassie from those sad, hungry eyes.

But she didn't welcome his protection. He grunted as he attacked another lump of dirt.

At least Pansy now welcomed his care. He recalled how she sat on his knee that morning while he read the Bible after breakfast and he breathed in the sweet, baby scent of her.

He'd tried time and again to win over the child but she would always turn away, bury her head against Daisy's shoulder or simply ignore Roper. But yesterday he'd succeeded in making friends. He'd hidden behind a tree and played peek-a-boo, letting her come closer and closer until she stood against the tree and giggled as he whispered, "Boo," just inches from her head.

He'd squatted to her level and let her study him closely, let her feel her own way, see he meant no harm to her.

When she lifted her arms and said, “Up,” he grinned clear through. After that she wouldn’t let him put her down until they were back with Daisy and Cassie.

His pleasure at holding Pansy yesterday had dimmed when he saw the way Lane watched Cassie. He didn’t have to have two eyes in his head to know the man wanted to spend all day mooning over her. And likely marry her and take her home before the week was out.

He threw spadeful after spadeful of dirt with unusual vigor. The muscles in his arms burned but not enough to make him forget Lane.

Neil leaned on the handle of his shovel. “How come you don’t like Lane?”

Had he inadvertently mumbled his thoughts aloud? He stopped digging, wiped the sweat from his brow. “I got no feelings one way or the other about the man. Hardly know him from Adam.”

“Yeah, but you don’t like him. I can tell.”

“Just don’t want him hanging about wasting our time.”

“Oh.” Neil returned to digging but didn’t even get his shovel into the dirt before he paused and looked about. “You think this hole is big enough yet?”

Roper stopped to consider. “You might be right. How did I miss that? We’ll smooth it out and tomorrow start work on the floor for the house.” Cassie’d be pleased at seeing some progress.

“I’m hungry,” Neil said.

“I expect Cassie will call us soon. You run along while I finish here.”

Neil scampered up the ladder and raced away, no doubt glad to be done digging.

He smoothed the bottom and tidied the sides. After he got the house up, he’d build shelves down here for Cassie to store her supplies.

A thought scratched at the back of his mind. When he finished here… When the youngsters' uncle collected them, he would have no excuse for staying. Not that he'd ever planned to. He recited one of his rules—*don't put down roots.* Another rule tagged along on the heels of the first. *Don't stay where you're not wanted.* How many times had he said that to half-grown orphans who were taken to a home to work? Work hard, he'd said. Aim to please. Be cheerful but if they are unkind, don't stay. He'd walked away from situations that made him feel small and useless.

Cassie would not want him to hang about helping. And he didn't have Lane's excuse that he lived nearby and appreciated home-cooked meals. Cookie made excellent meals and the ranch was not a shout and holler away.

He leaned on his shovel handle and contemplated his predicament. To think of leaving her alone hurt like a boil on his skin where it touched the saddle. Cassie was easy prey for young cowboys. And old mule skinners. Besides, who would gather her wood and make sure there were no snakes? How would she keep the water buckets full? It was a steep climb up from the river with two full buckets.

"Neil says you're done with the cellar." Cassie's voice over his head jerked him about so fast his neck cracked.

"Just tidying it up." He tipped his hat back as he peered up at her standing near the edge. "Careful you don't fall."

Her look informed him his warning was unnecessary and unwelcome. Then she turned her attention to the cellar hole. "It looks roomy." She brought her gaze back to him.

Standing in a hole staring upward, the sky bright behind her, he couldn't see well enough to know for sure why she studied him so.

"I want to apologize for complaining when you said you wanted to dig a cellar for me—I mean, for the house."

Was it so hard for her to acknowledge he'd done it for her? Well, he wasn't about to let her get away with that.

He climbed the ladder.

She edged back, keeping a healthy distance between them.

He jabbed the spade into the ground and closed that distance until he stood two feet away, able to see the uncertainty in her eyes. "Cassie Godfrey, I dug a cellar because I knew it would make your life easier. I did it for you." He stared at her.

Her gaze shifted to a spot beyond his shoulder but he didn't relent. He wanted her to acknowledge he'd done it for her.

But her gaze darted to him and shied away again twice before she drew in a sharp breath and kept her eyes steady on his. "I know you did. Thank you." It was barely a whisper and no doubt made a large hole in her pride but it signified a small victory for him.

He reached out and brushed his knuckles along her jawline. "There. Did it hurt so much to admit it?"

Her eyes widened at his touch and she swallowed loudly but didn't pull away. In fact, if he let himself read a whole book into a glance he would say his touch made her aware of a hunger for everything she denied herself. He didn't know exactly what that was and didn't bother to figure it out as his rules rang loudly inside his head. But he didn't back away. Not yet. Not for another moment.

Her eyes shuttered. "You will never know how much it hurt," she murmured, hurrying back to the table.

Later that night he sat under the stars, listening to the night call of the birds, the rumble of the water and the occasional murmur of voices from up the hill. All he wanted was a chance to help Cassie learn that it was all right to accept help. That she didn't need to stand alone. There were friends all around. He knew Linette, Eddie, Cookie, Bertie and even Macpherson would willingly help Cassie at any time.

But that wasn't exactly what he pictured.

What he saw, if he allowed himself to be honest, was Roper Jones, orphaned, nameless, with nothing of substance to offer, helping Cassie as she welcomed guests and fed them.

A groan rumbled from his chest.

He didn't put down roots. He didn't stay where he wasn't wanted. He helped people find their happiness. Which wasn't the same as interfering with their business as Cassie had said.

He ducked his head. "Dear Jesus, You know who I am. I just wish I did. I have nothing to offer any woman except my help. Please enable me to do that, to protect her and the kids until their uncle comes." It was all he wanted or expected from this arrangement.

The next morning he opened Cassie's Bible for their customary reading. He slowly read the story of the rainbow. He'd heard it many times while in the orphanage, but somehow today, reading the words to Cassie and the children, his heart swelled with assurance of God's love and protection. He finished and was quiet a moment, letting sweet thoughts fill him. Then he reached for Cassie's hand on one side and Neil's on the other. This was his favorite time of the day—them all together and united under God's love. He prayed for their safety. "Amen."

He didn't immediately release either hand.

Neil pulled away first and was about to leave when Daisy told him to bring water and help with the dishes.

Neil grunted. "I'm going to help Roper."

But Roper was in no hurry to return to work. He studied Cassie's downturned head. Was something bothering her?

When the children left, she extricated her hand. "Do you think about God's promises?"

"Not as much as I should."

"Do you think they are meant equally for everyone?"

He thought of the deaths noted in her Bible and guessed she wondered if the promises were for her. He didn't know what to say. "God told Noah He would remember His covenant and gave us the rainbow to remind us. It assures me that God won't forget me."

Slowly her head came up and she searched his soul. He let her, wishing he had something more to give her than a faltering trust.

"Seems I mostly remember the times when I thought He had forgotten me." Her voice faltered. "I saw no rainbow in my life then."

"What did you see?" How he ached to comfort her, hold her, bear her pain.

"Nothing. No one." She looked into the distance. "I learned to stand alone."

"God promises to never leave us or forsake us."

She jerked her gaze to him, doubt and defiance blazing from her eyes. "So where was He when I needed Him?"

"Did you look for Him?" Before she could answer, he spoke again. "Too often I've wandered about on my own, wondering where God had gone. It took way too long for me to realize God didn't move. I did." He'd learned the lesson at a young age. When—

When didn't matter. He no longer dreamed of the things he wanted when he was young. Home and family were out of his reach. He accepted that and looked for satisfaction in helping others.

She looked hard and long at him. But her resistance did not fade. "Maybe there are times when God expects us to stand alone."

It wasn't what he hoped she'd say. He saw her alone, afraid and hurting. "Oh, Cassie. You never have to be alone. I'll stand with you anytime you need it."

Her eyes narrowed. "No one can be always available."

He wanted her to reach out to him and accept his offer to be with her. But she was right. He couldn't always be there. "God is."

"I try to believe that but sometimes it's hard. Maybe even impossible."

"I'm no Bible scholar so I don't have any answers for you." He paused as an assurance grew in his own soul. "Except to say I believe God is always with us. Even when we feel most alone."

"When do you feel most alone?"

The question stripped away a barrier he wasn't even aware of until now. "You remember the Christmas party at the OK Ranch?" The whole crew of Eden Valley Ranch had been invited to the neighboring ranch to enjoy a beautiful meal and play games.

She nodded.

"Remember how we went around the table saying our favorite Christmas memory? I always picture Christmas as family gathered around the tree. That's when I feel the loneliest." He glanced about the table, now empty apart from himself and Cassie.

Daisy washed dishes. Pansy played at her feet. The boys struggled up the hill, water sloshing from the buckets they carried. "This is the closest to family I've ever had. It's temporary, I know. No roots for me." Maybe if he said it often enough he would believe it as deeply as he needed to.

Cassie's warm hand on his arm brought his attention back to her. "I'm sorry." Her voice burrowed into his struggling thoughts.

Their gazes locked. Hers went on and on, past swirling waters of doubt and hurt, straight to a hungry, needy spot he hadn't been aware of until now. No. He'd known it existed but he'd long ago learned to ignore it. Now he felt as if dusty doors were creaking open and refreshing air and bright sunlight poured in. As her look of concern continued, he struggled in vain to push the door closed.

Then she jerked away and bolted to her feet. "Thought you might be in a hurry to start building my house."

Her sudden movement enabled him to slam the door back in place. He took his time getting to his feet. "I'll get at it right away."

She was afraid of her emotions, he realized. She hadn't had as much time and practice at building solid doors, unlike the barriers he'd built long ago and reinforced as needed.

Cassie hurried to help with the dishes. Why had she lingered at the table and admitted to feeling alone at times?

Better to be alone than under someone's cruel thumb.

But Roper's words circled her brain. *God is with you. He will never leave you.*

But where was He when Grandfather made her life and Mother's life miserable? When her babies died? When George died, leaving her alone and penniless in Montreal?

He sent Linette. Made it possible to come to Edendale. Enabled her to start her own business.

Cassie straightened her spine. Yes, thank God, she had a fledgling business. It wasn't an opportunity she intended to waste. She put away the clean dishes and checked the bread. The loaves had risen so she put them in the oven to bake. She'd made biscuits after breakfast and taken them over to Macpherson. He'd thanked her and noted the amount in a ledger book.

"Heard a mule train is on its way. You'll have a meal ready for them?" he'd asked her.

"I will indeed." As she prepared a meal large enough to feed the hungry mule drovers, she listened to the sound of sawing and hammering. If she'd known more about construction work she could have done this on her own. Of course, the children's need for a safe home changed her need to do it herself.

A harsh truth gripped her thoughts.

It had changed many things.

She stared at the pot on the stove. Her chest tightened enough to make breathing difficult. The circumstances were changing her. Changing how she did business.

A few days ago she'd arrived here with her goals clearly formed. She would build a house, work and create a business on her own. She would ask no one for anything.

She knew no other way to ensure she would be independent.

Why had she allowed that to change? Not because of the children. She could take care of them fine on her own.

All she needed from Roper were instructions on how to build a house.

The food for a big meal was as ready as it could be until she heard the men cracking their whips as they reached town. She went outside, toward the shell of the house Roper was constructing. She watched every move. How he measured and cut. How he drove in the long spikes, making it look easy. He measured again from corner to corner.

"Why do you do that?" she asked, following him back

and forth as he had Neil hold the tape at one corner and stretched to the opposite one.

"To make sure it's square." He wound the tape measure up, apparently satisfied.

She needed to know how this ensured him it was square and what he would do if it wasn't but he trotted away for another board. She practically hung over his shoulder as he meticulously measured.

Slowly he straightened and faced her. "Did you want something in particular?"

She nodded. "I want to know what you're doing."

"Why?"

"I might need to know some time."

He shook his head and turned back to the board. "Muddbottom, if you ever need something built, you give me a holler, hear?"

She jerked back, almost tripping over a lump of dirt. A myriad of horrible feelings raged through her at the memories accompanying the sound of that name. "Don't ever call me that." She could barely squeeze the words through her tight throat.

He looked into the distance, exhaled noisily then slowly faced her. "Why not? Isn't it your name?"

She fought to push away the impact of that name. "It's a vile name belonging to my grandfather."

He set the pencil and tape measure on the board and edged closer. "Wouldn't it also be your father's name?"

"My father is dead and so is everything good associated with that name."

He was only inches away, his look endless and searching.

She scowled at him. "How do you know about it?"

He hesitated, then shrugged. "Read it in your Bible."

"You have no right to snoop." The births and deaths of

her babies were also in the Bible. He'd seen them. Seen fit to mention it when all she wanted to do was forget.

She stuffed her fist to her mouth to keep from crying out a protest and ran.

The only place she could hope to be alone was in the trees and she clamored through the underbrush unmindful of thorns tearing at her skirt.

"Cassie, wait."

There was nothing she wanted to hear from him. Nothing. He couldn't take back the words that brought painful memories from the deep pit where she'd buried them hoping they would never be resurrected.

She didn't stop running until she tripped over a root, and then she lay facedown in the leaves and needles, panting.

Her insides felt hollowed out, scraped cruelly by some sharp instrument. Her babies. Born two years apart. Perfectly formed. But neither of them had ever drawn a breath. They went from her warm sheltering womb to the cold lonely grave.

Oh, God, where were You then?

George hadn't blamed her in words but she was never in doubt that he silently thought she'd done something wrong.

But no more so than did she.

Oh, God, am I not to be allowed anything? Must I stand alone?

She knew the answer. *Yes.* Whatever she wanted or needed in life she must provide it herself.

No point in trusting God or a man to do for her what she could do for herself.

She scrambled to her feet, brushed the debris from her clothes, swiped at her face and smoothed her hair. No doubt she looked a wreck but that was immaterial.

She had a business to run and hiding in the trees, feeling sorry for herself would not lead to success.

She tramped back through the trees.

"Cassie?"

She practically bolted out of her shoes and stared at Roper half hidden in the shadows, sitting on a tree stump waiting.

"Are you okay?"

"I'm fine," she lied. She didn't know if she would ever be okay.

"I didn't mean to upset you."

"I'm fine." She didn't want to talk about her babies. Didn't want to ever mention them. The only way to deal with the pain was to push it so deep it would never surface.

And she'd done so successfully. Except for times like this when someone encroached into forbidden territory.

"I know you're not fine and I blame myself."

"Forget it."

"I don't think I can. I don't think you can. I seem to have an unfortunate knack for mentioning things that bring you pain."

She gave him a good hard stare, daring him to poke his nose any further into her business.

"I guess you don't much care for your grandfather."

She snorted. He had no idea. Suddenly she realized they weren't talking about the babies but about her grandfather. Her breath wheezed from tense lungs.

"I'm sorry about your losses." He spoke cautiously.

He did well to be guarded. She closed her eyes as a wave of pain clutched her insides.

"Never mind." She couldn't bear to say anything more.

"If you ever want to have a good cry I have two

shoulders you're welcome to use." He grinned somewhat crookedly.

"I've done all the crying I intend. Now if I'm not mistaken, there is a house to build and food to serve." She stomped on. Let him follow or sit like a bump on a log. Made no difference to her.

But she tipped her head a little and relaxed marginally as she heard him clumping after her. Unbidden a picture came to her imagination of her resting her head in the hollow of his shoulder and crying out her pain and sorrow and confusion as he rubbed her back and made soothing noises.

She shook her head. She needed no comforting. All she wanted…needed was to get on with her plans.

Chapter Eight

A short time later, Cassie welcomed the sound of the mule train. One thing Grandfather had been right about. Work didn't allow time for self-pity.

The children stood beside her as the drovers pulled up to the store yelling and cursing at their animals.

Daisy covered Pansy's ears and gave her brothers a warning look. "If I ever hear you say those words I'll wash your mouth out with soap. Mama would want me to."

"You listen to your sister," Roper said. "A man doesn't need to talk like that to accomplish his work."

Cassie felt him behind her but didn't turn. She couldn't look at him, couldn't even think about him without being reminded of painful things. Instead, she counted the men. "Six?"

"I'm guessing they'll eat more like a dozen."

"I'm prepared for it."

As the men unloaded supplies for Macpherson she rushed to get the meal ready to serve.

Daisy followed, shepherding her brothers ahead of her. "There's no need to stand around listening to that sort of talk."

Roper, as usual, hovered. "I'll give you a hand."

Cassie closed her eyes. Must they go through this again? She noticed Neil straining toward the activity at the store and it gave her an idea. "Why don't you take the younger children some place until the men have eaten?"

"Oh, yes, please," Daisy said, and handed Pansy to him. The little girl went eagerly, and Roper grinned.

"Glad to. Come on, boys. Let's go exploring."

Roper broke into a rough trot, bouncing Pansy until she giggled. The boys pushed at each other as they followed him down the hill.

He welcomed a chance to get away from Cassie's angry looks. He hadn't meant to upset her. But everything he did, every word he spoke brought forth her ire rather than her approval.

Playing with the kids would be a welcome relief from the sting of his failure.

"Where are we going?" Neil asked, falling in step on one side of him.

Billy trotted at his other side. Roper shortened his strides so the boy didn't have to work so hard to keep up.

"I bet there's treasure around here," Billy said. "Didn't Pa say he might find gold? Roper, where can we find gold?"

Roper chuckled at the boy's intensity. "What would you do if you found some?"

Billy picked up a handful of rocks. "I'd buy us a home."

The words fell into the air like hailstones, forceful, bruising.

Roper pulled Billy close. "I promise you will have a home." He had to believe going to a relative was the best thing for them.

Neil moved closer. "Daisy said you're an orphan like us."

"That's right." The boys considered him, as if checking to see if being an orphan had branded him.

He chuckled and playfully knuckled Neil on the arm. "It isn't the worst thing in the world, you know."

"What's worse?" Billy asked, his voice so mournful Roper's smile disappeared instantly.

"I can think of a few things. Being in a home where people are cruel. Not having anything to eat or a safe place to sleep." Losing two babies. He shook his head. He had to stop wanting to salve Cassie's pain. She didn't welcome it in the least.

Billy's breath released in a long sigh. "We sure 'nough have lots to eat. Cassie's a good cook. Don't you think so?"

"I surely do. I expect she's good at whatever she does."

Neil laughed. "Except putting up a tent."

Roper laughed, too. "Or building a house."

"Or digging a cellar." Neil laughed so hard he had to sit on the log beside Roper.

Billy didn't even smile. "You guys are mean laughing at her."

Roper sobered. "Ah, Billy. We aren't being mean. Just having fun."

Neil jumped to his feet and faced them. "We wouldn't be mean to Cassie. We like her, don't we, Roper?"

Roper could honestly say he did. More than was wise, considering her reaction to him.

"Why don't you tell her?" Billy asked.

The boys waited for his answer. Pansy played with his collar.

"I don't think it would be a good idea."

Neil plopped down on the log again. "I guess if you say being an orphan is okay, I'll believe you."

"You'll be fine. All of you." A person couldn't change the facts but he could enjoy the good things of life. "Let's go look for treasure."

The pair dashed off, pausing to examine shiny rocks then running on.

A little later Roper lifted his head and tipped his ear toward Edendale. "Listen, I think I hear the wagons leaving. We better go back and help Cassie and Daisy. They'll need water and wood." It took concentrated effort to keep from jogging back to the camp.

Home.

Cassie.

Don't put down roots. Don't expect you can have family. Never stay where you're not wanted. She clearly didn't want him. But he could not drive the traitorous word *home* from his mind. The best he could do was ignore it.

He crested the hill, and drew to a halt. She stood at the end of the table, smiling widely. His lungs drew in air with a whoosh and he realized he'd been worried about her alone with rough men. Her and Daisy. To see the pleasure in her expression eased his concerns.

She glanced up. When her smile didn't falter, his worry disappeared. She'd forgiven him for his earlier comments. Or forgotten about them, at least.

"You look pleased."

She nodded. "I am. The men each paid double what I asked." She shook the can. "I can hardly believe how well things are going. Every penny earned is a penny more I can pay Macpherson toward what I owe him."

"That's good."

"I don't like owing anyone."

"I kind of figured that out." He was glad to see her

good humor returned. Too bad it couldn't be because of something he'd done. Perhaps he should start a list of things that upset her, topics he must avoid. Talk of her babies, which he could sympathize with. Use of her name, Muddbottom. That had something to do with her grandfather. Offers to help. He stopped because he couldn't avoid that. He'd never stop trying to help her.

He'd simply have to find more subtle ways of doing it.

He grabbed up two empty buckets and trotted to the river. When he returned he filled the kettle and the basins and the pots she used for washing up dishes. He made certain there was plenty of wood, then returned to the construction of the house, measuring, sawing and hammering at a steady pace, Neil assisting him.

Hoofbeats signaled the approach of riders. He straightened to consider the visitors.

"Who are they?" Neil asked.

Roper tossed aside the hammer and headed for the trio. "Cowboys from Eden Valley Ranch."

Slim, a thin man who lived up to his name. Roper had found him to be quiet and helpful. Ward, solidly built with a ready smile and a quick sense of humor. He often tread where angels feared. And red-haired Blue—shy but thoughtful.

The trio swung down from their mounts.

Cassie put aside the paring knife and the potato she'd been peeling and hurried forward. "Welcome."

Ward pushed back his hat and looked about. "So this is what the pair of you are up to. Kids, a house…looks like a real home shaping up here."

Roper watched Cassie's shoulders stiffen and tried to signal Ward to stop his comments but Ward's attention had shifted to the children. "Hey, kids, these people treating you all right?"

Daisy and Neil had formed a flank with Pansy in Daisy's arms and Billy firmly between them. Daisy studied Ward then nodded. "They're good to us."

Neil added, "We help."

Slim held a package toward Cassie. "Cookie insisted we bring you cinnamon buns."

Roper chuckled as the children lost all wariness.

Cassie laughed, too. "Thank Cookie and tell her we truly appreciate them."

"I'll do that," Slim said. "But I'm to tell you she wants to know when you plan to visit."

"I'd love to." Cassie glanced about, her expression going from relaxed to stubborn. "Tell her I'm pretty busy now."

As Ward talked to the children and Slim talked to Cassie, Blue followed Roper to the construction site.

"This will be Cassie's home and give her a place to serve meals indoors in poor weather," Roper explained.

"She's really intent on this, isn't she?"

"Yes, I am," Cassie said as she hurried toward them. "Macpherson says I'll do well."

"Looks like you could use a hand." Blue waved to the others. "Come on, boys, let's help Roper with this floor."

Cassie sputtered a protest but no one but Roper seemed to hear.

The cowboys clattered to where Roper had several beams measured and cut. In a few minutes they had them in place and the spikes driven to secure them.

Roper saw Cassie's expression darken, and knew she resented their help. But she couldn't make herself heard above the hammering. She turned and stomped away. Out here people helped people. He vowed to speak to her about it before she offended someone.

A little later the three cowboys left.

This was his chance. "Cassie, you can't refuse every offer of neighborly help without offending someone."

"I don't want to be owing."

He'd expected her reply but still it clawed at his thoughts. He pushed to his feet. "Cassie, when will you learn not everyone demands repayment for kindness?" He strode away not wanting to hear her answer, sure it would be the same as always.

It had been a long and challenging day and Cassie couldn't wait for the forgetfulness of sleep.

Her emotions had been up and down all day. Up when the drovers paid her so well, up when the cowboys brought greetings from the ranch. Down when Roper scolded her for trying to turn away help from the cowboys.

A suspicion burst into her thoughts. Maybe he resented his part of their agreement, resented the amount of work he had to do. It wasn't as if she did anything in return. Their agreement had been for her to look after the children but she would do that, anyway, so it really didn't count. She must tell him he wasn't obligated to stay.

She could manage on her own. She wouldn't be lonely.

Especially for someone who had the bad taste to remind her of her babies.

Cassie tried to push the memories from her mind, tried to fall asleep so she could forget but every time she closed her eyes she saw her babies. Each wore a white dress as they were laid out in a satin-lined box. She stared into the dark, tried to focus on the sound of a fly buzzing against the canvas. The noise echoed in her head, annoying her.

It was too hot to sleep.

She pushed from her mat, pulled her dress over her head and stepped outside to the murmur of night noises.

She filled her lungs until they ached. Still the unsettled feeling of loss and loneliness would not depart.

"Cassie?"

She jerked toward the sound. "Roper?"

He climbed up the riverbank and came to her side. "Yes. Can't you sleep?"

"Too hot." He didn't need to know the real reason even though he was to blame. But at the moment, she lacked the energy to confront him.

"I have something to show you."

"What?"

"Come and see." He signaled for her to follow him back down the bank.

She hesitated. But anything was better than staring into the darkness of her past.

He fell in at her side, took her hand. "It's hard to see."

She started to pull away and stumbled. Only his grasp kept her from falling so she let him guide her down the bank toward the river.

"Over here. Sit down." His blanket had been spread against the sloping bank.

She sat. He lowered himself beside her, crowding close as they shared the blanket. He lounged back as if in a chair. "Look up."

She did, seeing a beautiful clear night with the sky full of bright stars. Her breath eased out of her strangled lungs.

Cool air came from the river. She sank back to enjoy the sky. The blanket smelled faintly of horse reminding her of the life Roper normally lived. "Don't you miss being out on the range, riding and roping?"

"Can ride my horse any time I want. Mostly I'm content being here. Building your house. Helping care for the youngsters."

He truly sounded as if nothing else mattered. She tried to convince herself it didn't make her feel a tiny bit special. Now was the time to inform him he didn't need to stay.

But before she could say anything a star flashed across the sky and flared into a sudden death. "Oh. A falling star."

"Yup. Seen six already. I guess it's a meteorite shower."

"Another." She pointed and adjusted herself more comfortably on the narrow blanket which meant she edged closer to Roper, felt the warmth of his arm against hers.

Then the sky was still. She waited, afraid to take her eyes from the sparkling canvas lest she miss a falling star.

One crossed the sky and before she could comment another. "Two," she murmured. "They come and go so quickly. They die almost as soon as they're born." The meaning of the words flared through her heart, searing a white-hot trail. Her throat tightened and a scalding tear escaped each eye. She wiped them away. She did not intend to cry over deaths that came too soon and sudden.

But a torrent threatened.

Another star blazed across the sky and burned out.

It happened so fast. Ended so quickly.

A sob ached from her throat. The tears scorched down her cheeks. She stiffened, determined to hide this embarrassing display of weakness.

Roper shifted to study her.

She prayed he couldn't see her tears or her twisted face in the darkness.

"Cassie, are you okay?"

She couldn't answer except for a muffled sound that even to her ears seemed more sob than denial.

He edged his arm under her neck and pulled her to his side. "I told you my shoulders are available anytime."

Heaven help her but she couldn't deny herself this bit of comfort, and she buried her face in the fabric of his shirt and let the tears flow. Once started she could not stop them. They tore from some secret place deep inside, a well of hidden, denied, bottomless sorrow. She clutched his shirtfront and hung on for dear life.

He made murmuring noises as he cradled her gently. It didn't matter that his sounds and words made no sense. They conveyed such a feeling of compassion and care that it made her cry harder.

Eventually, she cried herself dry. Too weak and spent to move, she remained in his arms as he stroked her hair. Gratefully he didn't seem to have a need to talk. She couldn't have said an intelligible word at the moment.

"Look." He pointed toward the sky. "Oh, you missed it."

But another flared across the sky. "That was a big one," she said.

"Good thing they burn up before they hit the earth."

She considered the idea. "Do you think there is a reason for bad things?"

He was quiet a moment. "I don't think God sends bad things. Wouldn't that make Him evil? But I think He can turn them into something good. Maybe He does so with such skill that we sometimes think He arranged the bad things."

She nodded. His words made more sense than the empty things well-meaning friends had said when her babies died. *This is God's will. They are far better where they are now...back with God.* "I don't see how God can make something good out of my babies' deaths."

His arm tightened across her shoulder. "Maybe the good is only found in God, not in our own hearts."

She tried to think what he meant but could not. "I don't understand."

He shifted to look into her eyes. He was close enough she could feel his breath on her cheek, but it was too dark to see his expression. "I think what I am trying to say is if I look inside, just at me, I see the hurt, the pain, the missing pieces. But if I look at God, maybe even let Him move into that area of my heart, I see wholeness, healing and love. Does that make sense?" He sat back. "I'm not much good with words."

She touched his cheek, liking the feel of his rough whiskers. "Your words are more than adequate and yes, it makes sense. I was somehow thinking God would make me forget the pain of my past. But you make me consider that maybe I can't forget, shouldn't even try. I can only let God cover it with His love." An awesome truth filled her heart. "God's love is bigger than my pain."

He gently caught her upper arms. "You say it much better than I do but that's exactly what I meant." He studied her, with her face toward the sky, seeing her better than she saw him. "Cassie, I am so sorry about your babies. I can't imagine your pain."

And yet the way his voice deepened, she felt he understood better than George had. "I've never before admitted to anyone how much it hurt." She pressed her palm to his cheek. "Thank you."

He captured her hand, turned to press his lips to her palm.

She saw he meant to kiss her. She hesitated half a beat and then she lifted her face toward him. It was only a kiss. A thank-you for his comfort. The final act of releasing her sorrow.

His lips caught hers, warm, gentle and yet…

Her heart lifted on gossamer wings and fluttered gently, soothingly, sweetly.

He hesitated as if he meant to end the kiss but she clung to him, not ready for it to be over. She'd been kissed many times. After all, she'd been married. But nothing before this had reached into a hitherto unknown corner of her heart and made her aware of a deep, bottomless longing.

Summoning every bit of strength, she forced herself to pull away. The kiss made something between them real. She didn't know what to call it. Friendship? Understanding? Acknowledgment of shared emotions?

For now she was content to remain cradled against his side.

That thought didn't seem quite right but she lacked the energy to examine it.

Half an hour later, they decided the meteorite shower had ended.

"I should go." Cassie scrambled to her feet.

Roper bounded up and caught her hand. "Thank you for a nice evening."

It was she who should thank him but how did one thank another for being allowed to soak the front of his shirt? Instead, she said, "It was nice." And with a hurried good-night she headed away.

But Roper would have none of that. "I'll see you safely back to the shack." Again he caught her hand and guided her up the hill. They paused outside the shack. He pulled her close and she willing went back into his arms. A harbor for her pain. She pressed her cheek to his chest and heard the steady beat of his heart.

When he caught her chin in his fingers and lifted her face to him, she again welcomed his kiss.

And then he turned her toward the door. "Good night, Cassie."

It wasn't until she was safely inside the shack that she realized she hadn't told him he wasn't obligated to stay. Did she really need to do so? Did she even want to?

She wouldn't answer the question. Not tonight.

Chapter Nine

Roper grinned up at the star-filled sky. *Thank You, Jesus, that I was able to offer comfort to Cassie.*

Back at his camp, he bent over his knees and groaned as pain chewed through him. Poor Cassie, losing her babies, then her husband. Oh, if only he could have spared her the pain. Or help her get past it.

But he couldn't. He had to accept and trust that God would use it to create something special in her life.

He settled down on his blanket, remembering how Cassie snuggled close to watch the stars, then turned into his arms. He'd offered his kisses as comfort and understood she'd welcomed them as such.

Only it wasn't comfort he felt in his heart. It was far more intense than sympathy.

He had nothing to offer Cassie except his two hands to build her house, his strength to drive in nails…

And his arms to offer comfort.

If only…

But he'd long ago accepted his reality. A man with no name. No past. And a lonely future. He'd learned to find satisfaction in making others happy. It was enough. His words to her echoed in his head. Did he truly let God fill the missing pieces in his heart? He had to. Nothing—no one—else could.

The next morning he climbed the bank with renewed determination to build Cassie's house as quickly and sturdily as he could.

But when she glanced up, a shy smile trembling on her lips, he faltered. All his fine intentions did not erase the emotions he'd felt last night. He had to fight his way back to his objective of expecting nothing more than the chance to help her.

"Morning," he called. "Everyone sleep well?"

He managed to act normal over the meal though his insides jumped every time Cassie moved, and holding her hand to say grace made his mouth run dry.

He took up her Bible, paused as he thought about the entries in the front. Of their own accord, his eyes sought hers.

They shared a silent memory of last night.

Realizing four youngsters watched him, Roper forced his attention back to the Bible. He opened to the bookmark and read, skipping over the names he couldn't pronounce.

Then he again reached for her hand so he could pray for God's safety and protection over them this day. Feeling her hand so firm in his own, gripping back as if she needed his strength, made him realize how much he wanted to be able to do this for her—and the children—day after day.

Don't put down roots. You'll only have them ripped out. He knew the pain of such uprooting. He meant to avoid it.

He said amen, and jumped to his feet. "Time to get to work."

Neil followed him over to the house and they set to sawing and hammering.

This was one thing he could do for her and one thing she would allow.

He bent his back to the task and worked with fervor. Only when Daisy called them for the noon meal did he realize Neil looked exhausted. Guilt blared through him. He'd worked the boy too hard. "After we've eaten we'll rest."

Neil almost folded with relief.

"Let's all go down to the river," he said as he sat down to eat.

"You and the children go ahead. I'll see to the dishes." Cassie looked hot and bothered as if she had worked at a frenzied pace all morning, as well.

"Seems we could all stand to cool off a bit." The sun sucked the moisture from the air and poured heat into every corner. "A break will refresh us all."

She didn't answer, simply waited for him to say grace. Even her hand felt limp. A bit of flour dusted one cheek. Her hair was damp about the edges. No doubt she'd spent the morning baking bread and biscuits. The heat from the cook stove would practically melt her bones on a day like this.

He would somehow convince her to go to the river and cool off.

As soon as they finished eating he gathered the dishes, and stuck them in the dishpan. He grabbed the kettle, and poured hot water over the lot. "Let them soak and they'll wash easier."

She didn't look convinced. "I need to get potatoes ready in case people come by for a meal."

"If the men want a meal they'll wait."

She considered the idea.

"It's not like they can go across the street to a competitor." He could see her begin to relent. "'Sides, everyone knows your meals are worth waiting for."

His praise accomplished its purpose and she nodded. "I wouldn't mind cooling off."

"Great." He led them to the river. The children took off their shoes and stockings and played in the water. He scooted out of his boots and rolled up his jeans so he could keep a hand on Pansy and protect her. "Come on." He waved toward Cassie. "This will cool you off."

She remained on the shore.

The youngsters called her to join them.

"How can I resist?"

The question teased Roper into wondering exactly what she meant. Resist the invitation to paddle in the river? Or resist all the things he wanted to give her?

She dipped her hand into the water and shivered at the cold shock.

Daisy giggled. "It feels good once you get used to it."

Neil splashed water on his face. "That sure cools me off." He cupped a handful and poured it over his head.

Billy and Daisy followed his example, and laughed.

Roper and Cassie looked at each other, the silvery water between them, Pansy at his side dragging her hands through the water. Roper held out his other hand to Cassie. "Come on in. The water's fine."

Her gaze darted to his hand then his face, searching his eyes as if the invitation held a hidden message.

Perhaps it did.

He wanted her to learn to trust him. Realize he would always protect her and take care of her if she would let him. She slipped off her shoes and slowly, hesitantly, she lifted her hand to him.

He pulled her closer, laughing when she squealed as

the cold water covered her feet and then rose to her ankles. She stopped inches away, her hand still resting in his. He smiled. "You're safe."

She nodded.

Neil flicked water at Daisy and soon the three older youngsters were soaked and laughing.

Pansy jumped up and down and squealed. She tugged at Roper's hand trying to escape to join the others but Roper held on, knowing she would fall down in the water.

Suddenly the trio turned toward Cassie and Roper. He saw the mischief in their eyes in time to jerk about and plant himself between Cassie and the spray of water the children sent their way. He pulled her to his chest. She drew close, hiding from the splashes. Pansy gasped then screamed.

The water attack stopped. Roper turned to stare down at the little girl. Her eyes were wide. Had she been hurt?

Daisy plowed through the water and snatched up her sister. "You boys stop spraying. You've frightened her." She pushed to dry ground and sat down, Pansy in her wet lap, crooning comfort.

The boys followed, and sat on either side of Daisy. "Sorry, Pansy," Neil murmured. "We didn't mean to scare you."

Billy stuck his face close to Pansy's. "I'm sorry, too. Please don't cry."

Cassie remained pressed to Roper's chest. He held her close, wanting to protect her from more than a spray of cold water. She clutched his shirtfront and her cheek pressed to his shoulder as if she found welcoming shelter.

Suddenly she jerked away, darted him a red-cheeked glance then headed toward the children.

He followed, making no effort to hide his grin. He'd seen the flash of awareness before embarrassment burned it away. And he knew without a doubt that she had enjoyed being protected in his arms.

It was enough for now.

Again, warning words flashed across his brain. *What happens later?* He'd have to leave. But he'd always known that. At least he could be at peace as he moved on, knowing he'd helped her.

His mental argument failed to provide the comfort he sought.

He joined them, knelt beside Daisy and stroked Pansy's head. "You okay, little one?"

She sobbed, and leaned out for him to take her.

His heart tightened as he cradled the child to his shoulder, shushing her and patting her back. Cassie watched. Was she remembering being comforted in the same way?

He shifted Pansy to one side and reached out a hand for Cassie.

Ignoring his outstretched arm, she said, "Guess it's time to get back to work." She sat down to put on her shoes. He realized he stood barefoot and scrubbed his feet on his pant legs and sat down to put on his own footwear.

Pansy scrambled away to retrieve her shoes and stockings, and handed them to Roper.

A few minutes later they climbed the hill. Roper, with Neil at his side, returned to work on the house. Billy trailed after them.

Roper hummed as he worked, satisfied Cassie had allowed him to comfort her.

The aroma of stewing meat and cooking potatoes filled the air with pleasant thoughts. A man should enjoy such comforts all the days of his life.

He straightened so fast he sent a board skidding away.

Here he was—a nobody—dreaming of a future that he couldn't own. Forbidden dreams and hopes pushed at the barred door in the back of his heart. Not only were they forbidden, they were impossible. His humming silenced. He bent his back and heart into doing for Cassie what he could—build her a house.

If he hadn't been so intent on driving away senseless dreams with every hammer blow he might have noticed the arrival of company before Neil said, "Lane is here."

Roper spun around. Yup. It was Lane. With a bouquet of wildflowers stuck in a tin can that still wore a label indicating the contents had been tomatoes.

Lane stood with the flowers in one hand, his hat in the other.

Roper eyed the hat. Black. Looked to be all new and fancy. What happened to the battered gray thing he wore the other day?

Cassie, in the shack, had not seen the man standing awkwardly in her yard.

Daisy came out with potato peelings and saw him. Her eyes narrowed and she backed into the shack. "You got company."

Cassie stepped out, drying her hands on her apron. "Lane?"

Roper tried to decide if it was only surprise that made her word sound breathless.

"Thought you might like some flowers." Lane took a step closer and held out the bouquet.

Cassie darted a glance at Roper as if silently asking him what this meant. He crossed his arms over his chest and watched without letting any of his emotions show in his face. He should be happy if a man wanted to court her. Didn't she deserve every bit of happiness she could find? But an emotion totally opposed to gratitude raged through his veins.

Cassie took the flowers and buried her nose in them. "Umm. They smell good. Thank you." She set the tin can in the middle of the table.

"F'owers." Pansy rushed forward.

Daisy lifted her, and let her sniff them.

"Like f'owers," Pansy declared.

Roper studied the flowers. Purple bells. Pink roses. White something or other. Yellow ones. Lots of them. Did the man spend his entire life gathering flowers? "Some of us have work to do." He grabbed his hammer and pounded a nail into place. What good were flowers? Except he'd seen the pleasure in Cassie's eyes as she admired them.

He kept his back to the others as he drove home nail after nail. He tried not to hear the murmur of their voices. Forced himself not to imagine Cassie smiling at Lane.

And faced a harsh truth.

He wanted to give her more than help and safety. And he didn't want Lane giving her anything. Somehow, without his notice, and certainly without his permission, his feelings had shifted beyond simply wanting to help. They had developed deeper than wanting only to make her happy. As if he could even dream of anything more.

Neil slipped away to join the conversation around the table leaving Roper alone to face his mental struggle.

He resented not knowing who he was. More than that, he abhorred his weakness in not following his own rules.

What had he told Cassie last night? That God provided wholeness and healing? But did God provide an identity? Because Roper felt like nobody at the moment. A nameless child with no past.

No future.

Nothing he could share.

Flowers? Cassie alternately looked from them to the face of the cowboy who brought them. Sure, flowers were nice. The bouquet brightened the table. But what did he want?

Roper continued pounding away on her house, the noise blasting against the inside of her skull. Lane sat with his elbows on the table telling her about his oat crop. His words rushed through her head with the insistence of raging water.

She glanced at Roper. If he would join them she'd feel she could go back to the shack without being rude. How was she to get the meal cooked if she had to entertain Lane?

But Roper hammered relentlessly. Her eyes bored into him. He so often went on about how he wanted to help her. Well, here was his chance. He could march himself over here and visit with Lane.

But her scowl landed on his back without causing him to flinch. Certainly without making him turn to see what she needed.

Fine. She'd manage without his help. Just as she meant to from the start. "You'll have to excuse me. I have work." She waved toward the shack.

Lane leaped to his feet. "Don't mean to be in your way. I'll just hang about until the meal is ready, if you don't mind."

"No. That's fine." Feeding people was what she did. She glanced at the flowers before she hurried to the shack.

Lane was still at the table when she heard others arrive and she hustled out to take count.

Six paying customers even though she knew the two drovers would each eat enough for three ordinary men.

Her business was growing. A glow of satisfaction warmed her insides.

She left Daisy to set the table while she went inside to get the food. As she turned, she came up short, almost slamming the pot of potatoes into Roper. She staggered, caught her balance and favored him with a narrow-eyed look she hoped conveyed more than surprise. She wanted him to know how annoyed she was with him.

He grinned unrepentantly as if pleased at getting her attention, even in a negative fashion. "I'll help you."

She hesitated, wanting to prove she didn't need help. The pot grew heavy in her arms as she mentally argued with her pride. But pride mattered little when there was work to be done and men to be fed. His assistance would mean half as many trips back and forth in the heat. She didn't have the strength to say no. Truth be told she was glad to see him after being ignored for the past hour. She would have scolded herself for such foolishness but she didn't have the time. The men wolfed down food as fast as it appeared. She'd held back enough to feed Roper and the children later or they would likely have cleaned her out. The children and Roper could have eaten with the men. Probably would have been simpler. But there was something cozy about the six of them eating alone, without these hungry men sharing their table.

Anxious to fill their stomachs and get on with their business, the men washed the food down with copious amounts of coffee that Roper kept pouring.

Except for Lane. He ate leisurely. Like a real gentleman. Every time Cassie's glance slid by him he watched her. Each time she jerked away, resisting an urge to run her hands over her hair. She tried not to let his attention unsettle her, but it did.

Almost as much as the way Roper studied him. His expression gave away little but she couldn't help wonder why he was so interested in the man.

"How's that crop of yours?" Roper's question seemed

sincere but Cassie watched to see if he had something else in mind.

"Good. Going to produce a bumper crop. I'm pleased with the way this new land has produced. Shows lots of promise. I'll have a good supply of feed for the winter."

Roper considered the comment. "A man can go far in this part of the country. Good grass. Good water. Good soil."

Lane leaned back, nursing his coffee cup. "Great place for a man to start his own place. Raise a family." His gaze brushed Cassie before he brought his full attention back to Roper.

Her cheeks burned. Did he think she would be part of his dream?

She spun away.

She had no intention of belonging to any man. Ever again.

Even if she had found sweet comfort in Roper's arms and from his kiss.

It had been a momentary lapse and it wouldn't happen again.

The men finished and departed, Lane at the tail, saluting a goodbye and promising to come again.

She wanted to tell him not to bother but he was a customer. She couldn't afford to turn him away so she smiled and waved, then started cleaning up the meal. She washed plates and forks so fast Daisy couldn't keep up then attacked the pots with vigor.

Daisy giggled. "You're going to wear a hole in it."

Cassie stopped scrubbing and straightened. "Guess I'm taking out my frustration on the pot."

"Don't you like Lane? I think he's handsome." She blushed and ducked away.

"I suppose he is." Though not exactly to her liking. She preferred—

Roper's face sprang to her imagination and she closed her eyes and willed it away. How had he wriggled so far into her thoughts? "I just don't care to belong to any man."

Daisy twisted the tea towel and considered Cassie's words. Finally she spoke. "My ma said she and Pa were one. Neither was more important than the other. They were equal and stronger for being together. She didn't seem to mind belonging to Pa."

"Your parents had a special relationship." Or else they hid their problems from the children.

"I thought all married people were like them." She looked toward her brothers. Slowly she hung the towel, picked up Pansy and went to join them.

Cassie put away the last pot and turned to see Roper standing nearby watching. "What?"

"Did you love him?"

"Who?" She knew he meant George, and when he waited, letting her know he knew, she mumbled, "We weren't like the children's ma and pa."

"What were you like?"

"Why?" She remembered his understanding and comfort about her babies and longed to feel it again. But her feelings regarding George were different than her feelings about her babies. More confused. Filled with a thousand different things. Anger. Guilt. Disappointment. Shattered hope.

He didn't move in close, forcing her to confront his gentle gaze. Instead, she felt it slip past the barricade her feelings formed.

"I married George to get away from my grandfather. George was never unkind." She tried to rein in her feelings. Stop the rush of words pushing at her tongue. "He just didn't take my feelings into account. Nor consider my wants or needs."

His gaze never faltered. Neither did it judge.

More words rushed uncensored to her mouth. "I don't know if I even understood what love was when I married George."

He waited, his eyes darkening with a deep emotion. She didn't try and analyze what it was.

"I thought we shared the same dreams."

"But you didn't?" he probed gently.

"Turns out no. I wanted only to settle in a safe home. George wanted to move West, try his hand at homesteading. Free land. Acres of it. We needed only to earn a little more money to buy machinery and supplies." She forced herself to take in a deep breath. Tried to calm the harsh words that revealed a truth she had never before confronted. "I tried to explain that I didn't want to move or start a farm in a new land but he said I was his wife and had no choice but to follow him."

His gentle smile contained sadness. "No wonder you vow not to belong to a man again."

She nodded. "There are many ways of owning and controlling a person."

He didn't speak for a moment. "What happened to him?"

"He got a job working in the woods to earn some money before our final leg of the trip out here. Got soaking wet one day." She stared straight ahead, seeing nothing as she relived those dreadful days. "His raging fever frightened me. We were in a new and strange country where I heard more French than English. I couldn't make anyone understand my need for medical help. In the end I was helpless to do anything except hold him as he gasped his final breath."

Her chest filled with a merciless weight. She thought she was in desperate straits under her grandfather's harshness. Thought things were bad when George dragged her to Canada. But when she sat beside his cold, dead body she realized that was nothing compared to being abandoned in a foreign land.

She shuddered as wave after wave of remembering pounded through her.

Roper's eyes filled with sorrow. Oh, how she ached to go into those comforting arms.

She hadn't realized he'd moved until he opened his arms and pulled her to his chest.

"Oh, Cassie. If only I'd been there to help."

She clung to his shirtfront as stored-up fear and sorrow washed through her.

"How did you manage?" His voice rumbled beneath her ear.

She sniffed back her tears. "I was all alone with no money. No home. I ended up sleeping in the train station, avoiding the conductors and station master who would have driven me out." Safe in his arms, she could almost smile at her predicament. "That's where Linette found me and practically forced me to come with her. I fought the idea, not wanting to be under another person's control again."

He laughed, the sound a gentle murmur inside his chest. "Good thing she did, otherwise what would have happened?"

"Turns out it was a move in the right direction. Out here in the West I can start my own business and stand on my own two feet with some hope of success without depending on a man…or woman, for that matter." She understood the irony of saying she had to stand on her own two feet while leaning against Roper, safe in his arms. But it was only for a moment while she gathered together her resolve. Then she pushed back and put a step between them.

"I learned a valuable lesson. I would never again be so dependent on another." She met Roper's gaze with determination. "I accept help only when I can pay for it in a businesslike fashion."

Roper crossed his arms and gave her a gentle smile. She knew he was thinking of last night. She'd accepted something from him that could not be bought or paid for.

And she could not bring herself to regret it.

Suddenly she remembered her own parents when her father was still alive. They honored each other without any obligation.

Except to love each other.

Where had those words come from? She must have heard them somewhere but she couldn't recall where. Perhaps a sermon at church. Or…

She shrugged.

Did it mean love was an obligation? A debt she had to pay? It made love sound petty and controlling.

She wished she could believe it was otherwise but she had no proof it was. Unless she counted her parents.

Roper shook his head. "Cassie, prickly Cassie."

She wanted to take offense at his words but they were spoken so softly she couldn't.

"Someday you will learn you can't reduce life to a balance statement of debts owed and debts paid. Some things are given freely. To try and repay a gift is an insult to the giver."

"Isn't there always an unspoken expectation?"

"I don't think so."

She tore her gaze from him only to see the flowers in the middle of the table. A gift. But certainly with expectations. If she wasn't mistaken Lane wanted to pursue a relationship. "My experience says otherwise."

He didn't move, causing her to look at him to see why. He watched her with a gentle, chiding expression on his face. "If you are completely honest with yourself you will know that isn't true."

No doubt he meant last night. And he was right. She couldn't deny she had nothing to give him in return and knew he didn't expect it. But she didn't know what to make of it.

She searched for an escape from his relentless look… from her confused thoughts. Her eyes scanned the site and lit on the basin full of water. "I need to finish my chores." Turning away, she lifted the pan, not caring that water sloshed over the sides and soaked her skirts.

"I'll do it." Roper reached for the basin but she jerked away, sloshing even more water over the sides. At this rate there'd be nothing to pitch out by the time she had gone three steps.

"I've got it." *Hear me, Roper Jones. I can do this on my own.*

He wisely stepped back.

Roper grinned as she stomped away, her wet skirts clinging to her legs. She could protest all she wanted but he hadn't forgotten how she'd allowed him to hold her and give her comfort last night. Nor would he ever forget it. His smile melted away as he thought of her words to Daisy, how she'd been alone with a dying husband, hiding in a train station. No wonder she'd been so prickly those first few months at Eden Valley Ranch.

Avoiding the muddy spot where she'd slopped water, he took six strides that brought him to her side.

She stubbornly kept her back to him, shaking lingering drops from the basin as if each silvery tear must water the ground.

He ached to pull her into his arms and comfort her as he had last night. "Cassie?" Would she hear the unexpressed invitation in his voice?

A shudder crept across her shoulders, and then they settled in a slight hunch. "Guess it's true what they say."

"What's that?"

"What doesn't kill you makes you stronger." She turned, the fierce look in her eyes almost blinding him. "I know I'm stronger for my experiences."

"Strong, yes. No one could deny it. But still a mite prickly." He grinned, hoping to convey a teasing tone even though he was deadly serious.

She spared him a defiant look. "Guess maybe the two go together." And she stomped away.

He knew strong and prickly didn't belong hand in hand unless a person chose to let them, but he reckoned now was not the time to argue with her. His gaze lighted on the flowers wilting in the tomato can and he figured his expression might match Cassie's. What did Lane want? As if it wasn't as obvious as the nose on his face.

The man would no doubt hang about courting Cassie, growing more and more open about his intentions. 'Course he had to tend to his work at least part of the time. Cutting his crop. Feeding his livestock. Gathering wood for the winter. Why, Roper figured, the man should be busy most every day of the week. Perhaps a little nudge reminding Lane of the upcoming winter would be in order.

His tension fled as quickly as it came.

Lane might bring flowers that died within hours but Roper was building Cassie a house. He figured the house to be more important than flowers any day of the week.

Whistling under his breath he sauntered back to the building site. He was satisfied with his work.

Still his gaze returned over and over to the wilted flowers. And his thoughts circled back to an endless regret.

He had nothing to offer Cassie, or anyone, apart from his help.

Cassie left the washbasin on the grass, and followed the sound of the children to the riverbank. Her conscience warned her she should be working—or was it only Grandfather's persistent voice? But she didn't want to return to the home site and see Roper. Even if she couldn't see him, she heard him working and was acutely aware of his presence nearby.

Prickly Cassie. He'd said it a number of times. She saw it as determination.

Some things are given freely. Like what? It hadn't been so in her experience.

She caught up to the children.

The boys picked through a pile of rocks.

Daisy sat on the sand, piling it into a heap for Pansy. She glanced up at Cassie's approach. "Do you need me?"

"No. Supper is ready. We'll eat a little later. Enjoy your play."

Daisy got to her feet. "I'll help if you need something done. It's the least I can do seeing as you're feeding the four of us."

"Oh, Daisy, I don't mind." She rather enjoyed wiping little faces after each meal, checking that there were clothes for them each morning. She liked baking things the children enjoyed. "I don't expect repayment."

The words echoed what Roper had said.

If Cassie could give without thought of repayment, was it possible others did?

She waggled her hand at Daisy. "You play with your little sister." She sat with her back to a nearby tree and watched the children. They were a sweet bunch and deserved a home where they were loved and allowed to be children. Their uncle better be a more appropriate guardian than her grandfather had been.

Pansy joined the boys examining rocks, ever under the watchful eye of Daisy who sat close by guarding her younger siblings.

Pansy picked up a rock and headed toward Cassie.

"Stay here," Daisy said.

Pansy shook her head. "I show her." She nodded at Cassie.

Daisy hesitated a heartbeat before saying, "Okay."

Cassie held her breath as Pansy walked to her, the rock cupped in her hands. The little one had never warmed up to her like she had to Roper. Or perhaps Cassie hadn't invited it, reminding her as she did of her own babies. But now she ached to be friends with Pansy and smiled encouragement.

"What do you have there?" she asked as Pansy stood before her.

"Treasure." She held out her rock.

Cassie took it and examined it carefully. "It's very pretty. See the pink here?"

"Pink."

Cassie held it out for Pansy to take.

"It for you."

"Me? Why thank you." She tucked it into her apron pocket.

Pansy edged closer until she stood at Cassie's shoulder. She patted Cassie's cheeks, her little hands soft and gentle. "I like you."

"I like you, too." The words caught in Cassie's throat.

Pansy plopped into Cassie's lap.

Daisy, watching the whole thing, smiled and turned back to her brothers.

Little Pansy snuggled close.

Cassie closed her eyes. She pressed her cheek to the sun-drenched hair, breathed in the smell of damp sand and baby skin. She held Pansy close, and let the feel of the warm little body fill her empty heart.

They sat quietly for several minutes, Pansy wrapped in Cassie's arms, then Pansy squirmed. "I go play."

Cassie reluctantly released her to run back to the others.

Daisy turned and smiled.

Cassie's answering smile came from deep inside, from a place that had been lonely and afraid a long time.

After a while Neil left, saying he needed to help Roper. The rest of them stayed longer as the children played happily.

Cassie was reluctant to leave this peaceful place and return to the realities of her life.

Eventually the children would go to their uncle. Roper would return to the ranch. Cassie would run a successful business. It was what she wanted, what she'd planned, but she'd miss them more than she dared contemplate.

Roper was still assessing the construction of the house, planning his work when an unfamiliar voice called, "Hello, the house."

He jerked about. "Constable Allen." The Mountie had crossed silently from Macpherson's. No doubt the ability to sneak about served him well in his job but it only made Roper wish he'd seen the man coming so he wouldn't have been caught dreaming.

"I said I'd be back to check on the children."

Neil had returned a moment ago and stood at Roper's side. He could feel the nervous tension vibrating from the boy.

"What's to check? Me and Cassie are doing just fine by them. Isn't that right, Neil?"

"Sure is."

The constable held up his hands in a no-need-to-get-fussed gesture. "I expect you are. However, my duty is to make sure these orphaned children are properly provided for." He glanced about. "Where's the rest of them?"

Roper tipped his head in the general direction of the river. At that moment, Daisy climbed the bank with a pail of water, Billy at her heels. Cassie followed, carrying Pansy.

That was a first. Roper wished he had more time to appreciate the sight.

Constable Allen had ears to match his footsteps and heard the others. "Good. I need to talk to all of you." He sniffed. "Are you about to have supper?"

Joining them, Cassie said, "You're free to join us."

"That would be ideal. Give me a chance to see how things are going."

Things are going well, Roper muttered silently. *Just like I said.*

Neil echoed the words in a faint grumble that likely the Mountie heard although he gave no indication.

Cassie put Pansy down. Daisy and Billy rushed to set the table for seven. Roper and Neil headed to the wash-basin, Allen on their heels.

Normally Roper would let a guest wash up first but he was in no mood for common courtesy and took his time scrubbing his hands even though he knew he only delayed the inevitable.

Somehow he'd forgotten the Mountie had said he would come back and decide if the youngsters could stay.

He dried his face and hands and handed the towel to Neil. Cassie stood in the doorway of the shack, a bowl of potatoes in her hands. He hustled over to take it.

"Is he going to take the children?" she whispered.

"Guess he has the right but I don't see any reason he should. Aren't we doing a fine job taking care of them?"

"I think so but he might see things he doesn't like."

"Such as?" He glanced around. Seemed everything was perfectly adequate.

"For one thing, we're pretty crowded at night. And the house isn't finished." She rocked her head back and forth. "I don't know what he might take objection to."

The Mountie dried his hands, and sauntered toward the table.

With a sigh that seemed endless, Cassie got the meat from the shack and carried it out. Roper helped her with the rest of the food.

"It's ready," Cassie announced. Her words were unnecessary as everyone sat around the table.

Roper made sure he took a spot across from Cassie and as far from the Mountie as he could. Though perhaps, on second thought, he should have positioned himself between Neil and the constable.

Out of habit and a need to feel connected to Cassie and helped by a power beyond himself, he reached for Billy's hand on one side and Cassie's on the other. "Let's say grace." After he muttered his simple, customary words, he added, "Help us be able to stay together and help each other. Amen."

Cassie slowly released his hand. He held her gaze long after their hands parted. Her eyes seemed to tell him she needed assurance, and he did his best to offer it even though the Mountie had the authority to do whatever he decided.

Constable Allen cleared his throat, making Roper realize how long he and Cassie had been sending silent messages to each other.

Roper glanced away and passed the food.

Chapter Ten

Cassie could hardly swallow her food. Why had the Mountie come now when she'd finally won Pansy's affection?

What would he see?

She'd done her best to provide properly for the children. They ate well. They had a dry place to sleep, though, as she worried to Roper, it was crowded. They were reasonably clean, more thanks to Daisy than to herself.

But when had her best ever been good enough?

This time more was at stake than her own concerns. These four children depended on each other and cared for each other yet they couldn't be allowed to live on their own. They needed adults to help them. *God in heaven, I don't know if I've done a good enough job but please make it appear so to the Mountie so the children can stay together with us.*

The Mountie paused from eating. "I saw Red Fox. He said to say hello to Mrs. Gardiner."

Cassie allowed a portion of her brain to slip back to the Indian woman and her children that Linette had taken into the cabin and fed. "How are Bright Moon and the baby?"

Constable Allen chuckled. "The baby is still wearing the little sweater Mrs. Gardiner gave him. They call him Little Shirt." The Mountie sobered. "The tribe had a tough winter. Not enough food." He shook his head sadly. "With the buffalo almost gone they're dependent on what the government provides for them to eat. They must learn to become farmers, but they don't understand the concept. For them, food is acquired by hunting. It's a hard lot for them. I fear many will suffer."

Cassie momentarily forgot her own worries and cares. "Red Fox and his family are okay, though, aren't they?" She hadn't shown them much kindness when they'd been at the ranch even though she understood they were starving. Now she wondered how she could have been so selfish and bitter.

"They're surviving."

She didn't much care for the hopelessness of the Mountie's words. "Did you see their older son?"

The Mountie nodded. "You mean Little Bear?"

"Yes. I first saw him hanging around the Fort when we arrived last fall. He was helping a man. And being treated cruelly." She should have done something then. But all she could think was how her grandfather had grown even more vicious if anyone intervened in even the slightest way. So she'd backed away. Not like Linette. "Linette found the freighter who had abandoned him and gave him a slicing with her tongue." She laughed as she recalled how the big man looked so angry. "She asked if he would starve his mules and still expect them to pull a load. He as much as told her to mind her own business." She smiled in Roper's direction, sharing a common knowledge that Linette didn't mind her own business if she saw someone needing help. Cassie returned her gaze to the Mountie. Linette wouldn't allow anyone to take these children and parcel them out to homes or a foundling home. But then Linette had a big house and the Gardiner money to back her up.

What could Cassie do? Besides pray again. Which she did.

The Mountie paused to enjoy some meat and potatoes before speaking again. "We could do with more people like Mrs. Gardiner." He shifted his gaze from Cassie to Roper and back again. "People willing to help those less fortunate." He turned back to his food.

Cassie thought the meal took an extraordinarily long time but finally everyone finished, the Mountie being the last to put his fork down and lean back. He cradled a cup of coffee. "You're a good cook, Mrs. Godfrey."

"Thank you."

"Macpherson tells me you are feeding travelers."

Uncertain how to answer, she stole a quick glance at Roper. Did the Mountie see her job as a good thing or a bad thing?

The Mountie continued. "It will be nice for people to be able to get a hot meal on their travels."

"I hope so." What was she supposed to say? Couldn't he simply let them know his decision and relieve the tension that crawled up her spine and dug talons into her neck?

Daisy excused herself, took Pansy and started washing dishes. Cassie went to help.

"What's he going to do?" Daisy whispered as they did dishes together.

"I don't know. We have to wait for him to say."

But the Mountie said nothing. Nor did he leave. He sat at the table, refusing a refill of coffee when Roper offered. Thank goodness Roper hung about. Her limbs felt like fragile sticks. She worried she might fall on her face if she took more than two steps in any direction.

The chores were done yet the children hung about near the washstand. Normally they would have gone to play in the lengthening shadows.

Roper slapped his hands on his thighs. "Sorry, Constable, but the youngsters like to have some fun about now. I see no reason to disappoint them." He pushed to his feet. "You make your decision and let us know." With a courtesy nod to the man, he turned to the children. "Who wants a game of tag?"

Daisy scooped up Pansy, and followed her brothers in Roper's wake as he headed toward the river where they often played.

Cassie hung back, uncertain what she should do.

Roper paused and looked over his shoulder. Like a chain reaction each child did the same. "You coming?" he asked.

She felt their silent pull on her. She stole a glance at the Mountie. Would he think it inappropriate for her to join in the fun? She tried to weigh her choices. Grandfather would have disapproved, but then there wasn't much he approved of. Linette, on the other hand, would have little concern about what the Mountie or anyone would say. If she thought it was the right thing to do, she'd do it without fear of consequences. Cassie couldn't be like that.

Neither did she want to let her grandfather continue to have so much influence on her decisions.

She tilted her chin, straightened her spine and marched over to the others who, seeing she was coming, filed down to the river.

Roper led them to the level ground by the river. As soon as he stopped, the children gathered around him.

"What's he going to say?" Daisy demanded.

"He can't make us go away." Neil crossed his arms over his chest and silently dared anyone to try.

Roper studied the worried faces before him. Pansy wasn't sure what was going on but she picked up on the concern of the others and stuck out her bottom lip.

Cassie did her best to hide her fears but her gaze begged support from him. If they were alone he would have pulled her into his arms and assured her he wouldn't let anything bad happen. Instead, he addressed them all. "There's no point in worrying about a future we can't control or a past we can't change. Better to make the most of the moment." He danced away, grinning. "Can't catch me."

Neil churned after him.

Billy yelled a battle cry and raced toward Roper. He tripped and fell facedown in the sand.

Roper paused, waiting to see if he would have to dry a pair of eyes, but Billy popped up, brushed himself off and continued pursuit.

Daisy and Cassie grinned at each other, gave some sort of signal then hurried to flank him. They had all somehow conspired to force him to the edge of the water, circling him so there was no escape. Daisy handed Pansy to Cassie. That should have been warning enough.

In less time than it took for him to go from "Nah-nah can't catch me," to "Oomph," the three youngsters tackled him, knocking him to the ground, the air whooshing from his lungs. He gasped but couldn't fill his lungs as all three planted themselves on top of him. He tried to hold them off but there were too many legs and arms flailing at once, tickling him all over. "Uncle," he rasped from his starving lungs.

They stopped tickling but remained on top of him in a warm heap. He finally sucked in air. But no one moved.

Neil finally spoke. "Can he really make us go away?"

"Of course he can, silly. He's a Mountie. They can do anything." Daisy's voice alternated between annoyance and admiration.

Roper had to admit he had similar feelings. The man had authority and, like all Mounties, used it wisely. But right now Roper resented it.

Pansy demanded to be put down and flopped on top of Roper.

He grunted. "Always room for one more." He grinned at Cassie letting her know it was an invitation.

She shook her head but not before she looked longingly at the spot next to his heart that he indicated.

Billy twisted and looked about. "He's watching us."

The Mountie stood at the top of the riverbank. He waved for them to join him.

Roper pushed the children to their feet then pulled himself upright. He scooped Pansy into one arm and took Cassie's hand on the other side. "Let's go see what he wants."

The morose bunch climbed the riverbank and marched over to the table where the Mountie sat waiting. They plunked down in unison and planted their elbows on the table, all except Cassie who folded her hands in her lap. She looked about as defensive as he could remember seeing her.

Roper looked about the table. "Where's Billy?"

They all turned toward the river. No sign of the boy.

Roper pushed to his feet. "I'll go see what's keeping him." He hurried back along the trail, reached the river without seeing him. He must have climbed by a different path. He rushed back to the waiting group. "He's not here?"

Cassie's eyes rounded then narrowed as if afraid the Mountie would see her concern.

"He's hiding." Daisy grabbed Neil. "We'll find him." She perched Pansy on her hip, and they spread out calling Billy's name.

"I'll help." Cassie made to dash after the children.

Constable Allen lifted his hand. "Wait a minute."

Roper sensed a warning in the man's voice and stepped to Cassie's side. At the worried glance she darted his way he would have taken her hand except he wasn't sure how the Mountie would take the gesture.

The Mountie studied them, a look of concern and knowing in his face. "This happen often?"

The way Cassie wrapped her arms about herself, Roper knew she'd heard the judgmental tone in the Mountie's voice.

Roper jammed his fingers into the pockets of his trousers. "If you're referring to Billy disappearing, it's never happened before." He made no effort to keep blame from his voice. "I promised the boy—all the children—they were safe with us."

"Then I suggest you make sure they are." The Mountie tipped his head toward the children who had disappeared from sight.

"Exactly what we had in mind until you called us back." He stalked away, Cassie so close to his heels he wondered how he didn't kick her. He didn't slow until he knew they were out of sight of the constable then he turned and reached for Cassie's hand.

"He's hiding somewhere. Thinks the Mountie will get discouraged and go away. Unfortunately, we both know that isn't going to happen so let's find him, and then we'll fight for them to remain here."

She nodded, her expression fierce. "I wish I could believe he'll let them stay."

"Billy's just given the Mountie a good reason to think he shouldn't leave them with us."

They reached the sandy riverbank. Neil and Daisy ran to them.

"He's hiding pretty good," Neil said.

Roper signaled them to silence. "Billy," he called as loud as he could. "Come out. You're only making things worse by hiding."

The only sound came from birds protesting at the noise.

Cassie nudged him, and nodded toward the campsite.

He jerked about. Eagerness gave way to disappointment as the Mountie watched them. "Let's spread out and find him."

They did so, looking behind every tree, beneath every bush and even going so far as to ask Macpherson to look in his store.

Then they gathered back at the campsite, defeated and discouraged.

Roper couldn't find a cheerful word anywhere as the Mountie plunked down at the table and indicated they should join him. "It seems we have a problem. One missing child."

Neil refused to sit. He poked Daisy. "This is your fault. You're supposed to make sure he's safe."

Daisy scowled at him. "So are you."

"You're the oldest. Ma said you had to be in charge."

At Neil's accusation, Daisy started to sob. Pansy gave her sister one look and wailed.

Roper and Cassie got up as one. He took Pansy and tried to console her. Cassie wrapped her arms about Daisy.

"It isn't your fault," she told the child. "You've done a fine job of watching out for your younger brothers and sister."

Neil glowered at them all.

Roper caught him by the shoulder and pulled him close. "It's not anybody's fault." Though he wondered if the Mountie believed that.

Pansy would not be comforted and flung herself at Daisy. Daisy jostled her and made comforting noises.

"She's tired," Daisy explained to the Mountie.

"Then perhaps someone should put her to bed."

"I'll help." Neil and Daisy headed for the shack.

Roper wanted to follow, too. So much for showing the Mountie how well they coped. The man signaled for them to sit but neither Cassie nor Roper made any move to do so.

"Whatever you've got to say will have to wait. We have to find Billy." Roper looked at Cassie. "Any idea where he'd go?"

"Did anyone look in the cellar?"

No one had. Roper lit a lantern and raced over to the partially constructed house. He lifted the trapdoor in the floor and hung his head into the hole, shining the light into every corner. "Billy?" He couldn't believe the boy wasn't there.

He replaced the trapdoor and sat hunched forward on the floor. "Where could he be?"

"We need to get a search party organized," the Mountie said. "I'll go to the store and enlist any help I can find. Tell the children to stay here while we look."

Cassie already headed for the shack. Neil stood at the door.

"I heard him. We'll stay here in case he comes back."

Ten minutes later a group of men had assembled.

"I'm going, too," Cassie said.

The Mountie nodded. "Then stay with Roper." He gave each man a direction to search. "If you find him signal with three shots. Otherwise return in an hour."

Cassie waited for the others to disperse. "Then what happens?"

Roper squeezed her hand. "We'll find him."

They searched to the north. Calling. Listening. Looking. But they found nothing.

Cassie sat down and sobbed. "What's happened to him?"

Roper sat beside her, and pulled her to his chest. "We'll find him." But his words were hollow. A thousand scenarios raced through his mind. The cold waters of the river. A body being carried along by the stream, bashed against rocks. Or a bear interrupted at her fishing expedition. A band of marauding men…

He slammed the door to such terrors.

"The Mountie will never let us keep the children now," Cassie wailed.

"Probably not. But what matters is they are all safe." He put a slight emphasis on the word *all.*

Her tears dried instantly. "Yes. We must find him." She leaped to her feet. "Maybe someone else has." She reached for his hand to help him to his feet.

He would never admit holding her hand made getting to his feet more awkward than if he'd done it on his own. Any more than he'd point out that if someone had found Billy they would have heard gunshots. Instead, hand in hand, they ran back toward the campsite, pausing often to make sure they didn't overlook any place Billy might hide…or fall.

The rest of the men had assembled—only a handful but every bit of help was appreciated.

The Mountie remained in charge. "At this point we must assume Billy has found an ally to help him get farther away. Macpherson, who's been by in the past couple of hours?"

"A freighter headed to Fort Edmonton. And a cowboy from the OK Ranch."

Two men were sent after them.

"The rest of you continue looking around here. The boy might be avoiding us." The Mountie headed for his horse. "I'm going to ride out toward a group of Indians that were hunting west of here. They might help us."

Cassie and Roper were alone. He realized they still held hands. She sent him a look full of desperate fear and he pulled her close and pressed her head to the hollow of his shoulder.

"Pray," she murmured against his shirtfront. "Pray he is safe and we'll find him before dark."

The shadows grew long and leggy. They didn't have much daylight left. Glad of the practice he'd had in praying aloud, Roper lifted his face toward heaven.

"Our Father in heaven. You see everything. You see Billy right now. Keep him safe and help us to find him. Please. Amen."

Cassie sighed softly and slowly straightened. "I'll let the kids know we're still trying to find him." She seemed reluctant to leave the shelter of his arms. A trembling smile caught her lips before she ducked her head and hurried to the shack.

Ten seconds later a cry rent the air. "Roper."

They were all gone. Cassie couldn't believe it. "How could four children vanish into thin air?" She hung on to Roper's arms afraid if she let go she would collapse into a sobbing pile of bones and flesh.

"They can't." Roper had lifted every blanket, moved every box as if they had shrunk enough to hide in such tiny places. "I need to think."

"They have no place to go." Every word tore from her throat leaving behind an aching trail.

"They'd go back to where they came from."

"Back to where their ma died?"

"I found them on their way to find their pa."

She reared back and stared at him. "He's dead."

"But he had a house of some sort. A bit of land. They might try and get there."

She shuddered to think of them alone. "Do they even know where it is?"

"They might. Or at least think they do." He broke from her grasp and headed for the door. "I'm going to hitch up the wagon."

"I'm coming."

A few minutes later they were driving from town.

Cassie perched on the edge of the seat, alert for any sign of them. "Wouldn't someone have spotted them?"

His laugh was mirthless. "Not if they didn't want them to."

She tipped her head in acknowledgment. "How are they keeping Pansy quiet, though?"

"Maybe they aren't." He stopped the wagon and they strained to catch any sound above the creak of wood and leather and the huff of the horse.

"Nothing." Roper flicked the reins and they continued on. He stopped twice more and they listened intently. "This is where I picked them up." He pointed toward a grassy spot. They listened.

They heard the sound at the same time. His eyes glowed with victory. "If I'm not mistaken that is Miss Pansy protesting."

He turned the wagon from the trail.

She kept her eyes wide for a glimpse of them. "There." She pointed at a flash of blue in some nearby trees.

And then they saw the children dashing from tree to tree, trying to get away.

"They're all there." She could finally get a full breath for the first time since Billy disappeared.

"This is just like last time." Roper pulled the wagon to a halt, set the brake and took off after the children, Cassie on his heels.

As he gained on them, the children split up. He veered after Neil, snagged the boy and dragged him after Billy.

Billy darted behind a tree, waited for Roper to approach, then sped off in a different direction.

Roper had his hands full holding on to Neil who yelled and tried to pull away.

Roper turned to Cassie. "Go find the girls."

Cassie went in the opposite direction and in short order she found them huddled behind a bush, Pansy pressed to Daisy's shoulder. Both of them sobbed so hard it threatened to tear Cassie's heart from her chest. She pulled them into her arms. "Shush. Don't cry." From somewhere came a lullaby and she sang it softly.

Daisy stopped crying. Pansy fell asleep. Poor baby was so tired.

"We aren't going back." Daisy hiccuped the words. "We won't let him take us."

"We were so worried about you. What if something happened to one of you?" The words stuck in her throat. "What if you run away and hide from everyone and something happens?" She recalled Roper's words. "Isn't it better to know that everyone is safe?"

Daisy sat up and dried her eyes. "You're saying it's better to let them take us away?" She hung her head.

Cassie stroked her head. "Honey, I don't want him to

take you. But it might be a little hard to prove we can take care of you after you ran away."

Daisy gave a shaky smile. "But we don't want to run away from you."

"Then let's go back and tell the Mountie." Their only hope was to convince him of the fact.

She helped Daisy to her feet, little Pansy still asleep on her sister's shoulder. Daisy covered the baby's ears and called, "Billy, Neil. It's okay. We're going back."

"I'm not." Billy's voice came from deep in the grove of trees. And then a little squeal.

"Yes, he is," Roper called.

A short time later they were back at the campsite. Dusk filled in the hollows and stole the green from the leaves.

Roper had fired off three shots at the wagon and he did it again. "I expect everyone is too far away to hear but just in case."

The children trooped to bed without comment but could be heard whispering inside the shack.

Cassie sank to the bench. "I am suddenly exhausted."

Roper sat across from her and took her hands, cradling them between his. "Go to bed. I'll keep watch."

To make sure they don't run away again. He didn't have to say the words; she knew. "We have to convince the Mountie to let them stay."

"We can try."

His words provided little comfort and she stifled a cry.

"It's late. Nothing will be decided tonight. Go to bed and get some rest." But he held her hands as if he didn't really want her to go.

She knew she wouldn't sleep. Not until she knew the children's future. Would they be allowed to stay? But there was no point in sitting in the growing darkness wishing things could be different.

"Good night, then." She eased her hands free and stood.

Roper stood, too. He came to her side, caught her by the shoulder. "We'll do our best."

"That's never been enough."

"It is for me. It should be for you."

She stared at him. Did he really mean it? Could she believe it? She always seemed to measure herself by her grandfather's standards. How foolish. She knew now it was time to stop it.

He lowered his head, caught her lips with his before she had time to think. Or protest. Would she have protested given the chance?

No, she wouldn't have.

She welcomed Roper's kiss. Found comfort and encouragement in it.

And more.

She wasn't prepared to deal with anything more. Not right now. The children were what mattered now.

She hurried to the shack.

"I'll be right outside the door," he murmured just before she ducked inside to crawl into bed fully dressed. She didn't sleep, aware that Daisy and Neil lay awake as if waiting for a chance to run again.

"Roper is right outside the door," she whispered. "You'll never get past him if that's what you have in mind."

No one answered but covers rustled as if they adjusted themselves. A few minutes later she heard deep breathing and wondered if they'd fallen asleep.

Or were they only pretending?

Roper jerked away at first light. He'd slept in front of the shack door. No one would have left without waking him.

Hoof beats sounded on the nearby road. Likely that's what had wakened him.

He sat up, stretched and scratched his head.

The Mountie rode up to the place and dismounted.

Roper hurried to his side. "The kids are all here. Safe and sound."

"So Billy returned?"

That's right. The Mountie didn't know the others had run away, too. Perhaps Roper wouldn't tell him and give him any more reason to judge them inadequate to care for the children.

"Found him in some trees down the road a spell."

"I see." The Mountie gave Roper a hard look but Roper was prepared and held his gaze without blinking.

Cassie stepped from the shack, the children at her heels. They all skidded to a halt and stared at the Mountie.

Cassie's expression grew hard. "Come along, children. Let's get breakfast ready."

The meal was strained. Roper almost decided to forego the usual Bible reading but the children waited, so he pulled out the Bible and read a chapter then prayed, though it felt awkward with the Mountie sitting next to Neil. Neil refused to extend his hand to the man. Instead, he reached across the table to take Daisy's.

As soon as Roper said, "Amen," the Mountie cleared his throat.

"I think it's time to think about the future."

Was he aware of three rebellious expressions turned toward him? Five counting Roper and Cassie?

The Mountie turned to Daisy. "Are you happy here?"

She nodded.

He turned to Neil. "And you?"

Neil pursed his lips and glowered at the man.

The Mountie smiled. "Is that yes or no? I can't tell."

"Yes." It was plain Neil didn't intend to say more.

"Billy, you ran away. That doesn't sound like you want to stay here."

The look on Billy's face should have made the Mountie cringe but the man looked unimpressed.

"You can't make me leave. I won't go."

The Mountie turned to Roper and Cassie. "Are you two prepared to continue doing this until the uncle comes?"

They both nodded.

"Very well. You two obviously know how to create a family environment." He pushed to his feet and leaned close to Billy. "If I say you can stay, will you promise not to run away?"

Billy glowered at the man then gave a slight nod.

"Then I'll be on my way. I'll let you know as soon as I contact the uncle." He turned to the children. "You kids be good."

"Yes, sir," three voice chorused.

As a postscript, Pansy echoed them.

He clamped his wide-brimmed Stetson on his head and returned to Macpherson's store.

Silence followed his departure until he was out of sight then Neil whooped. "Yahoo!"

Billy raced away to run mindless circles. The others headed toward the river and Billy followed. Happy sounds came from the direction they'd gone.

Cassie rose and gathered up the dirty dishes.

Roper didn't move.

"Roper? Is something wrong?"

He shook himself. "Did you hear what the Mountie said?"

"Of course. I was right here. He said the children could stay until their uncle comes for them."

"He said we knew how to be a family. How can that be? I've never been in a family. Not once."

Chuckling softly, she sat down beside him and patted his arm. "You seem to know how to be a family better than I do. Maybe because you've never seen the unfortunate side of family life."

In her words there were a thousand sad stories. Would she ever tell him any of them? He turned to study her face in the bright morning light. Regrets mingled with joy. He expected the regrets were from her memories, her joy from knowing the children could stay together.

Then she swallowed hard, and worry filled her eyes. "Roper," she whispered. "What if the uncle doesn't want the children? What if he refuses to come?"

It wasn't something he'd considered. "It's not possible. He's family. He'll come."

"See how you view family as an ideal? I can tell you that being family doesn't guarantee love."

He stroked her cheek. "Oh, sweet Cassie. Who has hurt you? Will you ever tell me?"

Her eyes grew so wide, filled with such longing that he thought the crackling of his heart would break the silence. He wanted to kiss away her pain. He lowered his head, paused in anticipation then claimed her lips. He felt her little sigh of relief and his heart righted itself. All that mattered was easing her distress, making her happy.

She leaned into him. Her hand crept up his arm, halted at his shoulder.

He lingered on the kiss, hoping she would put her arms about him but she continued to cling to his arm. It was enough. For now. But he wanted more. He wanted her to hold him like he'd never been held before.

She broke away, withdrew her hand but stayed in the shelter of his arms. "If the uncle doesn't want them, will they end up in a foundling home…or worse, as servant—slaves—in someone's house?"

"We won't let that happen."

"The Mountie won't let them stay here indefinitely. It wouldn't be right."

He knew what she meant. They weren't married. Come winter he couldn't continue camping by the river. But there was a solution. "There is a way we can keep the children."

She searched his face for clues to his meaning.

His first thought was to kiss her again but he had to explain his idea before he forgot all his good arguments. "We can make this arrangement between us permanent."

She searched deeper. "I don't understand."

Lost in the delight of her open look, wanting to see even deeper, he almost forgot what he meant to say. "We could get married and provide the children with a home."

She pressed a hand to her chest as if trying to still turmoil. "I told you. I don't intend to be owned again by any man."

"Hang on a minute. You aren't listening to what I said. It would only be a business agreement, a continuation of what we have already. You'd run your business. I could help where needed. Hunt for food. Maybe get some land nearby and run a few cows. It could work, Cassie."

"A business arrangement." She rubbed her chest with the flat of her hand. "No strings attached? Equal partners?"

"Only if the uncle doesn't want the youngsters." Of course he would. No man in his right mind would turn down a ready-made family.

And if he did take them, Roper and Cassie would have no reason to go ahead with a marriage.

He tried to make himself believe it would be okay.

"I could handle a business arrangement."

Did her voice sound hopeful, as if she welcomed the idea and not just to ensure the children were kept together? As if she secretly longed to maintain what they had here? He couldn't tell and didn't ask, not sure he wanted to hear the truth.

It was enough that she agreed. But he had to make sure she truly understood. "If the uncle won't take the children then we will marry and keep them?"

She nodded slowly, her gaze watchful, guarded. "A business arrangement." She ducked her head. "I agree."

He must see her face, read her expression. He caught her chin with his finger and tipped it toward him, waiting until she brought her gaze to him. "We'll be good together."

They looked deep into each other's eyes, plumbing for truth and on his behalf, something more, something he couldn't—wouldn't—name because he hadn't forgotten who he was.

A nameless orphan.

Could he learn to be a family with her and the youngsters? According to the Mountie they already had. The idea wound through his thoughts, caught hold of his heart and rooted there like an old oak tree. Family. With Cassie. He sighed.

He bent and caught her mouth with his own, silently sealing their agreement, giving an unspoken promise he meant to uphold.

I will show you what I believe about family.

He would do his best to care for them all, protect them and make them happy. A distant bell tolled in the depths of his brain. *This can't last.* But he ignored the warning, lost as he was in the warmth of her kiss.

He took her response as her own silent promise though he couldn't guess what words she would put to hers.

Cassie tried to concentrate on her tasks.

Marriage as a business arrangement. Was it possible?

He'd kissed her again. Not once but twice. Surely only to mark their agreement. But something inside her shifted a little more with each kiss. To be honest she found sweet comfort in the touch of his lips.

Suddenly she realized why. He demanded nothing from her when he kissed her. He simply gave. Was it possible…?

Of course not. This was only about the children.

And if they didn't need her, she would be free to pursue her original plan. But rather than make her feel better, the realization filled her with an acute sense of loss.

She would miss the children but it was best they go to family. Her insides warred. The loss would be more painful than she dared contemplate.

She shouldn't have let herself care so much. She smiled. She'd tried to protect her heart but what chance did she have against them? Daisy, so helpful with a sense of responsibility Cassie understood so well. Neil, determined to imitate everything Roper did. He'd even begun to walk like Roper—a rolling cowboy gait. Billy, so innocent, so mischievous. And Pansy—sweet, little Pansy.

Carrie pressed her palm against her chest where Pansy's head had rested. She'd thought she would never enjoy the feel of a warm little one in her arms.

Now that she'd enjoyed it she couldn't bear the thought of losing it.

But the children's future was not in her hands.

Whatever happened, Cassie would survive. Battered

and bruised but as she told Roper, what didn't destroy her made her stronger. She'd grow stronger.

That night she fell into an exhausted sleep only to be jerked awake by a noise. Her heart kicked into a gallop. Were the children running away again? She lay motionless waiting for the sound to recur so she could identify it.

"Daisy, are you asleep?" Neil's hoarse whisper was barely audible.

"Yes. Shh. Be quiet."

The covers rustled. Cassie guessed Neil crawled to Daisy's side.

"I miss Ma and Pa." Neil's whispered words reached her ears.

"Me, too."

One of them sobbed, the sound muffled as if they tried to cover it with their hand or bury it in the covers.

"Mama." Billy's voice joined the others, louder, more intense.

Daisy scolded, "Now you woke up Billy."

"I miss Mama and Papa," Billy wailed.

More rustling and Cassie guessed Daisy drew the younger boy close. She knew it for certain when she heard Daisy hushing Billy.

"I miss them, too." Daisy's voice was full of unshed tears.

Cassie lay quiet, wide awake now. Crying in Roper's arms had healed something inside her. Something she didn't even know was broken. Nor could she say if it was the tears or the comfort of his arms that accomplished it.

All she knew for certain was the children needed someone to hold and comfort them while they cried. She turned toward them. They heard her move and sucked back sobs.

"It's okay to cry," she murmured as she moved to

Daisy's bedroll. She reached for Neil and pulled him to her arms. Billy climbed to her lap and pressed her face to her shoulder—the same place where she had found such sweet comfort with Roper. "Of course you miss your mama and papa. Shh. Shh." She patted and stroked and made comforting noises until, one by one, the children lay quiet and spent in her arms.

"I think Billy has fallen asleep," she said.

Daisy eased the boy back to his sleeping mat.

Neil shifted away, too. "How long before Uncle Jack sends for us?"

He and Daisy waited for her answer. "I purely can't say. But you've no need to worry. You're safe here with Roper and me. I promise we'll take care of you until your uncle makes arrangements." Silently she added to the promise. *Even if he doesn't want you.* She would not say the words aloud, though. The children did not need to worry about such things.

Neil seemed satisfied and returned to his bed.

Daisy hugged Cassie then settled under her covers.

Cassie slipped over to her own mat and relaxed once she heard all the children breathing deeply.

Was she wrong to offer them assurances about the uncle? Even if he did come, who could guess at what he would expect in return for taking four children. Likely instant obedience, willing hard work and more. More than a child could be expected to know to do unless someone told them. It was in their best interests to be warned of what they might expect.

And who better to do it than someone who knew as well as she did.

She would speak to them in the morning.

Chapter Eleven

Roper whistled as he climbed the hill for breakfast. Cassie had agreed to marry him. Of course, there were certain conditions but somehow that didn't dampen his spirit. A wife. A family. A home. It was more than he'd ever dared hope or dream since he was nineteen years old and full of blind optimism.

He ignored the persistent warning bell in the back of his brain. Ignored the words of his rules. *Don't put down roots.*

He heard her speaking and silenced his whistle. The children sat at the table facing outward. Cassie stood before them, her back to him. The expression on the three older children's faces let him know this was a serious discussion. He drew to one side, not wanting to disturb them.

Cassie twisted her apron as she spoke. "Expect nothing for free. No matter what your uncle might say."

Poor little Billy looked confused but from the wide-eyed horror on Neil's face and the way Daisy pursed her lips, he guessed this was the tail end of a little speech and could almost guess what it involved—insistence that every kindness had a price tag. He ached for whatever experience had led her to believe this way.

"You're sure you understand?"

Three heads nodded. Pansy watched curiously.

"Good. It's best you be prepared."

Roper stepped into sight. "You youngsters go play for a moment. Cassie and I need to talk."

They scampered away as quickly as frightened fawns.

Cassie watched Roper, alerted by something in his voice he hadn't tried to conceal.

He shook his head as he studied her, reading the hurt in her eyes, the defensive way she crossed her arms over her chest. "Cassie, Cassie, who taught you there is a price tag to love?"

He expected she would deny it, refuse to answer but her face crumpled and tears clung to her lashes. With a muffled groan, he reached for her. She hesitated but a moment.

"Tell me who, sweet Cassie."

She choked back a sob. "My grandfather."

He'd expected as much. He edged her toward the bench and gently pulled her down to sit beside him. "He made you pay for love?"

She kept her head down but rested it on his shoulder as if the contact kept her from drowning. "He made us pay for the privilege of having a roof over our heads. He made it clear he owned us in exchange for every begrudging bit of charity."

"You and who?"

"My mother. When Father died—Grandfather's son—the old man took us in but he made us pay. Every day and every way. I married George against his will. He knew he was losing a slave."

The bitterness in her voice drew knife-sharp gouges in his heart. "What happened to your mother?"

"I tried to get her to come with me but she was afraid.

I wrote her but she's never written back. I doubt she's even got my letters."

"Oh, Cassie, my sweet Cassie. No wonder you are prickly sometimes."

"When the children cried about missing their ma, I couldn't bear it. I miss my mother. She could be dead for all I know."

"Can you not contact a neighbor and ask about her?"

She didn't answer at first. "I suppose I could send a letter to Mrs. Ellertson. She was always kind to us at the market. She'd know."

"Then you should do that."

She nodded.

He turned her so they faced each other and waited until she lifted her face to him. "But love does not have a price tag."

"How can you be sure? You've never had a family."

The truth of the words scraped the inside of his heart. He used to dream of belonging. Had learned he couldn't. Only being part of a pretend family unit with Cassie and the children had made him forget it wasn't possible for him. "I remember a passage I memorized many years ago in which Jesus said to love your neighbor as yourself. Seems to me that means there is no charge, no expectation other than to wish the best for others."

She clung to him with her eyes, as if wanting to believe what he said.

"There's nothing better than to love others and make them happy."

Her eyelids fluttered. "I understand that's your philosophy. Mine is 'Owe no man anything,' which I know is in the Bible, too."

"Someday, sweet Cassie, you will learn not everyone exacts a price like your grandfather did."

For a moment he thought she believed him, and then she shook her head.

He pressed her to his shoulder again and kissed her hair. "Someday."

Neil poked his head over the bank. "Can we eat yet?"

Cassie sprang from Roper's arms and bolted for the shack. "Call the others. The food will be right up."

Roper moseyed over to the shack. "I'll take the coffee." He reached for the coffeepot and she jerked back a good two feet.

"No need to be all jumpy around me."

She squinted at him. "I'm not. You're imagining things."

He studied her a long, hard minute wondering if she would turn away but she admirably held his gaze. Sheer determination, he figured. But then Cassie was good at holding her own. Even when it wasn't called for. He took the coffeepot and headed for the door. "Someday, sweet Cassie. Someday."

Her defiant snort made him chuckle.

"What's so funny?" Neil asked.

"Oh, nothing."

Daisy giggled behind her hand. "He and Cassie are arguing. A lovers' quarrel."

Neil grimaced. "Yuck."

"'Fraid it's no such thing." What he wouldn't give to have a lovers' quarrel. It would never happen, though. He'd lived without love all his life. He immediately corrected himself. He'd learned to count only on God's love. He figured he could continue to do so. Though never before had his heart twisted at the idea.

The day passed in fits and starts. Pansy cried for no reason and clung to Roper. Daisy and Neil argued reducing Daisy to tears. Billy threw a temper tantrum because the fence he had built for his pretend cows crashed down in the wind. He blamed Neil even though everyone knew Neil had been helping Roper on the house.

Several times Roper caught Cassie with a distant look on her face, her hands idle, her task forgotten.

So much for knowing how to be a family.

He must do something before they were all reduced to a pile of misery. He knew just the thing to remind them that life should be enjoyed.

Over supper he outlined his plan. "Let's go see a buffalo jump. It's not far. We could leave early in the morning and be back by evening."

"What about feeding the men?" Cassie's look informed him he must be missing a few brain cells to even suggest it.

"You're the boss. You can decide if you want to work or not." He said it knowing what her reaction would be, and chuckled when she got all huffy.

"Seems if you want to succeed, people need to be able to count on you." Her scowl matched his grin for intensity.

"I knew you'd object so here's what I figured out. You leave something cooking real slow in the oven and Macpherson could check on it for you..." He held up a hand as she opened her mouth to protest. "If that doesn't sit well with you then have a meal already cooked. We'll leave real early, spend most of the day and be back to serve the food. Might be a little later but you can leave a note informing the men they can come back after we return."

Cassie shook her head but Billy bounced up and down on the bench eagerly. "We can see buffalo skulls?"

"You sure can."

Neil didn't bounce but he was equally as eager. "I've never seen buffalo bones. Heard they were really big."

Daisy watched Cassie. "I'd help you get things ready. A picnic sounds real nice. And you've been working awfully hard. You deserve to take some time off."

"I'll help, too," Neil added.

"Me, too." Billy jumped from the table all set to start immediately. Cassie shifted her gaze from child to child, over to the half-built house and then to Roper. "Very well. So long as we're back in time for supper."

The children had convinced Cassie when he couldn't. He admitted a bit of resentment that she didn't jump at the chance to spend the day with him. Which didn't make a lick of sense. They spent every day together.

She'd agreed to go. That's all that mattered.

They cleaned up in short order then Roper got the youngsters making sandwiches while Cassie prepared and cooked meat and potatoes. He built a wooden safe, put the pots safely in it then set the box in the river and secured it. "The food will stay cool while we're gone."

The next morning Roper was up before dawn and hitched the horse to the wagon. The noise must have wakened the others for they soon clambered from the shack.

Cassie fried up breakfast and made a pot of coffee. They sat in the cool air of the purple dawn to eat. Roper read from the Bible, then took Cassie's hand as he prayed for safety, adding silently a request for a refreshing time.

As he prayed, he built memories in his head. The morning greetings of the wakening birds sang the melody of creation. The whisper of the river added a duet voice. He inserted his own words for this moment—*pleasure, satisfaction, anticipation.* In the future he'd rejoice over this day.

They were soon in the wagon, the lunch tucked safely away, the children singing in the back.

They left behind the trees and hills and meandered over deceptively flat prairie. The breadth of the land quieted the children's voices and they crept forward to watch the trail ahead.

Roper pointed to the right. "Antelope." The golden-colored animals lifted their heads and watched.

"Why don't they run away? Aren't they afraid?" Neil asked.

"They can outrun a horse so they aren't too worried."

The animals watched them pass then resumed grazing.

A jackrabbit skittered away in front of them. Overhead a hawk circled with a whistling cry.

Cassie let out a long sigh. "It's so peaceful."

Far to the right he saw a twist of smoke and made out a rock chimney. "Looks like another homesteader. Soon they'll be breaking the sod and ruining the land for cattle." He didn't welcome the notion. "Seems to me some of this land should be left as it is."

"People need to be able to provide for their family." Cassie continued to stare at the wisp of smoke as they continued along the trail.

Did he see longing in her gaze? It made him wonder what Cassie really wanted—a business so she could support herself or a real home? Like the one Lane had built? The idea soured in his stomach.

Sometimes he wondered if *she* knew what she wanted.

Did he? He couldn't say. But he would make the best of this day.

The children leaned forward, eagerly pointing out one thing or another and he focused his attention on them.

A few minutes later, Roper turned the horse from the trail and they bounced across the prairie for a bit then he pulled on the reins. "We're here." The children tumbled from the wagon. Roper held out a hand to assist Cassie.

When she would have ignored him he caught her around the waist and lifted her as easily as he did Pansy.

She giggled a little, surprised and perhaps a bit uncertain at his boldness, especially when he didn't immediately release her. She glanced up at him. Her lashes fluttered and she lowered her gaze.

Good. She understood he intended this to be more than a business trip. He leaned close and whispered, "If we are to be married we should practice acting like a couple about to get married."

She pushed his hands away and drew back. "Roper Jones, you know very well that isn't the kind of marriage we discussed."

He chuckled. "A marriage is a marriage, don't you think?" Undeterred by her dismissive sniff he took her hand. "Better let me help you. The ground is pretty rough."

Indeed it was, but he wondered if she tripped over a clump of grass or if his attention unsettled her.

The children, arms out like wings, ran shrieking across the prairie.

Cassie stopped to watch them, easing away from him and crossing her arms at her waist so he couldn't take her hand again.

"They look so free and happy." She sounded wistful and he moved closer until their shoulders touched.

"It's good for them to be unfettered for a day."

She sucked in air preparing to say something but he didn't want to hear how they might never be free again, how they would owe their very lives, perhaps their souls, to their uncle. "Come on. I'll show you the jump." He reached for her hand and she pretended not to notice.

"Come on, kids." The four roared toward him and fell in at his side, eager to accompany him.

They walked to the rim of the cliff, revealing a deep gulley. "Stay back from the edge." He showed them how the Indians drove the buffalo up the incline to this spot leaving them no escape.

"Can we go down there and look for bones?" Neil asked, leaning forward.

"Neil, stay back." Cassie's voice rang out in warning.

"We'll go in a bit. Now you kids stay away from the edge. We don't want to look for your bones down there."

Billy giggled. "Our bones are covered with skin."

"Let's keep it that way." He led them away. "Play for a while."

They resumed racing about.

Roper had plans. If Cassie wanted flowers he would show her some in full bloom. He'd spotted several bright displays on their arrival. "Got something to show you."

She hesitated.

"What? You think I have something sneaky up my sleeve?"

"Do you?" One eyebrow quirked. Something he'd never seen her do before, and he liked it. But her playful mood caught him off guard. He'd expected resistance. Prickliness. "You do manage to surprise me again and again." He couldn't tell if she was annoyed or pleased at this observation.

"In a good way. Right?" She quirked her eyebrow again making him chuckle.

"You'll like it. I promise." He held his hand out in invitation.

She studied it for several heartbeats, then put her hand in his.

He tucked his satisfied grin into a corner of his heart and led her to a patch of wild roses.

"Oh, they're beautiful." She leaned close to smell the full-bodied scent.

"There are more flowers over here." He took her to another area with bluebells and unusual purple, white and yellow flowers.

"Oh." Her exclamation of wonder was all the satisfaction he needed. "What are they called?"

He pushed his hat back. "I don't know. Never gave it much thought."

She knelt in the midst of the flowers, her hands brushing the blossoms.

He stood back and admired her. She was so beautiful when she relaxed like this. She practically glowed with happiness.

Finally she turned to him, her uplifted face alight with pleasure. "This is wonderful. Like a refreshing drink to my soul." She pushed to her feet and faced him, separated by no more than six inches. "Thank you."

He caught her shoulders and pulled her to his chest. "You are most welcome. God has put the flowers here for everyone's enjoyment. No charge. No obligation."

She eased back. "We better check on the children."

She'd withdrawn at his comment but she allowed him to take her hand as they returned to the shrieking, racing youngsters. And she seemed lost in thought.

He hoped and prayed she was beginning to see how many things were freely given. He shepherded the youngsters into the wagon and drove to the bottom of the cliff. He barely stopped before they jumped out and raced over to the spot where hundreds, perhaps thousands, of buffalo had met their death. He'd never seen a herd coming over the cliff, or watched the Indians skinning the animals and preparing the meat and hides. But an old cowpoke who'd seen it had told him what happened and he explained it to Cassie.

"This is where the women cut the meat into strips and hung it on racks to dry. It provided plenty of food for the winter months."

She looked about. "Yet they are now starving to death. Forced to steal cattle to keep their families alive."

He knew they both remembered how Red Fox had almost been hanged for trying to rustle one of Eddie's cows because his family was starving. "Eddie did right to give him part of the cow."

"You do know it was Linette's idea, don't you?"

He shrugged. "It was still his decision."

"T'would no doubt be a shame to give the credit where it's due."

"I don't expect Eddie would object to giving the credit to his wife."

"They weren't man and wife at that point."

"Eddie wouldn't object even then. He's a fair and reasonable man."

She shrugged. "He's also a hard, demanding man."

For a spoonful of dirt Roper would argue but he figured Cassie was just itching for a chance to point out all the follies of marriage. "He's a good boss. Never had better. What are Billy and Neil up to?" he asked as he noticed the boys.

She switched her attention to the boys and he let out a relieved sigh.

"Looks like they'd found something."

The boys tugged and pulled at an object.

Cassie and Roper sauntered over to see.

"We found a skull and horns." Neil leaned back, using his weight to try and get the skull from the overgrown grass.

"Let's have a look." Roper squatted to examine it. "That's a good one." Both horns were still attached and the skull was not even cracked. He wriggled it free and stood it up.

"Can we keep it?" Neil begged.

"Please, please," Billy added, bouncing up and down.

"It's up to Cassie." They all looked at her. Roper expected his eyes were as pleading as the little boys'.

She studied the skull. "I've never seen such a big head." She rubbed the ragged, rough horns. "It's quite a treasure."

The boys rocked back and forth, impatiently waiting for her answer.

She smiled. "Certainly you can take it back."

The boys whooped and Neil grabbed one horn, directed Billy to take the other and they carried it to the wagon and loaded it carefully.

"That was very generous of you." Did she realize she'd given a gift without expecting repayment? But she looked worried. Why?

"What if the uncle comes and won't let them take it? Won't they be disappointed?"

"Who knows what will happen with the uncle? We can only take one day at a time and leave the rest in God's care."

"I know I should but sometimes—" She shrugged. "God is good and loving but people aren't always."

"Nor are they always unkind and begrudging."

She considered his statement, her gaze following the two boys. Slowly she turned toward him, her eyes round. "Trouble is," she whispered, "how can you tell who and when? Seems best to prepare for the worst. Then anything else is a happy surprise."

"Am I a happy surprise?" His throat tightened around the words.

Her study of him went on and on. He wanted her to see that he gave freely, expecting nothing in returning, wanting only to make others happy. "I guess maybe you are." She spoke so softly he wasn't sure he heard her correctly.

He read fledgling trust in her eyes and wanted to whoop with joy just as Neil had. He wanted to dance across the prairie like the girls did. Instead, he leaned close and planted a quick kiss on her nose. "It's a beginning, sweet Cassie, a very good beginning." He tucked her arm through his. "Let's have our picnic."

He had never tasted such good syrup sandwiches in his life. Or better oatmeal cookies. Even the water had a sweet taste to it.

Cassie had given him her approval. It meant more to him than a gold mine. Dare he hope he could gain with her the very thing he didn't believe he deserved? Him, a nobody? Could he have a forever family? For today he would let himself believe it possible.

The children wolfed down their food and raced back to explore but he took his time, wanting this afternoon to last forever. He couldn't stop grinning at Cassie for no apparent reason and knew he was making her nervous.

Finally she leaned close, her eyes challenging. "What is so amusing?"

He sat up straight and pressed his hand to his chest in mock surprise. "Are you addressing me? Because if you are, you mistake my being pleased for amusement."

She almost managed to hide her confusion. "You aren't laughing at me?"

He touched her chin. "Cassie, I don't laugh at people."

She lowered her lashes. "What are you pleased about, then?"

Laughter bubbled up from his heart. "Because, sweet Cassie, you admitted I was a happy surprise. That means you are starting to see that what I do for you, how what I feel about you is given without a price tag."

Her gaze dipped deep into his as if she sought something more. She pressed her lips together. "What do you feel about me?"

"I—" He sat back as a rush of emotion raced up his insides and grabbed his throat. "I—" His throat tightened and he couldn't speak. *Don't put down roots.* The words blasted through his brain.

"Never mind. It was a stupid question." She grabbed the tea towel and box that had once held sandwiches.

"I care about you." The totally inadequate words burst from his lips. It was all he could offer her. And it was not enough. She deserved so much more. The heart of a man with a past and a future.

He had neither and his insides burned with regret.

She continued to grab at things and needlessly arrange and rearrange them.

He would not hurt her by word or action. Not for all the water in the ocean. "Cassie, let me continue to be a happy surprise. Know my friendship has no price attached to it. I only want to see you happy."

A couple of hours later Cassie sat on the wagon seat beside Roper as they headed home. It had been a fine day. The children had played freely and were thrilled at the skull they brought back.

She'd enjoyed the flowers and a day with nothing to do but take pleasure in the sunshine. But her delight was tinged by unsettling thoughts. He kissed her, then offered friendship. He grinned foolishly and endlessly because she admitted he was a good surprise and then he declared he only wanted to make her happy.

What would it take for her to be happy? Not so long ago she thought she knew. Have her own business, be independent. Now she wasn't sure. Her uncertainty left her unsettled. And when had she gone from prickly Cassie to sweet Cassie? Prickly sounded strong and independent. Sweet sounded weak and—

Heaven help her. She seemed to have lost the ability to control her thoughts. All she could think was sweet sounded exactly like something she'd secretly wished for most of her life. She clamped down on her teeth and reminded herself how vulnerable it made her to let people inside her boundaries. She must keep Roper outside them.

Was it already too late to barricade every opening?

The squat buildings of Edendale came into view. She leaned forward welcoming the diversion. Had men come by expecting to be fed? Would they return or decide if they couldn't count on her they'd stop coming? They passed Macpherson's. Several men perched on the hitching rail, and a couple squatted with their backs against the wall. All of them turned as the wagon approached.

"Supper be ready soon, Miss?" Rufus, the smithy, called.

"Give me half an hour." Her thoughts slid into place. All she needed to do was keep her eyes on her goal.

Momentarily her heart resisted. Was there more to life than she allowed?

Over the following days, the question repeated itself, becoming especially loud and demanding at unexpected times. Like when Roper reached for the coffeepot to carry it out to the men and his arm brushed her shoulder. Or when he took her hand as he prayed at the table, his grasp so solid. So steady.

Her thoughts were so tangled.

Yet he seemed content to continue their normal routine. Surely it was only her imagination that made her think he grinned at her more frequently or that his gaze lingered on her just a fraction of a second beyond ordinary when they talked.

Evenings were the most confusing for her.

He liked to remain after the children had gone to bed. Sometimes he suggested they go for a walk and she agreed. Out of curiosity about what he wanted, she reasoned. Not because she longed for his company. They would saunter up the short street of Edendale and back. Or they'd follow the road from town until the deepening dusk forced them to return.

Other times he invited her to the river and they would look at the stars or listen to the murmur of the water.

She discovered he liked to talk. He had many stories about the places he'd been and the people he'd worked with.

"I was left on the step of the orphanage when I was very tiny," he said as they sat in the same spot where they'd watched the falling stars and she'd found comfort in his arms.

Her attention intensified because he seldom talked about himself.

"A tiny baby wrapped in a piece of flannel. No basket. No note. But my blanket had been secured by a bit of rope." His laugh lacked bitterness. But it also lacked humor.

"The maid who found me named me Roper because of that bit of rope. Jones was the last name of the month, I guess."

She reached for his hand. "Seems a perfectly good name. Better than Muddbottom."

They both laughed a little though she wondered if either of them was amused. "I lost two babies. I can't imagine having to give up one. I wonder what happened."

He shrugged. "I used to make up stories. But I will never know the truth. I'm not complaining. Life wasn't unpleasant in the orphanage, especially if a person tried to make it pleasant."

"And you, being Roper Jones, tried to make it pleasant for everyone." A thought began to take root. "You might not have a past but everyone who knows Roper Jones knows who he is and what he stands for. Seems to me that's a pretty good heritage."

He gave no indication that he heard or understood except for a telltale twitch of the muscles in his arm.

She squeezed his hand, hoping he would acknowledge the value of what she'd said.

"I liked to take care of the other children."

So he was going to ignore her comment. That was all right. Sooner or later she would convince him his lack of family history did not detract from who he was.

"Most times I could cheer them up no matter how sad they were."

She understood it had become his mission in life to make others happy. Was she only a mission for him?

"Who makes sure you're happy?" she asked as the stars draped the night.

"You do." And then, as if he'd said too much—or was it too little?—he quickly added, "So do the children."

"Happy enough to marry in order to give them a home?"

"You made the same agreement. Is giving them a home enough to make you happy?"

She said it was. But it was yet another question to echo through her head in the quiet of the night when she couldn't escape her thoughts.

Her plans had seemed so complete and satisfying at one time.

Why did they now feel fractured and disintegrated?

The question rattled about in her brain so she couldn't sleep.

Chapter Twelve

The next morning, the rattle of a wagon drew her attention to the ever-deepening trail at the edge of her property. Early customers? Her worries disappeared at the sight of her company. “Linette. Eddie. And Grady. Why it’s about time you came to see me.” She ran to greet them.

Eddie helped Linette to the ground and Grady scrambled down on his own.

“We would have been here sooner but it’s been busy. I finally told Eddie if I didn’t see you soon I would simply die of loneliness.” Linette laughed merrily. “Cookie sent cinnamon rolls and a few supplies.”

Cassie glanced into the wagon and groaned. “You can’t keep sending me so much stuff.”

Linette hugged her. “Why not? We can afford it. Can’t we, Eddie?”

Eddie pulled his wife to his side. “We have more than enough. But I’d have more than I deserve if I lived in a tiny cabin with two women and a child.”

They shared a laugh. That’s exactly how they’d spent last winter when Linette and Cassie had first arrived.

Eddie planted a kiss on Linette’s nose. “I’ll be back after I pick up the mail and supplies.” He turned to Roper who had come from the house to see who it was. "Come and give me a hand," Eddie called and Roper jogged over to join his boss. They unloaded the supplies, stacking them in the shack where there was a little more room now seeing she had used up much of what Roper had brought previously. Then they headed for the store.

Eddie waved at Linette. "Enjoy your visit."

Linette watched him go, her eyes brimming with love.

Cassie wondered what it would be like to know such love, to be so certain of it. She thought of Roper but he offered only friendship. Besides, she didn't trust love. *Obligation to love.* The words again sprang from her memory. If she could remember the source maybe they would make sense.

She shook troubling thoughts from her mind. "Grady." She held out her arms and the boy threw himself into a hug. "How are you?"

"Papa gave me a horse." The boy had called Eddie papa ever since he and Linette married. "I can ride it."

"Good for you." Not so long ago the boy had been afraid of horses and Eddie.

"Come and meet the children." She introduced Linette and Grady to the children, and they immediately included Grady in their play.

"I want to show you my house." But as soon as they were alone she turned to her friends. "Roper informed me you have a little one on the way. Congratulations."

Linette considered her, her palm pressed to her stomach. "I wasn't sure how you'd feel about it."

"Why, I'm happy for you."

"I'm sorry my joy reminds you of your sorrow."

Cassie did not want to rob her friend of any of her deserved joy. "My sorrow is in the past. Your joy is present. I'm nothing but happy." She drew Linette into the building. Roper had put up the walls with the help of the men who came by to eat. A roof stood overhead. The rooms inside were marked out.

Linette wandered through with Cassie pointing out where the big table would go and where the stove would stand, and showed her the trapdoor to the cellar. "This room will be mine." The far end of the house would be her bedroom.

"I'll build a solid door," Roper had said, giving her a look she could only describe as possessive.

How could she think it might be such? He certainly gave her no reason.

Suddenly the house, her pride and joy, seemed so primitive and inadequate compared to the beautiful, big house on the hill where Linette and Eddie lived. "I know it's not much but I can feed men here. I can bake bread and other goods. I can support myself."

Linette linked arms with her. "It's going to be lovely. What kind of curtains are you going to make?"

"I thought red gingham. I want to make tablecloths to match. Though I'll likely use oilcloth most of the time." The men wouldn't care what she covered the table with, only what she served, but on the rare occasions a woman visited she planned to set a nicer table.

She edged Linette toward her quarters. "Maybe something a little finer in here." In truth she hadn't thought too much about how she'd outfit her room, her main concern being the eating area. "I think I'll do a quilt during the winter."

"I have some fabric scraps you can have."

For a bit they talked about sewing and decorating. Cassie caught up on news of happenings at the ranch.

"Have you had any news from Grady's father?" Linette had vowed to get the man to acknowledge his son. She'd acquired the child on her trip across the ocean when his mother died. Her task had been to deliver him to his father in Montreal but the man had turned his back on the boy, saying a four-year-old child was of no use to him.

"I have sent several letters. Last time I drew a likeness of Grady and sent it along. I pray that someday he'll realize what a gift he has in a healthy son."

Cassie crossed her arms across her middle and pressed tight. A living healthy child, boy or girl, was a gift not offered to everyone. How could the man be so ungrateful?

Linette noticed her reaction. "Cassie, I'm sorry. I shouldn't have said it like that and reminded you of your loss."

"No. You're absolutely right. The man doesn't deserve what he has."

"I hoped Grady would forget the scene with his father but he hasn't. The other day he asked if he was an orphan. When I said he has a father he got all sad. Said his father didn't like him." Linette shook her head. "I am determined to get the two of them together, appreciating each other." She glanced toward the store. "Maybe there will be a letter from him today."

"Maybe I'll have a letter soon, too." She warned herself there might never be a reply. Her grandfather would prevent it if he could. "I wrote to a lady back home asking about my mother. I would like to at least know if she is dead or alive."

Linette sighed heavily. "I can't imagine not knowing. I will add to my prayers a request for you to hear from your mother."

"I don't expect to hear from her directly. My grandfather would never allow it."

Linette turned toward the sound of the children screaming with laughter. "What's to happen to them?"

She meant the four Locke children. Cassie explained the Mountie was trying to contact their uncle. "I guess their future depends on whether or not he is prepared to take them on."

"I guess we've seen how it doesn't always work out that way. Then what?"

"Roper and I have agreed to a businesslike marriage so we can care for them."

Linette grinned widely. "I'm guessing you'll marry him whether the uncle comes or not."

"Oh, no, it's only a business agreement for the children's sake."

"Your eyes say otherwise."

Cassie squinted, hiding anything Linette thought she saw. "What could you possibly think they say?"

"That you care about the man." Linette sounded terribly pleased about her observation.

"Certainly I do. He's a good man and a good help."

"I agree, but be honest. Don't you have deeper feelings for him than that?"

Cassie shook her head. She couldn't admit it. Even to herself. "You know I am not about to chain myself to a man ever again." But it wasn't chains she pictured when she thought of Roper. It wasn't obligation and owing. What she saw was his wish to make her happy. She chomped on her back teeth. She dare not trust such thoughts.

"Raising children is a lot of responsibility," Linette continued. "Sure you want to take it on?"

"I'm sure." She could give these children what her grandfather had withheld from her—care without cost. Kindness without strings attached.

Linette seemed to be considering something. "Even without adding four children to the community we desperately need a church and a school. They only make it more imperative. I will speak to Eddie about it again."

Suddenly Cassie realized how many things four children required…schooling, clothing, room to sleep. She could conceivably outgrow her little house before she even moved in. Linette was right. Four children was a lot of responsibility. Good thing she and Roper would be caring for them together should it turn out that way.

Eddie called out a greeting. Linette turned eagerly and picked up her skirts to rush to his side. "Did we get a letter?"

"Several but not the one you're looking for." Eddie handed her a stack of correspondence.

Linette checked through it as if Eddie might have made a mistake.

Roper had paused to rearrange the supplies in the wagon box and now sauntered over to join them. His gaze sought and found Cassie and a smile brightened his face.

As if he were glad to see her.

She smiled back automatically, barely recognizing this strange feeling in her heart. Once, in a time almost beyond her ability to recall, she'd been glad to see a man return. Welcomed it. Understood it meant she would receive love and attention…when her father was still alive. Before she'd learned there was a cost to attention. A payment due for everything given.

Linette announced they must leave, pulling her away from her dark thoughts.

Cassie hugged her friend. "It was nice to see you."

"I'll be back. We need to work together on getting a church. I think that's most important. Depending on how things work out—" Her gaze flitted to the nearby children. "We'll have to set our sights on a school, as well."

"At least you have your Sunday services at the ranch."

She couldn't believe how much she missed Cookie and the others and the time of worship they conducted in the cookhouse every Sunday.

"You're welcome to join us any time you want."

Eddie lifted Grady to the wagon and helped Linette up. Cassie hated to see them go. They left behind a hollowness.

She wished Roper would move closer.

As the wagon rumbled away, she pushed such foolishness out of her mind. She had a business to run. Children to care for. And she headed to the shack to prepare a meal.

A few days later, minutes before mealtime, Lane appeared for the dinner. This was his first appearance in nigh unto a week.

"I've been putting up firewood. Got a good supply for the winter." He slid into place at the table but bounced back up before his jeans touched the wooden bench. "My oat crop is beyond expectations. See for yourself." He handed her a small bundle of green oats, tied with a bit of twine.

She examined the offering and made what she hoped were appropriate comments. Truth be known, she had little knowledge about farming and crops as she'd tried to explain to George when he was so keen to head west and stake a claim on free land. She wondered how much he knew having been raised in town and having always lived in town. His response had been to dismiss her concerns. Say it was the very reason he was determined to get a piece of land with his name on it.

When she handed the oat cluster back to Lane he waved it away.

"Keep it. Have a look at it every so often and think what promise this land has."

"Thank you." She stuck it in an empty Mason jar, not knowing whether she should water it.

"The land is rich and generous," Lane said.

His raving gave Cassie an idea. "Do you have a garden?"

His enthusiasm waned slightly as he watched her. "I put in a few root vegetables. Enough for a single man like me." He grew more intense. "I would think a man could raise enough garden produce to feed a whole family."

Cassie ignored the way Lane looked at her. She had no intention of being part of his plans no matter how wonderful he made them sound. Besides, she had a tentative agreement with Roper.

Several others joined them for the meal. As she dished stew into each man's dish, she stole a look at Roper. His eyebrows thundered together and his eyes shot silent arrows at Lane. What on earth was the matter with him?

She ignored him and returned to the conversation about gardens. "It's too late in the season for me to plant this year but next year I'll raise my own vegetables. I wouldn't mind getting some hens, as well. Does anyone around here have some to spare?" She looked about the table for an answer.

Rufus wiped his chin. "Petey could bring some from the Fort on the stagecoach."

"I'll speak to him and I'll get Macpherson to order me some chicken wire." Satisfied with her plans, she served the rest of the meal.

Lane lingered after the others left, sitting at the table, drinking cup after cup of coffee while Cassie and Daisy did dishes.

Roper went back to work on the house. A few minutes after he'd left, he returned. "Need a drink." He guzzled a dipper full of water and stared at Lane hard enough that

Cassie wondered if the man wore armor under his shirt to protect him from the heat of Roper's displeasure. Then Roper stalked off.

Again she wondered what Roper was upset about. Seems she should be the one bothered about a man occupying space without lifting a finger to help.

"My family has a dairy farm back in Toronto," Lane said. "Big place. There are four sons. I'm the second youngest. I could have stayed and worked but it seemed there were more opportunities out here. With my parents' blessing here I am."

Yes. Here you are. Drinking a pot of coffee and interrupting my work. "I'm sure they're pleased with what you've accomplished."

"Yes, indeedy."

Indeedy? What kind of English is that? She scrubbed the table right up to his elbows, forcing him to lift his arms. "I suppose you'll be going back East soon to spend time with them."

"Oh, no. I'm here to stay."

Seems like it.

Roper rushed to the water bucket. "Thirsty again," he muttered, and downed another dipperful. Neil stood at the house watching, looking startled by Roper's sudden and intense thirst.

Roper swiped at the water dribbling from his chin, rocked his gaze from Cassie to Lane and back to Cassie then loped over to the house, muttering under his breath about something.

Cassie looked longingly at the little shack where she might find some peace and quiet. She'd endure the heat from the stove in order to escape these crazy men. "Excuse me," she said to no one in particular. "I have to tend to supper for the children."

Daisy looked about, obviously confused by all the coming and going. "Do you need me?"

"Not for a little time. Go play with Billy and Pansy."

She scurried away.

Lane didn't move. Cassie began to wonder if the man was glued to the bench. Suddenly it dawned on him he was about to be left alone and he finally found his feet. "I'll be back tomorrow. Say, maybe you'd like to see some pictures of my family. I could bring some when I visit."

Visit? Is that how he saw it? But if agreeing would get him moving…

"That would be nice." She ducked inside the overheated shack before he left and leaned against the wall exhaling a loud sigh. Apparently Lane considered himself a good catch. Somehow she had to convey to him she wasn't interested in any man. Good catch or otherwise.

Besides, she and Roper had an agreement.

One dependent on the actions of one unknown Uncle Jack.

Roper pounded the nail so hard it dented the wood. He stepped away, grabbed a board and measured it, sawed it in record time and carried it to the wall.

Neil held the other end.

"Bring it this way." Roper tugged it into place.

"It's too short."

"Shoot. I measured wrong." He tossed the board to the shrinking pile of wood.

"Why didn't you just tell him to leave?" Neil asked.

"Who?" As if there were anyone other than Lane who lingered as though he didn't have anything else he should be doing. Like weeding his garden or admiring his oats. "What are you talking about?" His voice was sharper than he intended.

Neil snorted. "I ain't getting in your road." He turned to examine something on the ground.

Roper sucked in air. "Sorry." He had no call to be so cranky. But why was Cassie encouraging Lane? She'd promised to marry *him.*

Only if the kids' uncle didn't show up. Otherwise there was no obligation on either side.

But even so, Lane was not her sort of man. He was a dandy. Used to a fine lifestyle. Cassie would never be happy living the life of a fancy lady. He ought to warn her.

No, that would only make her angry. She would not welcome any interference from him.

Besides, how could he be so certain she wouldn't welcome the sort of life Lane would offer? A fine lady in a fine house.

Because, he told himself with utmost conviction, it would remind her too much of her grandfather. He knew Lane would expect her to keep up certain standards. How he knew this he couldn't say. But he would not admit he might have misjudged the man.

There had to be another way to make Cassie see the truth.

He recalled the recent conversation. She wanted a garden and some chickens. He could help her with that.

"Supper is ready," Daisy called.

Roper and Neil headed for the table. Roper squeezed Neil's shoulder to let him know he wasn't angry and was relieved to feel the boy relax beneath his palm.

At the table, he reached for Cassie's hand to say grace. After his amen, he continued to hold her hand for a beat. Two. Then he released it without once looking at her. He knew if he looked at her, she'd see in his eyes more than he wanted to reveal. More than he understood. More than he could promise.

"Is Grady an orphan like us?" Billy asked.

Cassie answered. "No, he has a father."

"Then why is he with the Gardiners?" Billy asked the question but Neil and Daisy watched Cassie with wide eyes, as interested in the reasons as Billy.

Cassie sent Roper a look that begged for help.

His smile of reassurance seemed to help her relax.

She turned back to the children. "Grady's father wasn't able to care for the little boy on his own."

There was more to it than that but Roper hoped the answer would satisfy.

None of the three returned to their meal but sent silent messages to each other.

"What is it?" Cassie asked.

"He's only one little boy." Daisy stared at her plate as she spoke.

"That's true. Ah. And you're worried because there are four of you."

Daisy nodded. "Four is an awful lot of kids when they aren't your own."

"Not if the kids are the best in the world," Cassie said.

Roper wanted to cheer at her kind answer. "Four kids like you aren't a lot of work. In fact, I'd say anyone would be privileged to make you part of their family." He didn't say what else he thought. That he wanted them and not just so Cassie would marry him. He glanced about the table. This felt like family. Real and forever family. *He didn't know about family.* The persistent thought demanded attention. This was different, he argued.

The kids grinned at the answers they'd been given and returned to their meal.

Roper met Cassie's look. They smiled at each other, content to have eased the children's worries. Her brown eyes revealed warmth and...dare he dream he saw admiration? He was quite sure she hadn't looked at Lane in such fashion.

His good humor restored, he said, "Let's clean up real quick, and then play hide-and-seek."

The lot of them sprang into action. Daisy gathered up the dishes. Cassie filled the washbasin with hot water. Neil and Billy grabbed buckets and headed for the river. Roper brought over wood.

"We're done," Daisy called before he had the last load of wood back to the shack. "Not it."

They all called, "Not it," while Roper dropped the wood into the pile close to the shack.

He was it. He didn't mind a bit. "The shack door is 'home free.' I'm counting to fifty, and then I'm going to find you." He pressed his forehead to the door, closed his eyes and started counting out loud.

He grinned as the kids scattered, and then all was quiet.

They played until dusk, laughing and enjoying one another. Twice he inadvertently crashed into Cassie and was rewarded by having to hold her tight to keep her from being knocked over.

After a bit, Cassie said, "I think it's time for bed. Poor Pansy must be exhausted." They'd taken turns carrying her as they played.

"Aww." Billy let out a protracted protest.

Daisy tapped his shoulder and gave him a warning look, then they all trooped into the shack, Cassie at their heels. Roper would have gone in and helped but there wasn't enough room.

He circled Cassie's almost-finished house. If the children stayed he'd have to add a couple of rooms.

He heard Cassie step out of the shack and hurried to join her. "Everyone settled?"

"Pansy feel asleep almost instantly but Billy is restless."

"I guess we should have wound down a little sooner."

"He'll be fine. Daisy is singing to him. They're awfully good kids, aren't they?"

"They certainly are."

"They deserve the best."

"And we'll do everything in our power to see they get it."

She sighed, a troubled little sound.

"What's wrong?"

"First, we have nothing to say about it. If the uncle wants them it won't matter if he is mean-spirited or not. They will go with him."

"Then we'll have to pray he is kind."

"And if he doesn't want them, doesn't even come," she went on as if he hadn't spoken, "they'll be stuck with us. Do you think we can give them the best? You, who never had a family and me—" She waggled her hands.

He caught her hands and stopped their fluttering. "Oh, sweet Cassie. You are completely blind to all you have to offer, aren't you?"

"As you say, I'm prickly and overly defensive."

He'd never said the latter. "You're gentle and kind. I've seen you hug the children, heard how you encourage them. I've seen the way you watch them, your eyes full of affection. You care about them."

"I don't deny it. But is that enough?"

"I'd say caring in the shape of kindness and affection is certainly enough. Wouldn't you?" He pulled her to his chest and looked down into her uncertain eyes. "Wouldn't you have been grateful for that?"

She gave a crooked smile. "I would have thought I'd died and gone to heaven."

"There you go." He placed a gentle kiss on her forehead and, before she could react, he said, "Now, where did you think you would plant a garden?"

She showed him.

He measured off a plot and drove in four stakes. "I'll start turning over the sods tomorrow."

"It's not up to you. I'll—"

"I'm thinking of the children. If we become a permanent family we'll need to feed them. The ground should be broken this summer so the sods can break down over the winter."

She looked so uncertain, he laughed.

"We're in this together."

Finally she nodded. "For the children."

Roper allowed himself a moment of joy at what the future offered.

Several times the next day, Cassie glanced at the stakes Roper had driven into the ground. He'd be a good father, always making sure the children were well taken care of. He'd do the same for her.

If she let him.

Part of her welcomed his gentle concern.

Another part feared she would turn out like her mother—selling her soul, forfeiting her freedom for someone to take care of her. She sucked in her bottom lip. She'd never do that.

She was still preparing the meal when Lane headed across from the store. One hour earlier than the posted mealtime.

Cassie groaned. "How am I to get the meal ready on time if he expects me to visit with him?"

Roper gave what passed for a grin. "If you encourage him he'll keep coming back."

"I don't encourage him. But he's a paying customer."

Roper shrugged and sauntered away. "Guess he wants to make sure he gets what he paid for."

"What do you mean? He pays for a meal. That's all I give him."

Roper glanced over his shoulder. "Seems to me you're letting someone own you for the price of a meal. Isn't that exactly what you're fighting against?" And then he ducked out of sight in the house leaving her with her mouth hanging open and Grandfather's words echoing through her head.

I provide for you. That gives me the right to say what you can and cannot do.

You plan to eat? Then you do as I say.

Truth was it wouldn't have been hard to do things for him if he was a kind man. Instead, he was cruel and seemed to delight in making sure the things he demanded were unreasonable, petty and downright objectionable. Like the time he insisted the laundry must be hung out in a bitter winter wind. He'd wanted Mother to do it on her own. It was one of the times Cassie defied him and insisted on helping. She made sure she hung three baskets to Mother's one.

But this was different. Lane was only— What? She understood there was more to his visits than a home-cooked meal. He no doubt fancied that he courted her. But she'd never given him an ounce of encouragement. Neither had she discouraged him.

Was that what bothered Roper?

In all fairness she must make it clear to Lane she had no interest in him. Even if the children's uncle came and got them and her agreement with Roper ended, she didn't intend to give up her independence.

Lane reached her side, his face beaming. "I thought

you might have time to look at these pictures before the meal."

"I'm sorry, Lane. But I must have the food ready when the men arrive."

"I'm sure they won't mind waiting."

"I'm not prepared to test them to see. They are working men who want to eat their meal and get back to work. You have to understand that I have a business to run here."

He edged closer, purposely rubbing his elbow against her arm. "You wouldn't need to if you had a husband."

She stepped back. "That's just it. I don't want a husband. I want to be independent."

He only grinned. "I think you could be persuaded to change your mind."

No doubt you think you're just the one to do so. For two seconds she considered asking him to leave but she couldn't afford to turn away customers. If word got around that she did so, others might decide to avoid taking the chance she would do the same to them. "Not today. Now if you don't mind, I must do my work." She turned away. But Lane didn't move. Cassie couldn't decide if she should invite him to sit while she worked or simply ignore him.

"Lane." Roper's soft voice scratched along Cassie's nerves. "The meal will be served in an hour. Come back then."

Lane sputtered and looked toward Cassie for direction. She found a frayed edge on her apron to examine. "Perhaps you'd like to see the pictures later?"

She nodded. "Perhaps."

Finally he headed back toward the store.

She didn't speak until he disappeared around the corner then she flung about to glower at Roper. "Don't get the idea you can start running my life. I don't intend to ever again give a man that right."

He gave her a look of pure disgust. "Well, excuse me if I thought you didn't want him bothering you while you made the meal but were too polite to say so." He dragged the final two words out as he stalked back to the house, Neil skulking at his heels.

Cassie tossed her hands upward. "Men." But she saw Daisy watching her with big eyes. And of course, Billy and Pansy played nearby and overheard the whole thing. They looked about ready to cry. "Don't worry." She did her best to inject a bit of laughter into her voice and guessed she missed by a mile. "We aren't angry. Just expressing our opinions." She couldn't vouch for Roper's feelings but it certainly wasn't a hundred percent true for her. She felt a lot of anger. She meant what she said. He had no right to think he could run her life.

A little later Roper came out to help serve the meal as he always did. But he refused to meet her eyes, which suited her just fine. So long as he understood.

When Lane remained after the others left, she smiled at him. "Just give me a few minutes to clean up and then I'll join you."

Daisy helped with the dishes though the girl seemed unwilling to talk. She dried the last dish and hung the towel to dry. "I'll take the little ones down to the river so you can be alone with him."

It wasn't what she wanted. Roper and Neil had left a few minutes earlier. She wanted to join them but she'd already promised Lane. Besides, it was time she made it clear that she stood on her own two feet.

She sat beside Lane and looked at the pictures of his home and family. He came from a seemingly well-to-do family of good breeding if he did say so himself. As she commented on the pictures and listened to his detailed description, she heard Roper's voice as he called to the children.

Yes, she echoed to herself, that's what she wanted—to be with the children…and Roper.

Chapter Thirteen

Even over the laughter and screams of the youngsters, Roper caught snatches of the conversation between Cassie and Lane. Lane had a family. A good family. He had something to offer. Cassie, smart woman that she was, no doubt recognized it.

Roper's only claim on her was on behalf of the children.

She'd made it clear she welcomed Lane's attention. And would allow no interference from Roper.

Why should he think it would be any other way? A familiar ache reared its head and squeezed his heart until he wanted to groan.

They played a rowdy, noisy, vigorous game of tag. He ended up on his back as the children tackled him. They pounced on him, tickling him unmercifully. Finally they settled down, hopefully as exhausted as he.

"Is Cassie going to marry Lane?" Billy asked.

"Of course not." Neil's voice was full of disgust.

Billy wasn't convinced. "I think she likes him."

"She's just being polite." But Daisy's voice conveyed a healthy dose of doubt.

Roper wished he could assure them Cassie was going

to marry *him.* But they'd agreed it was best not to tell the children of their plan. Besides, their agreement came with no assurances.

"I don't think he would make her happy." Neil had drawn his own conclusions.

Roper grabbed the notion and clung to it. He only wanted Cassie to be happy. Seems the only thing that would make Cassie happy was being independent.

He'd never noticed before how dismissive the word sounded.

Peeling the children off him, he scrambled to his feet. His horse might welcome a flat-out ride but he couldn't walk away and leave the children.

Neil poked his head over the bank. "The man is gone."

"Let's go home." *Home is where I kick off my boots.* And yet this rough little plot of land—with the shack made half of wood and half of canvas, the table only a rough slab of wood out in the open and an almost-finished house nearby—was as close to home as anything he'd known.

The children followed him up the hill.

He'd only meant to help her. But he had no right to interfere. As soon as the children were tucked in, he approached Cassie. "I apologize. I didn't mean to suggest I had any right to order things in your life."

"Apology accepted." She said the words and yet he felt as if a great barricade of logs and rocks and dirt had been piled high between them.

Soon after, he said good-night and returned to his camp.

Over the next few days he devoted every minute to completing her house. The only thing that kept him from putting in longer hours was consideration for Neil who tried to match Roper's efforts. He would not drive the boy that hard.

Cassie was everlastingly polite, but distant, and he missed the closeness they'd shared for a few days.

And every day Lane came by with more and more evidence that he was a fine, upstanding young man with family roots and something to offer. He brought flowers, a picture of his family that he gave to Cassie. He told of attending school. From all accounts—his own—Lane had been an excellent student.

Roper knew his cynicism was unfounded. Understood it was due to the fact that Roper had not had such opportunities. He hadn't even completed fourth grade because he was always needed to help at the orphanage, or when he was a little older, hired out to local farmers and businessmen. Schooling, after all, was not important for a nobody kid left behind when he was only a few days old.

A wagon approached. Roper looked up and recognized Linette and Eddie. He set aside his tools.

"Neil, no more work this afternoon. Run and play with the others." Roper barely waited for the wheels to stop rolling before he jogged over to the wagon. "Need a hand, boss?"

"Yup."

Roper climbed to the seat and waited as Eddie escorted Linette to Cassie's side and Grady joined the other youngsters.

Eddie returned to the wagon and took the reins. "How are things going?"

Roper almost blurted out how bad things were but it seemed foolish to be sulking because a better man was interested in Cassie. "Be done here soon. House is almost finished."

"Good. I hope that means you're coming back to work."

"Depends on what we hear from the uncle."

"Right. Linette told me about it. It's good to know the children will be taken care of properly. I suppose then you wouldn't be coming back to the ranch?"

"Cassie has her business to run. It's important to her."

"But are you prepared to give up your life? What's important to you?"

Roper shrugged, though the question ricocheted about in his head. He hadn't let himself think that far ahead. "We work well together and more important, the youngsters seem happy enough to be with us."

"I see. Well, if you change your mind please come back. I'm thinking I might need a foreman to help run the ranch. You'd be my first choice."

"Thank you." He'd like the job. Eddie was a good man to work for, and the ranch was growing. Roper wouldn't mind having a hand in that. "I'll give it some thought but it will depend on the uncle." And if Cassie continues to show interest in Lane.

The first stop was to pick up the mail. Eddie glanced through the handful of letters, paused at one in particular. "If I'm not mistaken this will be from Grady's father. Linette has been waiting for it. I fear she will again be disappointed by the man's response."

"He still refuses to acknowledge his boy?" Cassie had said Roper didn't understand the dark side of family. This certainly proved it. He couldn't understand how a parent could abandon a child. Yet he was living proof such things happened.

The men continued to talk about ranching things, the others at the ranch and general news as they loaded up supplies. Before they headed back to Cassie's place, Eddie drove down the road to a pretty spot close to a bend in the river. "Linette is keen to see a church established in the community. At first I didn't see any need. There were too few people, too scattered about. But every time I turn around, I see more people coming in. That young fellow, Lane Brownley, and a young family over there—" He pointed in the general direction of the place Roper had seen when he took Cassie and the youngsters to the buffalo jump.

He smiled as he recalled the event. Then his smile slid away. How had he gone from the happy contentment of that day to this restless uncertainty in such a short time?

"I haven't met them but I'm told their name is Schoenings and they have four very small children. As Linette points out, we need to draw together in worship. She says this will be an ideal place."

Roper agreed it would, though he wondered about the possibility of drawing together. From what he'd seen, even in the orphanage, differing religions often caused division rather than unity.

They turned back toward Cassie's place and Eddie collected his wife and Grady then headed home.

He noticed the stark longing on Cassie's face as she watched the wagon depart. Did she miss the ranch?

A suspicion mounted in his brain. One he wished he could deny. But it refused to be ignored.

Did Cassie see the love between Eddie and Linette and wish for the same for herself? Was she ready to forget the many cruel years under her grandfather and accept love? Believe in it?

Another unwelcome notion took root.

Perhaps what she wanted was what Linette and Eddie had—a nice home, a ranch to support them—all the things Lane could offer her.

He spun away and stalked down to the river, murmuring something about taking care of the horses.

Cassie watched Roper disappear. The man had gotten so moody the past few days she feared to talk to him. He helped when it came time to serve the men a meal but without the usual joking and teasing. And it seemed he couldn't wait to be out of sight as soon as the men finished eating. Had she offended him so badly he couldn't even bear the sight of her? Had he expected her to change her mind about who she was, what she wanted? Was that why he was angry?

Not that she could change her mind even for the sake of peace with him.

Thanks to Roper, her house was almost finished. Her dream was about to come true.

But she didn't want to be friendless. They must mend this rift. For the sake of the children who watched them warily when they were together. And if the uncle refused to take them, they must learn how to be a family.

But she didn't know how to fix things. Every time she started to bring up the idea that there seemed to be a problem between them, Roper found an excuse to leave. He couldn't seem to wait to get away from her. About all she could do was pray things would improve.

Roper returned a while later and Cassie watched for a chance to speak to him, but the afternoon slipped past without her finding an opportunity. Not that she didn't try. Roper just ducked away every time she took a step in his direction.

As usual, Lane came by early and brought something. Sometimes it was a gift. Other times it was a letter or something from home he wanted to show her. Today he had a bit of burgundy fabric. "What do you think of this for curtains for the front room?"

She sighed back her impatience at his repeated interruption of her work. "It's very nice. Do you like it?"

"It's similar to what Mother has at home so it should be appropriate."

"I expect it's fine."

"If you saw the place you could better judge. My description is very inadequate."

She refrained from saying it was more than adequate.

"Why don't you let me take you out for a visit? Say Saturday afternoon?"

"I'm sorry, Lane, but who would cook for the men?"

He studied her long and hard.

Cassie thought his look very demanding and she had to stifle a reaction. He was not her grandfather. He had no hold over her.

"Seems you could arrange something. Let the others take care of it."

She kept her voice as gentle as possible but felt the sharpness in her words. "It's *my* job. *My* responsibility."

"You should be taking care of a home and family, not feeding a bunch of strangers."

She forced herself to give a little laugh. "Most of them aren't strangers. Take yourself for example."

"You know what I mean."

"Yes, I do. Need I point out that this is what I want to be doing?"

Lane made a noise of exasperation. "You'll change your mind some day."

She thought it best not to deny it. "I need to tend to the meal." She waved her hand in the general direction of the table where he would sit and wait as she escaped into the shack. She wished Lane would take her hints and leave her alone.

She would have to be clearer with him. Somehow convince him she wasn't interested in his attention. And she had to find a way to ease the tension between herself and Roper.

The next afternoon she still sought for a way to accomplish the latter. She prayed. She contemplated a dozen different scenarios. She even approached him twice but both times he'd suddenly found something he needed to do twenty feet away. Once it was to arrange some wood in the woodpile.

"Thought I saw a snake," he explained.

The other time he held a tape measure and kept consulting it. "Sorry. I have to mark a board before I forget the measurement."

He was making it very difficult.

But when he stepped out of the house and stood back to study it she decided this was the time. She put down the basin of potato peelings and headed across the yard. She barely reached his side when she heard footsteps heading their way. *Oh, please. Let it not be Lane. Not this early in the day.* But it was Constable Allen.

Daisy had been tidying up the little yard and straightened to watch him. Billy, assisting her, jerked about as if feeling the tension in the air and stared at the Mountie. Neil stepped out of the house, holding a hammer against his chest like a shield. Only Pansy, playing nearby, seemed oblivious to the importance of this visit.

"Hello," the Mountie called out.

Cassie couldn't find her voice to respond.

Roper jerked into action and reached out to shake hands. "Howdy."

"I expect you all know why I'm here." No one answered. “Why don’t we sit down?” He sat at the table, put his Stetson before him.

They slowly joined him. Cassie pressed in close to Roper needing his comfort. Thankfully he didn’t slide away. The children crowded in beside Cassie and Roper, all of them sitting across from the Mountie.

Roper cleared his throat before he spoke. “I think we know why you’re here but perhaps it’s best if you just say.”

“Very well.” He directed his gaze toward the children. “I was able to contact your uncle.”

None of the children appeared to breathe. Cassie twisted her hands in her lap, aching to reach for Roper, to hold tight and find courage.

He must have felt her nervousness for he wrapped a hand about hers. She flashed him a tight smile then concentrated on what the Mountie said.

“He responded immediately saying he wished to come and see you.”

Cassie couldn’t swallow. Her muscles clenched. It was the news she’d hoped and prayed for. The children should go to their relatives. But she’d miss them terribly. And now there would be no reason for her and Roper to marry.

The Mountie continued to speak and Cassie forced herself to focus on his words.

“He wants to meet you right away.”

“Right away?” Daisy squeaked.

Cassie knew her voice would sound every bit as strained if she tried to talk.

“Yes, he’s at the store waiting.”

Daisy and Neil turned as one toward the store. Billy watched his brother and sister, gauging their reaction to see what his should be.

Constable Allen leaned forward. “He realizes this is

scary for you. He said he doubts any of you remember him."

"I do," Daisy managed to squeeze out.

"He doesn't want to make any of you uncomfortable so he said I was to inform you. He'll wait until you are ready before he comes over."

No one spoke. Cassie knew this must be the children's decision. She must have turned her hand into Roper's at some point because they were palm to palm, their fingers intertwined. He squeezed her hand encouragingly. Despite the strain that had been like a wall between them the past few days she glanced up and held his gaze, seeking and finding a common interest in the well-being of these children.

And something more. Something that pinched the back of her heart with unspoken yearnings, impossible hopes. Something that made her wish she could be different. That she could be the person he needed her to be.

What did she mean by that? Who or what did she think he needed? She tried to make sense of her thoughts but Roper shifted his gaze back to the children and she decided she was simply confused, her equilibrium upset because of the uncle's arrival.

Daisy and Neil silently consulted each other again. Then Daisy nodded. "Tell him we're ready."

The Mountie rose and positioned his hat on his head. He didn't immediately leave. "I think you'll like the man. I know I do." With that he departed.

Cassie stared after him.

Her life was about to take a sharp turn. She couldn't imagine what lay around the corner.

A few minutes later, Cassie watched the man accompanying the Mountie across the yard. He bore a startling likeness to Billy. Or rather, she supposed, Billy looked like him. He had a gentle expression but Cassie wasn't about to trust first impressions. Sure the Mountie liked him but the Mountie wasn't a child about to be at the mercy of the man's moods. No, she would be observing him closely. If she saw even the faintest sign the uncle would be cruel and unreasonable, she would offer the children a home with her, whether or not Roper intended to continue with their plan for a businesslike marriage.

"I'll be watching him," Roper murmured close to her ear.

"Me, too," she whispered.

The pair of men drew to a halt before the table.

"Children," the Mountie said, his hat in his hands, "this is your uncle Jack."

The uncle removed a fine woolen cap. His hair was white and thinning. His skin pale and translucent with a thousand tiny wrinkles. Cassie tried not to stare but the man looked old. And thin. Whoever provided his meals needed to be more generous.

The Mountie nodded toward Cassie and Roper. "May I present Jack Munro." Then he introduced Roper and Cassie to the man. "They've been caring for the children since they arrived in this neck of the woods."

Jack spared them a glance. "I owe you a debt of gratitude." He smiled at the children. "Daisy, I remember you when you were no bigger than this." He indicated Billy who pressed to Daisy's side. "You were much like Pansy. And Neil, you were only a baby. Billy, I've never had the pleasure of meeting you before." One by one, he greeted them and shook their hands.

The children murmured a response, obviously overwhelmed.

So far the man seemed friendly, Cassie acknowledged.

Would he be so after a few days of dealing with children who needed more than a roof over their heads? And certainly more to eat than this man appeared to consume.

Cassie pushed to her feet. "I'll make tea." When Daisy rose to help, she shook her head. "You stay and visit."

Roper gave her a little nod. He wasn't going anywhere until he saw how this visit went.

She ducked into the privacy of the shack, and while the kettle boiled she put cookies on a plate and she prayed.

Oh, God. Let this man be kind. And if he isn't, help us see it before he whisks them away. Though she wondered what she could hope to do about it. It would likely prove futile to fight against the uncle's claim to the children.

She would not think how any decision either way would affect her future. She would only think of the children and what was best for them.

The kettle whistled. She poured the boiling water over the tea leaves and put the pot, the plate of cookies and cups enough for everyone on a tray and carried it out.

Uncle Jack was telling the children that he lived alone—"Apart from my housekeeper," he said—in an apartment in Toronto.

A city man. Cassie knew it shouldn't matter but she couldn't imagine the children living in such surroundings.

Jack asked each child what they liked. The children answered politely, loosening up a bit over tea and cookies.

Cassie glanced over her shoulder toward the shack. She needed to prepare a meal before half a dozen hungry men descended on them.

Roper understood why she kept fidgeting. "Why don't we go down by the river to talk so Cassie can get at her cooking?"

"I'll help," Daisy said, jumping to her feet.

"No, you go with your uncle and the others." Cassie

shifted her gaze to Roper. "I'll manage on my own." She hoped he understood she wanted him to go, too. Surely he'd notice if there was anything amiss.

He nodded, and led them away to the sandy bank where they often went, and she turned her attention toward meal preparations, even though part of her followed the others down the bank. She would like to be able to observe from some hidden spot without the uncle's knowledge. Almost always, unkind, cruel things happened in secret places out of the public eye.

Memories flooded her mind. Times when she knew if she revealed the pain across her shoulders where Grandfather had strapped her, she would get more of the same when they were back home. Occasions when visitors commented on how fortunate she and Mother were to have such a kind benefactor. How she'd struggled to answer sweetly and falsely.

She didn't hear Roper return until he spoke.

"They are having a good cry in Uncle Jack's arms."

She spun toward him. "You left them alone?"

"Constable Allen is with them." He leaned closer. "Are you crying?"

"No, of course not."

"Then what is this?" He caught a tear with his fingertips.

"Nothing." She turned away as anger and sorrow and pain crowded close.

"Oh, sweet, sweet Cassie."

The compassion in his voice threatened to unlock the dam of tears. It was something she didn't want to happen. But when he caught her shoulders and turned her about, she could not refuse the invitation of his comforting arms.

"What has upset you so?"

She couldn't speak past the knot in her throat.

He patted her shoulder and rubbed her back.

Oh, how she'd missed the comfort of his friendship. "I'm afraid." She could go no further.

He waited, as if he understood there was more.

"He could pretend to be kind and good while there are others around."

Roper nodded, his chin gently bumping against the top of her head. "He said he wouldn't take the children right away. It will give us time to assess him. Besides, both Daisy and Neil are being cautious. They intend to protect the younger ones."

"Who will protect *them?*"

Roper edged her back so he could look into her face. "I think he is a good man but we will make sure they know they can contact us if they ever need to."

She nodded. "I have never heard from my mother."

"I know. Perhaps you will one day, though."

She clung to his steadying look and sucked in a cleansing breath. Then she straightened. "Maybe I worry too much."

He squeezed her shoulder. "Could be because you remember what happened to you."

"I will never forget."

"But maybe one day you'll be able to leave it behind."

She bristled. "What do you mean?"

He brushed her cheek, his touch soothing, calming. "Nothing, sweet Cassie. Nothing at all. Now what can I do to help?"

The table needed setting. The meat needed slicing. He did both while she tended the vegetables and iced a cake.

When they took the food out to the table, half a dozen men waited, including Lane. He watched Cassie's every move. He said something about the weather but she barely heard him as she tried to listen for any sound from the river. Were the children okay?

She sent Roper a desperate glance and he smiled encouragingly. As they passed each other, he murmured, "Relax, the Mountie is with them."

As soon as the meal ended, she left the dishes and hurried to the river.

The children clustered about their uncle Jack, talking eagerly. He seemed demonstrative, reaching out to touch one of the children on the head, squeeze a shoulder and smile encouragement.

Cassie's throat tightened. She was only beginning to understand how much affection such touches offered and realized how much she'd been deprived of as a child. Her gaze sought and found Roper—a man who freely offered such gestures. Roper turned, caught her look, read something in it she meant to hide and smiled softly.

She jerked away returning her attention to the children and their uncle. Jack turned toward her. He looked weary, no doubt exhausted from his travels and the emotion of seeing his orphaned nieces and nephews. She allowed herself a bit of sympathy but on the other hand, when a person was tired, they often lacked the strength to pretend. It was a good chance to observe him and gauge his true attitude toward the children.

The Mountie was sprawled out, his hat over his face. So much for someone watching the children. But the man lifted the brim of his hat, peeked out to check on their arrival then resumed his stance.

Everything appeared fine but she wasn't ready to believe appearances.

A little later, she served a family meal, the table more crowded than usual with both the Mountie and Uncle Jack in attendance.

The Mountie sauntered off after a slice of cake. Uncle Jack said he wanted to spend a few days with the children before they made any changes so Roper invited him to camp with him.

"Thank you. I'm very weary. Do you mind if I retire immediately?"

"Of course not. Come along. I'll show you." Roper led the way to his camp.

Cassie stared after them as the children clustered around her.

"He seems nice." Neil's words sounded tentative.

"He says I look like Mama." Daisy sounded as if nothing else mattered.

Pansy lifted her arms to Cassie and Cassie hugged the little one close. She'd grown to love all of them. How would she survive without them?

Why was everything she cared about snatched from her?

Daisy sighed. "I guess we might as well go to bed." She headed for the shack. The boys followed without arguing.

Cassie helped prepare Pansy for the night, delighting in the way Pansy lifted her face to be washed and how she had to unfurl each chubby finger to wash it. She wouldn't get many more opportunities to enjoy this.

Daisy wriggled between her blankets. "Cassie, did you like my uncle?"

Cassie scrambled to think how to answer. The children needed to face their future with strength and optimism, yet they also needed to know they had alternatives if things didn't turn out well. "He seems nice enough but I think it's too soon for me to make any firm assessments."

Daisy nodded. "That's kind of what I think, too." She turned to Neil and Billy. "We need to remember what

Cassie told us about not giving our uncle any reason to regret giving us a home. That means no arguments, no punching each other and be quick to do whatever chores there are."

Both boys nodded.

Cassie regretted her words on the matter. If they acted naturally, being rowdy and argumentative at times, she'd get a chance to see how Jack reacted. But it was too late to change things. She kissed the children goodnight.

It was too early to go to bed and her mind was in too much turmoil for her to expect sleep to come so she went outside.

Roper sat at the table and without hesitation she went to his side. Their plans for a marriage no longer existed. She would soon be alone, but for tonight she would allow herself this bit of comfort and she rested her shoulder against him. "I wish I could keep them."

He touched her hand. "Me, too, but this is the best for them. He's their uncle. He knows their history." His voice grew soft and she saw that he stared into space. "It's important to know who you are."

"And yet I wish I could forget."

His attention jerked back to her. "Do you? Do you really want to forget your mother and father?"

She instantly repented of her words. "Never."

"Then you understand how important it is for the youngsters to hold on to what is left of their family."

She nodded slowly. Yes, she knew it was for the best. "We've done well together, though."

When Roper didn't answer she turned to study him. Deep lines gouged his face. His mouth drew back in a fierce scowl.

She'd seldom seen him without a smile. "Roper? What's wrong? Didn't you say this was best for the children?"

He nodded, his gaze fixed on a spot in the table. "They deserve family." The words ground out as if every letter scratched his throat. He jolted to his feet like he'd been shot from a cannon. "They are fortunate to have an uncle who wants them." He headed toward the river and paused. "Good night."

She stared after him long after he disappeared. He'd never acted so strangely. Did it hurt him so much to know the children were leaving?

An ache the size of all her tomorrows grabbed her gut and she groaned. The children would leave with their uncle. Their business agreement ended, Roper would leave, too.

She would get the independence she wanted.

Shouldn't she be rejoicing?

Chapter Fourteen

Roper had done his best to reassure Cassie that Jack was to be trusted but as he lay on his bedroll under the stars he strained to make out the words as Jack tossed and turned and talked in his sleep. But he could make no sense of the mumbling.

The man was older than Roper had pictured but that didn't automatically make him unsuitable. Constable Allen assured him Jack's credentials were flawless.

"He's a well-respected businessman. My superior in Toronto says he's a fair man with a healthy bank account."

Roper had no bank account. He wasn't any sort of businessman. Most of all, he had no claim to the children. But despite his words to Cassie he wished the man had not come.

How was he to say goodbye to the children?

His plans for marriage to Cassie ended with the uncle's arrival.

He would continue on as a cowboy with no family ties—empty and alone.

It was a familiar position for him. He would make the best of it as he'd always done. But would he be happy?

Next morning, he was up early, impatient to be at work

finishing the house. He knew Cassie would refuse help once the children left so he meant to get as much as possible done in whatever time he had.

Jack staggered from the tent, pale as butter and shaking.

"Are you okay?"

Jack nodded. "I'll be fine as soon as I have coffee."

"Cassie will have it ready when we get there." He'd normally have been at breakfast before now but had waited for Jack.

The other man washed at the river, shivering at the coldness of the water then they climbed slowly to the top of the hill.

The children watched their approach, caution filling their eyes.

"Good morning, Uncle Jack," Daisy called. She nudged the boys and they added their greeting.

Jack paused, breathing hard. "Good morning, children." He made it to the table and collapsed on the bench, letting out a weak sigh. "I'm not used to sleeping on the ground."

Roper studied the man. He looked worse than when he went to bed. Cassie watched him, too, and she and Roper exchanged glances. Was the man up to caring for four children? Of course, he wouldn't have to do it personally. He could doubtlessly afford a nanny.

But after two cups of coffee, Jack seemed to revive. He asked to be shown around.

"Go ahead," Cassie said in response to Daisy's questioning glance.

"I'll be back to help with dishes," the girl promised.

Cassie waited until they were out of earshot then gathered up the dishes. "Daisy will soon enough be gone. I can manage on my own."

Roper could point out that she wouldn't be feeding and washing up after six or seven. Only herself.

It sounded mighty lonely and unnecessary.

After they'd eaten the noon meal, Jack said he'd like to have a nap. Daisy tucked Pansy into bed, then hovered about the house where Roper and Neil worked. Roper considered the girl. "You look worried."

Billy sidled up to his sister. "She doesn't want to go."

"Billy!" Daisy grabbed the boy and shook him gently.

"You can pretend you do, but I don't. I like it here." He confronted Roper. "Why can't we stay?"

Roper put his hammer down on the window frame, using the time to gather his thoughts. He must ignore his own feelings. Not let them know that he wanted them to stay as much as Billy said he did. They had a future with their uncle that was likely full of all kinds of good things. Somehow he had to convince them of it.

He sat on the doorsill and waved them to join him. They crowded together. For a minute he let himself enjoy the way they sighed and pressed tight to each other. They expected words of strength and understanding from him. He uttered a quick prayer for wisdom then began to speak.

"You all know I was raised in an orphanage. I never knew who my father and mother were. Yet I was happy. Not everyone was, though. I remember when the Trout children came to the orphanage. You kind of remind me of them. There were four of them and they were so scared. The oldest one was a girl so she had to go to the girls' side. The others were boys so they were separated from their sister. It was really hard on the girl, Judy. She told me time and again that if she could be with her brothers and keep caring for them she would feel so much better. You see, she'd promised her mama to always watch out for them."

He paused to look into each intent face.

"What happened to them?" Billy asked, worry lines furrowing his forehead.

"Well, Judy grew up. She was offered a job working for a nice family."

Daisy gasped. "She had to leave her brothers?"

"She could have. That's what was expected." Roper let the words sink in. "But Judy had never forgotten her promise to her mother and she begged the matron to let her stay. Said she would do anything—cook, clean, help teach."

All three watched him with eyes wide. He guessed they had all forgotten to breathe.

"Did the matron—" Neil couldn't complete his question.

"The matron was very understanding. She let Judy stay, and then her oldest brother was big enough to go out to work. Last I heard Judy and Mike had made a home for their two younger brothers and they were all together."

The tension eased from the three children. Daisy and Neil exchanged a look.

"We'll be together," Neil said.

"And soon we'll be grown up."

Billy jumped up. "And then you'll bring us back here and we can live with Roper and Cassie."

Daisy laughed. "We won't have to live with anyone then."

Billy plunked down again and sat with his chin in his hands. "I want to live with them."

Roper gave them a big hug. "Let's promise to keep in touch."

"We will," Daisy said, and with that they all had to be content.

Roper returned to his work, Neil at his side.

"I hope we'll be happy," Neil said.

"You can learn to be no matter what."

For the first time he didn't believe it. Not even for himself. His only hope of family gone, he would have to fight to be happy after the children left.

He crossed the floor and pretended an interest in the door frame for Cassie's room.

He couldn't imagine returning to his solitary life.

No children.

No Cassie.

A groan tore from his throat.

Neil rushed over. "Did you hurt yourself?"

"Just a pinch. I'm fine." This pinch was internal and he wondered if he'd ever be fine again.

Roper concentrated all his thoughts and energy on finishing the house. Later in the afternoon, he glanced up as a familiar voice came across the yard.

Lane.

Roper had seen how Lane resented competing with Cassie's distraction over the children yesterday and wondered if he'd return. But he was there, a look of determination branded on his face. To his credit he did not come early but neither did he leave when the meal was over. Instead, he followed Cassie around as she worked, doing everything on her own as Daisy and the children had gone to the river to visit with their uncle.

Roper was torn between accompanying them and staying behind to keep an eye on Lane.

He tipped his head toward the river but the children were quiet. No doubt Uncle Jack lacked the energy to play any sort of active game with them. The man still seemed rather peaked in Roper's opinion.

He brought his attention back to Lane's lingering presence. He wanted to tell the man to leave but Cassie had made it clear she would be the one to tell him if she so desired. Obviously she didn't mind his attention.

Roper ground about on his heel and stalked back to the house. He couldn't abide to watch them together.

Yet he seemed to find himself at the window at every turn.

Lane hovered at her side as she washed dishes. Roper stared at Lane's back. Didn't the man see the tea towel and the dishes needing to be dried? Apparently not. Instead, he constantly got under foot forcing Cassie to take extra steps.

Any minute now she would reach the end of her patience and suggest he take himself on home.

The man twisted his hat in his fingers and said something that brought Cassie up short. Roper wished he could see her face but she had her back toward him.

Lane smiled. Rather uncertainly, Roper thought. Or was it just hope? And then as he watched, Lane lowered his head.

Roper lurched closer to the window. It looked for all the world like Lane meant to kiss Cassie. Surely now she would step back. Tell him to be on his way.

But she didn't move so much as an inch. She allowed Lane to kiss her right on the mouth. Did Lane linger? Sure seemed like he did.

Roper ground his teeth together. He should never have left the pair alone. Should have been there to protect Cassie.

He narrowed his eyes. Cassie didn't slap the man. Didn't even seem upset. She sort of hung her head, all shy and uncertain.

The wind felt as if it were sucked from his insides, leaving him weak as a newborn kitten. He leaned against the wall.

Seems Cassie didn't need or want his protection.

He grabbed his forgotten hammer and returned to his work. He'd constructed a frame for her bed, built a table and benches for the house. The heavier table and benches they'd been using he meant to leave outside to use in pleasant weather. He'd also put shelves up for her to store things on, built bins and more shelves in the cellar. Tomorrow, as soon as the stove cooled, he'd get it moved inside. That left him time to do a couple of extra things that he'd been planning.

He would do them for Cassie and expect nothing in return but her happiness, and if that meant giving Lane the right to kiss her…

He had nothing to offer her but the work of his hands. No fine home. No parents and brothers. No history. Not even a name. He'd always known he could never be part of a family. It shouldn't surprise him that this attempt was no different.

That night, for the first time since he and Cassie had started this business agreement, he could hardly wait for the evening to come to an end so he could retire to his camp.

Jack accompanied him. The man was full of talk about his plans for the future with the children. "I know how much my sister loved them. Even as I loved her. I'll do everything in my power, God helping me, to raise them like she would want." The man choked and couldn't go on.

Cassie needn't worry about the children. They were going to a good home. He'd give her this last bit of assurance tomorrow.

The next day was a repeat of the previous one except Jack looked even more worn out and chose to spend most of the day sitting. Cassie suggested the children play near their uncle.

Roper followed her to the shack, helping return the food and dishes.

Cassie planted her hands on the worktable and leaned over as if consumed by pain. "I'm going to miss them," she said, her voice thick.

"Me, too." He wanted to take her in his arms and comfort her. But shouldn't he leave that to Lane?

"I hope and pray they'll be okay." A sob ripped from her throat.

Lane wasn't here and he was, so he opened his arms and pulled her to his chest. "Jack is a good man. I believe he'll give them the sort of home that neither you nor I knew."

She eased back to look into his face. "I never thought of it before but we do share that."

And so many other things. Long talks in the dusk. Laughter and play with the children. The work they'd both contributed to getting this house and business built. And a few hugs and kisses. He couldn't say what they'd meant to Cassie—and he wouldn't admit they meant the world to him.

He withdrew his arms and backed away. "Let the stove cool so I can get it moved." Without one glance backward, he returned to the house where he put the final touches in place. He'd added an unnecessary detail he hoped would give her sweet enjoyment.

He stood back to assess his work. The place was pleasant. He hoped she'd enjoy many hours of happiness here.

He had only two things left to do—dig the garden, which he would do before he left, and put in the stove. By noon he had that in place.

Only then did he open the door and wave Cassie inside. He'd asked Jack and the children to give them a moment alone.

She stepped across the threshold and her eyes and mouth widened with pleasure. "My own place." The way she clasped her hands together at her throat was enough thanks for Roper. Walking around the house, she examined each detail. Her gaze lighted on the little extra he'd added, a tiny shelf next to the stove and the pretty vase he'd found in the depths of Macpherson's store. He couldn't help wonder what she thought of the meager collection of wildflowers he'd stuck in the vase but if she liked flowers so much, he thought she should at least have a nice place and a nice vase for them. Even if, after this, he wasn't to be the one to bring them to her.

He planted a hand to his chest to stop the pain and sucked in air to calm his inner turmoil. It hurt to give up his plans even to a fine dude like Lane.

She continued her inspection of the house. She tried the door to her bedroom. Then came full circle back to face him. "Thank you so much. I feel like I owe you something for this."

"It was part of our agreement. There is no owing." *No owing for my work or my friendship.*

She nodded, uncertainty erasing her pleasure.

He heard her silent question. Now what?

"We did well together, didn't we?" He wondered if she heard the uncertainty and longing in his voice or did it exist only in his heart?

She smiled into his eyes. "I'd say we did."

Her agreement eased his tension. "Seems a shame to end a good thing."

Her smile disappeared and sorrow filled her gaze. "But the children will be leaving soon."

He hadn't meant the children. He knew one way to test whether or not she had any interest in continuing their arrangement. "I figure to dig the garden this afternoon."

She jerked to full attention. "I know you planned to do it for the children's sake. But that's no longer necessary. They're leaving. Our agreement is over."

"It doesn't need to be." He looked intently into her eyes hoping she would see all he meant. That she would understand he didn't want this to end.

She marched to the window and stared out, her shoulders drawn up with tension.

He waited, hoping to see the tension soften. "Cassie, I—"

She spun around, her features iron-hard. "I only let you help because of the children. Don't get me wrong, I appreciate all you've done but I think I've made it clear that I don't need or want anything more. This—" Her hand circled to indicate the room. "Is all I need. My own business. Independence."

The back of Roper's eyes burned. His throat tightened so he knew he couldn't force out a word. Not that he had anything more to say. She'd left no doubt about what the future held for them.

All he could do was nod and stride from the house. His steps didn't slow until he found escape and solitude by the river. He sat on the damp sand, his legs out before him like poles clad in denim. He stared at his boots and slowly his mind began to function.

The boots said it all. He was a cowboy. He belonged in a saddle behind a herd of cows. And Eddie could use his help. It was time to return to what he did best.

Cassie closed her eyes and held on to the window frame as wave after wave of shock lapped through her. Roper had offered to stay—to continue their business arrangement.

Like he said, they had done well together.

But to continue without the children made her heart clench until it hurt to even breathe. She guessed he meant they would marry as they had discussed. But wasn't marriage the ultimate form of control?

It wasn't for Linette and Eddie. Surely they were the rare exception. They loved each other enough to sacrifice, to allow the other to follow their heart.

On further consideration, marriage wasn't the ultimate form of control.

Love was.

Or was it the ultimate form of surrender?

What was the difference?

She moaned as her thoughts twisted and knotted with questions she couldn't answer.

Why was she even thinking such foolishness? It wasn't as if Roper had suggested he loved her. And she wasn't ready to make that ultimate sacrifice. No, sir. She finally had her freedom and meant to keep it.

Her mind was made up, but rather than peace she knew only the sensation of her insides rushing out the soles of her feet, leaving her painfully empty.

"Cassie, Cassie." The shrillness of Neil's cry jerked her from the quagmire of her musings and she rushed outside.

Neil grabbed her hand. "Come quick. Something's wrong with Uncle Jack."

Forgetting all else, she lifted her skirts and raced across the yard to where Jack lay on the ground, the children clustered around him. She knelt beside the man who was curled into a fetal position, his teeth chattering.

"I'm so cold," he choked out.

"Daisy, get a blanket. Neil, bring a drink of water. Billy, take Pansy over to the table and keep her occupied."

The children scattered to obey.

"Now tell me what happened," she said to Jack.

"I tried to stand but my legs refused to work." Saying those few words left him panting.

"Have you been sick before?"

He shook his head.

Daisy returned with the blanket and they helped Jack sit up. He drank the water Neil brought.

"I'm feeling better now." He smiled weakly, but he made no attempt to get to his feet.

"Where's Roper?" She regretted the words as soon as she spoke them. Hadn't she assured him she could manage on her own? And yet the first time she had a problem she looked for him.

"I'll find him," Neil said, and he took off before Cassie could say not to bother.

Not that she would have. Jack's weakness worried her.

Would it mean the children stayed longer? Wouldn't Roper then stay, as well?

Angry with herself for such selfish thoughts she turned back to Jack.

"I'm hot." He tossed aside the blanket and his face grew bright pink.

"What's going on?"

She'd never been so happy to hear Roper's voice.

"He's sick." Her answer was unnecessary considering the way Jack mumbled and plucked at the edge of the blanket.

Roper knelt beside her. "We need to get his fever down. Get some tepid water and a cloth. We'll sponge him."

She rushed to do his bidding. Daisy shepherded the children to the table where they sat watching. Their fear was palpable. Cassie paused in her haste to get water and cloths.

"We'll do everything we can to help him," she assured the children.

"If he dies we have no one," Billy said.

Daisy took his hand. "We have each other."

"And you have us," Cassie added, then returned to Jack's side with the supplies.

It didn't take any effort to put aside her selfish thoughts and concentrate on Jack for the next few hours.

His fever broke and he was able to sit up, though obviously weak and shaken.

Roper pulled her aside. "He's not well. Sleeping on the ground, living like this is not doing him any good. I'm taking him to the ranch to recover."

"I expect that's for the best."

"I'll take the kids, too."

"But—"

"They need to be with him and no doubt he'll rest better if they are nearby. I'll be leaving as soon as I hitch up the wagon."

She nodded, feeling the blood drain from her face.

"Of course. I'll help the children get ready." Her voice sounded like she'd ground the words with shards of glass. How long would he be gone? She spun around and announced Roper's decision to the anxious children hovering nearby.

Roper soon drove the wagon to the side of the house, his horse tied at the back. He helped Jack into the back where he'd made a pallet of his bedding.

Cassie stood beside the children. "Your uncle will be well cared for at the ranch." The words she wanted to say stuck in her throat. *I don't want you to leave. I thought we'd have a few more days together. Please don't go back with your uncle without a proper goodbye.*

Roper carefully arranged the children's belongings beside his own. "Ready?"

No one moved.

"Your uncle is waiting."

Daisy turned to Cassie. "We have to go." A sob escaped and she threw herself into Cassie's arms.

Cassie blinked back tears as she hugged Daisy and wished her all the best. "I'll be here if you need me."

Daisy nodded as she stepped back.

Cassie hugged each of the boys, then scooped Pansy into her arms. It took every ounce of self-control not to hug the child hard enough to make her squirm. She kissed the chubby cheeks several times, then handed the little one to Daisy who waited, teary eyed, in the wagon.

Cassie swallowed hard and turned to Roper.

He twisted his hat round and round in his hands. "I'm going back to my job with Eddie."

Each word dropped into Cassie's heart like a heavy river rock. Then the meaning of them grew clear. "You're not coming back?"

"Like you said, our agreement is over."

She'd said the words without truly understanding the full consequence of them. He was leaving. She crossed her arms across her chest and pulled them tight. "I guess this is goodbye, then."

He nodded. "It's time to move on."

She groped from one heartbeat to the next. Tried to recall how to breathe in and out. Forced words from her starved lungs. "Goodbye and again, thank you."

He touched the brim of his hat. "Goodbye, Cassie. If you ever need anything—"

"I'll be fine."

She didn't move as he drove away. Long after the wagon disappeared from sight down the long, dusty trail she stared after them.

Then she shook herself into motion and headed for

the house. Yes, she'd be fine. She'd stand alone and independent.

She stood in the middle of her new house. She hadn't expected them to leave so soon, hadn't expected him to go so quickly, but there was nothing to make him consider staying. She'd seen to that.

She forced her attention back to her surroundings. Everything was perfect. He'd added a few special touches. He'd built a platform for her bed.

Her gaze lighted on the little shelf with the vase of pretty flowers. What kind of business agreement involved flowers? She grabbed the vase and headed to the door intent on pitching the contents into the woods, but she made only three steps before she stopped and slowly retraced her steps. No point in throwing the flowers out while they were still so bright and cheerful.

She set the vase back on the shelf and considered the room again. She had the fabric for curtains. Time to get them made.

Work would put her thoughts to right again. Work was the antidote to foolish emotions.

Chapter Fifteen

Roper concentrated on the road ahead of him. He needed to get Jack to a proper bed and proper care as soon as possible. The man looked ready to pack it in. What would the children do if their uncle died?

He and Cassie would give them a home.

But he would never wish ill on anyone for his own benefit.

He ached at the idea of leaving Cassie. But it was for the best. The sooner he left the easier it would be for them both. With the children gone, Lane would no longer see Roper's presence as a necessary evil.

He couldn't even think it without his insides churning.

If she'd given him even a hint that she wished to continue this agreement—

But her dismay over his suggestion to do so couldn't have been plainer.

Thankfully they reached the ranch and his thoughts were consumed with getting Jack into bed. Linette took over immediately, ordering Eddie and Roper about as they settled Jack and got the children moved into two nearby bedrooms.

"I'll take the kids out and show them around," Roper

said when Linette seemed satisfied that everyone was organized.

"We'll talk later," Linette warned.

Roper didn't answer. He had no desire to face a bunch of questions about Cassie and guessed that's what Linette had in mind.

He took the children down the hill. The first place he stopped was the little log cabin. "That's where Cassie and Mrs. Gardiner and Grady spent the winter." He opened the door. Daisy and Neil stepped inside.

"It's nice," Neil decided. "We could live here."

Daisy looked about. "Uncle Jack lives in Toronto." She sighed heavily. "We'll make the best of things."

"Good choice." Roper drew them outside and turned them toward the cookhouse. "Cookie will want to meet you."

She'd have his hide and skimp on his share of the cinnamon rolls if he passed by without taking the children in.

He led them into the cookhouse. "Cookie, these are the Locke children Cassie and I have been looking after."

Cookie lifted her hands in a jubilant gesture. "Well, just look at you. It's a joy to have more children on the ranch."

He introduced each child, relieved when Cookie spared them her normal hearty slap on the back.

"Good to see you." She sent him forward with her pat. "But where's Cassie?"

"Back in Edendale. She's got a business to run."

Cookie scowled at him. "And you just left her there? By herself? Roper Jones, you're about as dumb as a hammer."

"You got no call to judge me."

Cookie sighed loudly. "That's the saddest part of all. You don't even know what you've done."

"I ain't done nothing but help her. Help these kids and bring their sick uncle here so he can get better." He'd lived up to his personal expectations, making sure everyone was happy and taken care of.

Cookie planted her hands on her hips and gave him a look fit to scald him. "Humph. Where does Cassie figure in all this?"

"Cassie is doing exactly what she wants to do."

"Men are so blind. Except for my Bertie, and he's one in a million." She leaned close. Roper dared not back up or show the least fear. "Have you ever taken a real good look at Cassie?"

"Of course I have." He could describe her in great detail if Cookie cared to hear it. From her shiny black hair that never quite stayed tidy to her brown eyes that could be so warm and yet sometimes so cold, to the way she hustled about, her hands and feet flying as she worked.

"I beg to differ. If you ever looked close you would see a woman aching to be loved. You don't deserve tea and treats but the children do." Her gruff voice grew cheery only as she served the children.

By the time they'd enjoyed milk, tea and Cookie's famous cinnamon rolls, Cookie acted as if she'd forgiven Roper for being so blind and stupid.

He stood. "Come on, kids. I'll show you the barns and pens. You might even catch sight of some baby kittens."

Cookie followed him to the door and grabbed his arm to hold him back. "If you hurt my friend Cassie you will answer to me."

He held up his hands in surrender. "I've done nothing."

"Likely that's the problem." She pushed him out the door.

Roper hurried away, taking the children on a tour of the barn, letting them explore the hayloft in a fruitless search for kittens. They visited the pigs, watched the colts romping and stood on the bridge catching flashes of silver minnows in the water of the creek. He talked to the children, answered their questions, pointed out things for them to look at and tried to forget Cookie's words.

Likely that was the problem. But he had spoken to Cassie, had said it all.

Or had he? Had he been honest about all that was in his heart?

Would it have made a difference except to scare her even more?

Over the next few days Cassie moved everything from the shack to the house. She decided to leave the shack as it was. Perhaps with what she'd learned from watching Roper she could build solid walls and a roof and use it for storage or a chicken house. She would ask Petey about getting hens from the fort.

She made meals for the men, serving them at her new table indoors. She fashioned curtains for the window.

And she congratulated herself on being an independent young woman. She ignored the inner restlessness that made her feel she worked for a task master as unkind as her grandfather had been.

Lane came by every evening, even though she had been less than welcoming since he'd the gall to steal a kiss right in front of the washstand as she did dishes. It had taken every ounce of her self-control to keep from slapping his face.

She shouldn't have curtailed her instincts because he now seemed to think he'd gained some sort of favor with that stolen, unwelcome kiss.

"Cassie, leave the dishes and sit with me."

"I like to get them done before the food hardens on

them." She continued to wash each plate and set it in a pan to drain.

Lane failed to hear the hint in her voice. "Aw, come on, Cassie. I don't enjoy watching you work all the time."

She handed him a towel. "If it bothers you so much then dry the dishes."

He looked like she'd suggested his mother was evil. "That's not what I meant."

She guessed as much. "Who washes and dries dishes at your place?"

"I do." It obviously pained him to admit it. "But when I get married, my wife will."

She practically boiled at the way he studied her, all possessive as if he already had her in the kitchen with a towel in hand. "Sooner or later the dishes have to be done. I prefer to make it sooner."

He tossed the towel aside and crossed his arms. His disfavor was evident. "They can wait."

Her temperature climbed dangerously. What right did he have to expect anything from her? None whatsoever. And if he thought stealing a kiss gave him the right… Well, he had better give the idea another thought.

Each dish bore the brunt of her anger. By the time they were washed and dried, she was about ready to blow a cork.

Lane stood up from his impatient wait. "Finally. Now let's go for a walk."

She faced him, keeping a safe distance away lest she smack him, as she was so tempted to do. "Lane, you are a good customer and I appreciate that."

He reached for her arm, grinning widely. "I hope to be more."

She sidestepped him. "I know you do. But you are mistaken in thinking that's what I want."

"But of course—"

Her eyelids flashed red. How dare he assume he knew what she wanted? "This is my life." She waved her arm about the room. "The one I want. It's what I've dreamed of for a very long time."

Clearly the idea didn't suit him. His lip curled. "You can't be serious. My house is far better."

"Lane, I'm not interested in running your house. Or any man's." Unless it was Roper's, an insistent voice protested. She pushed aside the idea. Roper wasn't interested in anything but a business agreement. And she didn't want a continuing business deal.

Then what did she want?

"I want nothing more than to be independent."

His mouth tightened in disapproval. "You will live to regret this decision." He grabbed his hat and reached the door in three strides, slamming it after him.

"I guess I lost a paying customer," Cassie murmured but she felt not one hint of regret.

She turned full circle, examining the room. It was empty. So empty.

And she was alone. So alone.

The walls crowded her. With a cry of protest she raced to her room and sank to the bed. *Oh, God, help me. I have my heart's desire so why am I so unsettled?*

Her Bible sat on the nearby shelf. She hadn't read it since Roper and the children left. With desperate fingers she picked it up, stroked the cover, remembering Roper's strong hands on the leather. She opened the cover to the page with her babies' deaths. A familiar pain snaked up her insides but it lacked the deadly power of the past. She'd been at peace about her loss since Roper held her and comforted her. She flipped the pages to Genesis and could hear Roper's voice reading the words. Guilt flowed through her veins that it was Roper she saw in each line …not God. Utter loneliness consumed her. This Holy Bible was her only companion, her only comfort. She turned the pages past Genesis, unable to bear the memory of Roper reading, Roper holding her hand as he prayed, Roper—

She flipped the pages to the Psalms. She'd heard them read at funerals. Seemed a fitting place to rest her eyes. Psalm 1. *Blessed is the man.* Guess that didn't fit her. She was neither man nor blessed. *He shall be like a tree planted by the rivers of water.* She sighed. She had all she wanted yet she felt neither blessed nor planted. But because she had nothing else she wanted to do and because doing so brought Roper closer, she continued reading the Bible.

As the days passed, she spent more and more time pursuing that activity. Her soul found healing and peace, even though a constant loneliness caused her heart to ache.

The days passed woodenly as Cassie fed a growing number of men. Some were passing through to the north in search of land. Others came to scout homestead possibilities close to Edendale. But mostly they were men conducting business with the local ranchers. All of them were happy to pay for a hot meal.

As usual, one morning several days later, Cassie headed to Macpherson's with her latest batch of bread. It sold well, as did her biscuits. All in all, she had a very successful business venture.

A wagon stood in front of the store. A very tired-looking young woman slumped on the seat. Cassie watched a moment wondering if the woman would fall forward but she rocked back with a groan, her eyes closed so she didn't see Cassie.

Cassie hurried onward and slipped into the store. A young man spoke to Macpherson, pacing before the counter as he talked. Not wanting to interrupt, she hung back.

"I don't think my customers would like having a sick woman here," Macpherson said, turning to see who had entered. "This is Mrs. Godfrey. She might be able to assist you."

Cassie waited, not about to commit herself to anything until she knew what it was.

"This young man says his wife is too ill to travel any farther. Wants to find a place where she can rest." He turned to the young man. "Mrs. Godfrey operates a dining place. She has a nice little house."

Both men turned toward her.

"Ma'am, I'm Claude Morton. My wife, Bonnie, is unable to continue. She's deathly ill. If you could help?"

Cassie had seen the woman and knew it to be true. But she wasn't certain she wanted to share her quarters. Not with strangers. She thought of how crowded she and the children had been in the shack—

The shack. "I can offer primitive accommodations. If you don't mind them, you're welcome to bunk there."

"Ma'am, any place dry where my wife could rest."

She turned the bread over to Mr. Macpherson then led the man outside. "Drive around the store. You'll see the place."

The man wasted no time in following her directions and stopped near the shack as she indicated. She showed him inside the little building.

"This is fine. Just fine. Hang on, Bonnie, dear. I'll have you settled in a moment." He trotted to the back of the wagon and pulled a bedroll from under the canvas tarpaulin. With barely a nod as he passed Cassie, he spread the blankets on the floor, then dashed back. "Come, Bonnie."

She tumbled into his arms.

He staggered under her weight, then carried her gingerly to the shack and made sure she was comfortable.

Cassie's eyes stung at the tenderness between them. She wanted that kind of caring. Her mind hearkened back to the comfort Roper had offered her again and again.

She spun away. She had her independence. It had to be enough. "There's lots of wood in the stack. And you're more than welcome to join the others for a meal."

Bonnie tried to raise her head. "Thank you so much for your kindness." She panted by the time she finished the few words.

The poor woman. "You rest. Get strong." She spoke to Claude. "If you need anything just holler." He barely acknowledged her, his attention focused on his wife, his face wreathed in such concern Cassie's eyes stung. She slipped away.

For three days, Bonnie lay on her blankets. Cassie began to fear she would die. Claude walked around in a cloud of misery yet he kept her wood box filled, took out ashes, carried in water and after the second day began to help serve the meal. Just as Roper had done.

Cassie appreciated the help but it made her miss Roper with an ache that tempted her to lie down beside Bonnie and wallow in misery.

On the fourth day, Bonnie got up. She struggled into the house and Cassie made her tea.

"It's good to see you feeling stronger."

"I'm ashamed of how weak I was. Poor Claude was so worried yet he never once complained. Even though it means we still haven't found a place to settle."

Cassie hoped they'd find a place soon and get a solid

cabin built before the snow came. How would Bonnie survive the winter?

Bonnie gave a weak smile. "I know you're thinking I'm not very sturdy to be going homesteading but it's what Claude wants. I'll get stronger with time."

"Claude is a farmer?"

"No. He just wants to own his own land and be independent."

It was too sharp a reminder of George's quest. If he hadn't died before he could claim a piece of land she wondered if he would have survived the first winter.

Bonnie looked about. "This is nice."

"It's a solid house." Thanks to Roper. Again, pain grabbed her breath. She missed him. She missed his company, their conversations, his understanding—

Stop! There was no point in wishing for things that couldn't be.

Claude and Bonnie stayed a few more days before they moved on.

Cassie missed them but she told herself she enjoyed the daily work. Told herself she was content. But she could not persuade herself she was happy.

At the end of the week she took her earnings over to Macpherson as payment on her bill.

"You're making quite a dent in your account," the storekeeper said. "What with your baked goods and the money from the meals you serve." As he spoke he checked the mail. "Something came for you in the latest mail bag."

Her heart skipped a beat. A letter from home? She took it, saw the return address bore Mrs. Ellertson's name and with a hurried "thank you" headed back to her house to read it in private. Her fingers shook as she opened the envelope.

Dear Mrs. Godfrey,
It's a surprise to think of you as a married woman and now a widow. I was some surprised to hear from you, I can say. I recall, I do, how you and your mother scurried about getting your things at the market. Always so quiet and cautious as if ye thought we'd bite. I've since put it all together and realize it's your grandfather you's afraid of. He's a hard man but I guess you already know that. You ask if I've had any contact with your mother. I'm pleased to be able to say she still comes to the market and I took the opportunity to mention your letter to her. She was some surprised, I could tell, and teared right up. She says to tell you she is fine. Just fine. Your grandfather has suffered a mild stroke. She didn't say anything more about that but I can guess it likely hasn't improved the man's state of mind but perhaps he's weaker so she finds it easier to put up with him. Your mother said to say she would write if she got a chance and please take care of yourself and be happy. It's all that matters to her. I hope this message has cheered you. I will be glad to receive another letter with news to pass to your mother.
Your servant,
Mrs. Ellertson

Cassie read the letter twice trying to picture the changes. Was Grandfather confined to bed? If so she didn't want to think how cantankerous it would make him, but if he was, at least her mother would be able to escape his constant supervision.

Take care of yourself and be happy.

She was doing the first reasonably well. The other? Perhaps happiness was too much to expect or hope for.

Except as she read the Psalms she got the impression God wanted His people to be happy with life.

She folded the letter and slipped it into the Bible for safekeeping. *Thank you, God, that my mother is alive and well.*

A knock startled her and she went to answer the door. "Linette. Come in." She reached out to grab her friend and drag her inside, then thought how desperate it made her look. She hadn't realized until now that she was that eager for a friendly face. The men she fed were friendly but it wasn't at all the same.

"Eddie and Grady are still at the store but I couldn't wait." She waved an envelope. "I got a letter from Grady's father." She closed the door and ripped open the letter, then read it quickly. "He says the child looks like his side of the family. Thanks me for caring for the boy."

Cassie waved Linette to the table.

"Not a word about coming for Grady. Not even an inquiry about how his son is doing." She shook the pages in disgust.

Cassie shook her head in disbelief. "How can some men be so unfeeling?"

"He just needs to get to know Grady but how will he if he never sees him? There must be a way to get him to come out West." Linette mused about what she could do as Cassie made and served tea.

Finally she gave a heavy sigh. "About all I can do is keep writing him and pray God will change his mind." She gave a short laugh. "Sorry to rattle on so. How are you?"

Finally Cassie could ask the questions burning her tongue. "How are the children? How is their uncle Jack?"

But she didn't voice the most pressing question. How is Roper?

"Jack is improving but still weak. He does his best to spend time with the children but admitted to me that he's happy they are able to amuse themselves. Grady is really enjoying having some children to play with. The children are so lovable." She launched into an accounting of everything the children did and said.

Cassie took it all in but wished for some news on Roper.

Linette pushed her empty teacup away and looked about. "Your place looks nice. How are you doing?" She rested her gaze on Cassie, waiting for her to answer.

"My business is going well. Macpherson is pleased with how quickly I'm paying off my bill at the store."

"And Lane?"

"Lane? What about him?" She couldn't understand how he deserved mention.

Linette studied her and Cassie met her look openly.

"Roper told me that Lane was courting you. Figured he'd be asking for your hand any day."

Cassie gave a short, mirthless laugh. "Lane thought the same thing but I told him I wasn't interested. Haven't seen him since."

"So you aren't encouraging his attention?"

"No and I never have."

"Ahh, I see."

"There is nothing to see."

Linette took her time answering as if considering her choice of words. "Roper seemed to think otherwise. He's been morose since he came back. I think he misses you."

"He's worried about the children. So am I."

"Strange. He seems at peace about the children but the minute your name comes up, he clams up tight."

Cassie assessed this information, trying to think what it meant.

"Cassie, he's lonely and hurting, and I think you're the only one who can fix it."

Hope hummed through her veins. Did this mean he cared about her? Reality set in. "He never mentioned anything but continuing our business arrangement."

"He's afraid you'll reject him because he has nothing to offer."

"He said that?"

Linette waggled her hands. "Not in so many words but I'm good at reading between the lines."

So it was only Linette's opinion. Linette, the eternal optimist, the dreamer.

She reached out for the post from Mrs. Ellertson. "I got a letter, too." She read it aloud to Linette.

"Isn't that good news?" Linette asked when she'd finished.

Cassie nodded.

"God answers prayer."

"Not always."

"He gives what's best." Her eyes resting on Cassie, she added, "I'm going to pray that you and Roper get together."

Cassie laughed. "Don't we have anything to say about it?"

"I'm expecting you will both come to your senses. It's plain as the nose on your face that you're lonely and missing him. It's equally plain that Roper is lonely, too, and missing you."

"Seems to me you're reading a lot into innocent expressions on a person's face."

Linette only smiled and nodded as if she had a secret.

Cassie decided it was time to change the subject. "What brings you to town?"

"Oh, I almost forgot. Eddie is arranging a meeting to discuss starting a church. Everyone is invited to the ranch next Saturday for it. You should come."

Before Cassie could reply, Eddie came to the door. "Sorry to rush your visit but we have several other stops to make before we go home."

Linette hurried to his side, pausing to thank Cassie and to press her point. "Come to the meeting about the church."

"I have no transportation."

"I'm sure Macpherson will be coming. You can accompany him."

She murmured something noncommittal and hugged her friend goodbye.

The room echoed with emptiness as the wagon drove away.

Why did Roper think he had nothing to offer her? If he thought she wanted a big house and fancy clothes, he hadn't learned much about her.

Had she misinterpreted his offer of a marriage based on business interests? *An obligation to love.* Why did those words again blare through her head? What did they mean? Where had she heard or read them? Would she find the answers to her confusion in the Bible? She'd learned it offered comfort and she opened the pages seeking something but not knowing what it was or where to find it. Then her eyes lighted on Romans 13:8. "Owe no man anything, but to love one another."

She sat back. The words that mocked her were from the Bible. How could love be a debt? Or was that what it meant? Slowly another thought worked its way into her mind. Perhaps loving wasn't a debt or obligation, perhaps it was a gift. She recalled where she had heard the words. At a sermon in her grandfather's church. It had been an admonition to put people ahead of possessions. Ahead of duty or profit. To give and accept love. She had rejected the words at the time because her grandfather was exactly the opposite.

Was she becoming like him? Putting work and obligation and money and her own interests ahead of all else? And in doing so denying her own needs? She finally admitted she wasn't joyful even though she had achieved her goal.

She did not want to end up unhappy and mean-spirited like her grandfather.

What did she really want? She knew the answer but wondered if it was possible.

She wanted to love and be loved. And she wanted it all with Roper.

She fell on her knees. *Dear God, I have been driven by the wrong motives. Forgive me. And help me plan my next move.*

Roper saw Linette headed across the yard to him. She and Eddie had been driving around the country announcing the meeting about starting a church. He knew they had gone to Edendale. No doubt they'd visited Cassie. Likely Linette was on her way to tell Roper that Lane and Cassie were growing more and more fond of each other.

He veered away to avoid her.

"Roper, hold up," she called.

He thought of ignoring her but she was the boss's wife. And he liked his job enough not to give Eddie cause to dismiss him so he ground to a halt and waited for her. "Howdy. What can I do for you?"

"I don't want anything except to tell you I saw Cassie.

Thought you'd like to know she told Lane not to bother coming anymore."

His heart clawed up his throat and stuck there. She had dismissed Lane? After kissing him? Had they argued? Or had she finally realized how controlling he was, how he was not her kind of man at all?

He knew what sort of man she needed.

His heart settled into place with a thud. At least Lane had provided some company. "She'll be a mite lonely, I 'spect."

"Maybe so but the trouble is, she has eyes for no one but you."

He wondered how words had the power to make him suck in his breath like he'd been punched. "She said that, did she?"

"Not in so many words but I'm good at reading between the lines." She waved and headed back toward the house.

He stared after her, his boots rooted to the ground. Eyes for him? Oh, he missed her. With every beat of his heart, with every breath he drew, with every move he made. If only she had accepted his offer to continue their plans.

But he didn't want a business arrangement.

He loved her and wanted a real marriage.

He wanted to protect her, help her, comfort her, be at her side every step of her future. But what did he have to offer her?

Only love with no strings attached.

He'd never spoken words of love because he didn't think he had the right to offer his heart. He was nobody.

Nobody but a man in love with her.

Was it enough?

Chapter Sixteen

Cassie heard a wagon approach and went to the door to see who had come. "Claude and Bonnie, how nice to see you. Come in and visit." She studied the pair as they climbed down. Both looked healthy enough but sent quick little looks from one to the other.

She waited until they were seated at the table enjoying tea and cake before she asked the question begging to be asked. "Is something wrong?"

Another secretive glance passed between them. Then Claude spoke. "We've been talking."

Bonnie edged forward on her chair. "Remember I said neither of us knows anything about farming?"

"I remember."

"Then perhaps you also remember that I said we only wanted to own our own little piece of land."

Cassie's curiosity grew as the pair continued to dart looks at each other.

"We have something we want to discuss with you." Claude swallowed nervously. "Don't answer right away. Hear us out, and then think about it."

"And pray about it," Bonnie half begged.

"Okay."

Claude sucked in air. "We thought about how alone you are here. We could see you missed your former partner and the children." He held up a hand to stop Cassie's protests. "You keep awfully busy and all. Our idea is we could become your partners." The last words rushed out.

Cassie couldn't believe her ears. "But this is mine. I've worked hard for it."

Claude deflated. "I thought you might say that but we thought we had to try."

"Won't you at least think about it overnight?" Bonnie asked. "We need to plan what we want to do next. Maybe we could rent the little shack again. Spend the night."

Cassie nodded. "You're welcome to its use."

The pair beamed at each other. Then Bonnie spoke again. "We'll help with the chores as payment."

Cassie couldn't refuse. The afternoon sped past as the pair regaled her with stories of the people they'd met, the places they'd seen and a particularly entertaining tale of encountering an old man in a tiny shack up in the hills.

"At first he ordered us off the place, then he changed his mind and insisted we sit down. Hard to refuse when he aimed his rifle at us." Claude chuckled. "I think he was lonely for someone to talk to. Said he had moved out there three years ago to get away from people. By the end of our visit he confessed he was getting a little weary of no one but himself to talk to. Then he laughed loud and long, and showed us that his gun wasn't even loaded. Said he'd never hurt anyone."

"Poor man," Bonnie said. "So lonesome. I told him he should leave his isolated cabin and move closer to people. He got all serious and said he didn't trust people." She sighed again. "I tried to tell him there were more good people in the world than bad. You just have to be ready to take the risk of meeting both but he isn't ready to believe it."

Travelers began to arrive then, and the conversation ended. But Cassie kept thinking of what Bonnie said. *You just have to be ready to take the risk.* It seemed the words could apply to Cassie's life, too. She had to believe not everyone was like her grandfather. She had to be willing to take a risk.

The words still circled her brain hours later after she'd bid good-night to Claude and Bonnie and retired to her room.

Some risks were worth taking. Like starting her own business. Like Linette coming from England expecting Eddie to marry her.

Was letting herself admit she loved Roper an acceptable risk? Her heart jolted with hot fear.

Fear of being controlled. Fear of disappointment. Fear of the unknown.

She examined each fear. Would Roper try and control her if they married? A smile tugged her lips. If so, he'd soon learn she wouldn't accept having his will imposed on her.

Would he disappoint her? She didn't even have to think about that answer. Never. Because she would be happy simply to have him sharing her life.

The unknown remained scary simply because it was exactly that. She couldn't control it. But reading the Psalms had filled her soul with deep conviction. God held the future. She could trust Him.

That left her one question to answer.

Did she have the courage to confront her fears?

Roper watched the buggies and horses drive in for the meeting about getting a church. He figured Linette and Eddie must have visited everyone within forty miles, judging by the number of people arriving. Seems only a year ago that there was no one but a few scattered ranchers and the people working there.

Guess it was inevitable that things would change.

He leaned against the corner post of the corral fence and watched. No doubt Cassie would come. He'd told himself he'd speak to her. He'd even practiced a countless number of speeches but he still had no idea what he would say. Only that he must tell her how he felt and see if he had a chance.

It scared him to think of confessing his love but anything was better than this endless misery of wishing, hoping, telling himself not to hope and going straight back to wishing.

The Mountie rode up to the house and dismounted. Roper hadn't expected him to attend the meeting but then he hadn't thought about much except Cassie.

Macpherson's wagon rumbled up and Roper pushed away from the post, unable to breathe. The man jumped down but rather than reach up to help a lady down, he headed straight for the house.

Roper stared. Where was Cassie? Was she ill? What else would keep her from attending?

He intended to find out. He jogged toward the barn as fast as his bowed legs and riding boots allowed. In minutes he had a horse saddled and raced from the yard.

If something had happened to Cassie—

He should have never left her there alone. It was his stupid pride that had made him walk away.

The horse was doing all the work but Roper sweated like he did the running.

Down the road came a tail of dust indicating another wagon headed for the ranch. Whoever it was should slow down. The meeting wasn't important enough to risk an upset.

He reined the horse off the trail to let it pass, caught a twinkle of a dark blue dress and a surprised expression as it flashed by. He blinked. Cassie? Why was she driving like that? The wagon rattled to a halt.

Cassie stood up looking as surprised as he felt. "Roper, what are you doing out here?"

He edged closer. "I could ask you the same thing." He saw what appeared to be all her worldly goods piled in the back. She was going somewhere? In a hurry? Without a word to anyone? Not even him? His heart threatened to leak out the bottom of his boots. "You planning on leaving the country?" Or had she changed her mind and was headed to join her life with Lane Brownley? He grabbed the top of his boots and tugged in a vain attempt to stop the way his insides sank.

"Not leaving. Going back." She watched him closely as if her words should mean something special to him.

How far back did she mean? "Back to Montreal?" His words were cautious. Maybe she was going back to England.

Her smile seemed a little crooked. "No, back to the ranch."

Her answer made no sense. "Eden Valley?"

She nodded.

What reason did she have to go to the ranch? "What's back there?"

She lifted one shoulder. "I thought you were."

The words wound their way through his head with maddening slowness. He couldn't grasp her meaning. "Me?"

She nodded, her gaze watchful, intent.

Understanding crept closer. "You were coming to see me?" He squeaked like a twelve-year-old boy. "Why?"

She looked away. "Maybe I missed you."

A visit? But the wagon was full. He swallowed hard. "How much did you miss me?"

"Enough to sell half my business to a young couple who are prepared to run it for me. Enough to pack all my belongings in a borrowed wagon. Enough—"

He leaped from his horse into the wagon, sending it rocking, and grabbed Cassie's shoulders. "Are you saying—"

"Roper, I'm not saying anything more. I think it's up to you now."

He squinted his eyes at the goods in the wagon box. "Just exactly what did you have in mind?" It tickled him to think she might have planned to ride up to the ranch and propose to him.

She looked away. "I knew Linette would always welcome me. I could work for her."

He choked back his disappointment. Where did he fit into the picture?

Then she smiled at him, tipping his world sideways with her blinding intensity. Was it only his hoping that made him think he saw love and acceptance?

"Did you—" His tongue couldn't seem to find the right shape for the words he wanted to say and he tried again. "Did you see me in your plans?"

"I guess that's up to you."

It was all the encouragement he needed and yet his mouth was so dry he couldn't speak. He couldn't make his brain work. He could only stare at a face full of hope and promise. A face he saw in his thoughts day and night. A face he'd missed beyond measure. "But I have no name."

"Roper Jones is a very nice name."

"I have no past."

She smiled and touched his cheek with fingers that soothed him like cool water. "Sometimes the past is best forgotten."

"I don't know who my family is. Maybe they're idiots or insane."

"Or maybe they're kings and scholars."

He chuckled at that. "What happened to being independent?"

"I think love doesn't mean owning, but honoring."

She'd thought of everything. So had he. He took her hands and studied her face, cherishing each feature. "Cassie Godfrey, I love you and if you'll have a nobody cowboy, I'd like to marry you." His lungs locked up tight and he couldn't continue. Maybe he'd misunderstood her. His heart ticked out the seconds as he waited for her answer.

She lifted their joined hands and smiled. "It would be my honor to marry you and share your life. I love you, Roper Jones."

His heart blasted into action, sending relief humming through his veins. It was beyond belief that she could love him but he wasn't about to argue and he pulled her into his arms and hugged her, wanting to keep her next to his heart forever. But he wanted even more than that.

He lowered his head and kissed her, his love flooding his heart until he had to step back and whoop his joy. The horses both snorted a protest but Cassie laughed.

He kissed her again, love pouring from his heart in a gushing waterfall.

A little later, she sighed. "I meant to attend the meeting."

"We can still go. Might be a bit late, though." He tied

his horse to the back of the wagon and they returned to the ranch.

As they stepped into the big room at the ranch house, Linette glanced toward them. Her eyes grew wide and she started to grin.

The others in the room followed her gaze and saw Roper with his arm around Cassie.

"About time you two came to your senses," Eddie said.

"Now we really need to get the church built so we can have a wedding." Linette would have it all planned out in a minute.

Roper murmured to Cassie. "Not sure I want to wait until they build a church and find a preacher."

"Me, either."

But they said nothing and slipped into two chairs at the back of the room.

Cassie had a hard time concentrating on the meeting. She could not think past the joy of the moment. Roper loved her and she loved him. Together they would create a new family. She would not let herself think of the four children she had grown to love. They'd been a family, but now the children had a new family of their own.

The meeting ended and Linette insisted Roper and Cassie come to the house. Cassie needed no persuasion. The children and their uncle had remained there, and she was anxious to see them again.

The children saw them coming and screamed her name as they raced down the hill. Only Roper's protective arm about her kept her on her feet as the children flung themselves into her embrace. She hugged and kissed them all and lifted Pansy to her arms. The little girl patted Cassie's cheeks and gave a watery smile.

"Oh, I've missed you all," Cassie said.

Daisy tucked her arm through Cassie's. "We've missed you."

"How is your uncle?"

The three older children all answered at once. From what Cassie could make out Jack was feeling better but wasn't strong.

Cassie stopped and drew them all close. "Roper and I are going to get married." Her heart overflowed, and she hugged them all close. Roper wrapped his arms around them as best he could, trying to include them all.

"I wish—" Billy started but Daisy's jab cut him short.

Me, too, Cassie agreed, feeling exactly as Billy. She reached for Roper's hand and strength, seeing in his expression the same regret none of them voiced.

They reached the house and Linette drew them into the family sitting room where Jack sat so he could see out the window.

Cassie hurried to greet him. "You look much better than last time I saw you."

He gave a wry smile. "I'm feeling much better, thank you." He eyed her and Roper. "Seems you two have finally allowed yourself to see what the rest of us saw from the beginning."

Cassie laughed. She didn't mind knowing others had seen their love before they did…or at least before either of them willingly admitted it.

"Children," Jack said, "would you run and play for a few minutes? I want to talk to Roper and Cassie in private."

Billy complained he hardly got a chance to see Cassie but Daisy shushed him and pulled him out of the room.

Jack seemed to consider his words before he began to speak. "I'm glad to see the two of you together. It makes it possible for me to make a rather large request of you." He stopped for a moment.

Cassie darted a glance at Roper. What was this all about? But Roper quirked an eyebrow, letting her know he didn't know.

"I love the children and would be glad to give them a home but I've discovered I am not strong enough. I guess I knew it before I even left Toronto but I wasn't about to let my sister's children be put in a home. Or given to begrudging people. But with you—"

Cassie held her breath not daring to believe he meant what she thought. What she hoped.

Jack studied each of them carefully. "I know it's a lot but I'm asking if you would be willing to care for my nieces and nephews."

Cassie heard Roper swallow. He gripped her hand tightly.

"Are you asking us to take the children?" he said, his voice full of uncertainty.

Cassie nodded, filled with the same doubts as to the meaning of what Jack said.

"If you would?"

Roper pulled Cassie around to face him. He grinned. "I don't even have to ask what you want. I can see it on your face as plain as day." As a pair they faced Jack. "Yes, we'll gladly give them a home."

"It will be our joy," Cassie said.

"Thank you. Now go tell the children. I think I know what their reaction will be."

Roper called the children back indoors. "I have an announcement to make." He waited until Billy stopped dancing about. "Your uncle Jack asked us to keep you and we agreed."

Neil understood first and whooped. The others followed suit, even Pansy. The noise of the joyous celebration brought Linette from the kitchen and Eddie from the yard where he visited the neighbors.

"This is wonderful news," Linette said.

Roper pulled Cassie into his arms, uncaring about the audience about him. "This is a day of good news. I am the happiest man on earth."

And in front of all those present he kissed her and their kiss brought a roar of cheers and clapping.

Epilogue

Roper drew Cassie into the crook of his arm and rested his chin on the top of her head.

"I wonder how many couples get married and adopt four children on the same day."

"Only a fortunate few, I venture to say." Cassie sighed her contentment. "Isn't that right, children?" she called over her shoulder.

"Yes," they chorused in unison.

Jack had wanted to sign the papers before he returned to Toronto so they had made the trek to Fort Macleod where they were married. With promises to write and Uncle Jack's assurance he would return to visit, they'd said goodbye to him as he began his journey back to Toronto.

The children stared after their uncle as he dcparted on the stagecoach.

"I wish he didn't have to go," Daisy said.

"Me, too, but I'm glad we don't have to go with him." Billy's comment made them all smile.

They were soon homeward bound. A little later, the children recognized landmarks and pressed close to watch.

"Are we almost there?" Neil asked.

"Almost. Look. You can see the ranch in the distance."

Suddenly the children sat back.

Cassie gave Roper a questioning look. He shrugged as he turned to consider the huddle of children.

"What's wrong?"

The children silently consulted each other then Daisy spoke for them all. "You adopted us. You're giving us a home. We have nothing to give you."

Cassie shifted and signaled them to come close. She hugged them. "You have given us the best gift anyone can give. Your love."

"Amen," Roper said. Then he turned the wagon up the trail toward home. Eddie had appointed him foreman before they left and promised him the little cabin. It would be crowded until they could build on a couple of rooms but they'd been crowded before and managed just fine.

Eddie and a bunch of the cowboys came from the barn.

Roper wondered at the way they all grinned, then he turned the wagon toward the cabin.

"Hold up," Eddie called.

"What's up, boss?"

"Here comes Linette."

Linette trotted down the hill, Grady at her side, and when she reached Eddie she laughed.

Roper thought it rather odd.

"Hop down."

"You're the boss." He jumped down and helped Cassie to her feet. The kids scrambled out on their own.

"Let's go."

Cassie raised her eyebrows and looked from one grinning face to another. "Where are we going?"

Linette grabbed her arm. "You'll have to come see."

En masse they marched down the trail, past the storage sheds, past the barn, past the corrals. They kept going and drew to a halt before a new building.

"That wasn't there when I left," Roper pointed out.

"We built it while you were gone."

Linette laughed again. "It's your new house."

Cassie stared. "You built this while we were gone?"

"We had it all planned and the material ordered. As soon as you left the yard we got to work." Eddie waved them ahead. "Have a look."

Roper let Cassie go ahead of him. There was a nice big kitchen, furnished and ready to use. Beyond that, a small sitting room with two rocking chairs.

"Jack provided them," Linette said.

Roper opened the doors off the sitting room to find two smaller rooms.

"Bedrooms for you and the girls," Linette explained. "There's a loft for the boys."

Roper stared at Cassie, saw the shock in her face and knew she was as surprised as he. "I never expected—"

Eddie chucked him on the arm. "I want my foreman to be happy."

"I couldn't be happier but it's not because of the house. Don't get me wrong. I appreciate the room. But it's Cassie—" He pulled her to his chest. "And the kids." He opened his arms and drew them all close. "They provide my happiness."

"We know that." Linette signaled to her husband, and they all withdrew, leaving Roper alone with his new family.

He kissed Cassie. "I love you."

"And I love you."

"Us, too," the children chorused.

Roper knew he had never before known such joy. Joys shared were joys doubled, and he meant to double his over and over.

* * * * *

Dear Reader,

I love children of all sizes and ages and temperaments so it was a joy to write about four children who were instrumental in bringing together a wary hero and heroine. As I wrote the story and created situations that involved the children I had fond memories of when my children were young. We made a sincere effort to create pleasant memories for them. That included picnics, game time, family dinners and reading the Bible together. I'm sure many times the children did not see it as ideal. So I'm happy that the children in my story regard their family traditions as worth maintaining.

Of course, the story is really about Cassie and Roper. I hope as you read it, you, too, find a measure of something positive, be it sweet memories of family traditions or the assurance that God cares about each of us even when circumstances would give us reason to think otherwise.

I love to hear from readers. You may contact me through my website, www.lindaford.org, where you can also hear about upcoming releases and learn a bit about me.

Blessings,

Linda Ford

Questions for Discussion

1. What is the reason for Cassie being so prickly? Do you think she is justified? How would you react in similar circumstances?

2. What has shaped the way Roper looks at life? Do you consider his viewpoint as positive or negative?

3. How did Roper keep people at bay so he didn't expect too much from them? Or did he? How did he protect his heart?

4. Why does Cassie refuse Roper's help when it is so freely offered?

5. What role do the children play in helping Cassie and Roper fall in love? Do other characters in the story play a role? How? Why?

6. Did you feel Lane should have won Cassie's heart? Why or why not? Did you like the way she dealt with Lane or should she have done things differently, in your opinion?

7. How did you feel about Cassie's mother? Do you think she should have stayed with her? Why or why not?

8. Did you think the children should have gone with the uncle? Why or why not? Would your answer be different if the man had been young and healthy?

9. What lesson did Cassie and Roper each learn that enabled them to trust love? Do you feel the way they overcame their past was realistic? Too simple? Too hard?

10. Was there any lesson in this story that you can apply to your own life?

11. Do you think Cassie and Roper's story ended happily? Is there anything different you would have liked to see them do? Do you think their lives together as a family will be happy?

Love Inspired HISTORICAL

In the fan-favorite miniseries
Amish Brides of Celery Fields

ANNA SCHMIDT

presents

Second Chance Proposal

The sweetest homecoming.
He came home…for her.
A love rekindled.

Lydia Goodloe hasn't forgotten a single thing about John Amman—including the way he broke her heart eight years ago. Since John left Celery Fields to make his fortune, Lydia has devoted herself to teaching. John risked becoming an outcast to give Lydia everything she deserved. He couldn't see that what she really wanted was a simple life—with him. Lydia is no longer the girl he knew. Now she's the woman who can help him reclaim their long-ago dream of home and family…if he can only win her trust once more.

Amish Brides of CELERY FIELDS

Love awaits these Amish women.

www.LoveInspiredBooks.com
LIH82959

Love Inspired